W9-ARR-027

HULA GIRL

LARA WARD COSIO

Copyright © 2019 by Lara Ward Cosio

All rights reserved.

No part of this book may be reproduced in any form or by any electronic or mechanical means, including information storage and retrieval systems, without written permission from the author, except for the use of brief quotations in a book review.

This is a work of fiction. Names, characters, businesses, places, events and incidents are either the products of the author's imagination or used in a fictitious manner.

Cover by: Chloe Belle Arts
Edited by: LaVerne Clark
Proofed by: Roxanne Leblanc, Rox's Indie Edits

Also by Lara Ward Cosio
Tangled Up In You
Playing At Love
Hitting That Sweet Spot
Finding Rhythm
Full On Rogue: The Complete Books #1-4
Looking For Trouble
Felicity Found
Rogue Christmas Story
Problematic Love
Rogue Extra: The Complete Books #5-8
Hula Girl: A Standalone Romance

Dedicated to my husband — my own fairy-tale romance.
Thank you to the Cosio side of the family for inspiration for parts of this story.

1

AVA

One week.

It doesn't sound like very long. Until you break it down.

Seven days.

One hundred and sixty-eight hours.

Six hundred and four thousand, eight hundred seconds.

I'm spending all that time in what most people would call paradise—the Hawaiian island of Maui. But for an admittedly type-A personality like me, the passage of these first two days has been agonizingly slow.

I've tried to make the most of what amounts to an *enforced vacation*, really, I have. I dutifully unplugged by leaving my lifeline—a top of the line MacBook Pro—at home. I haven't called into the office to check with my assistant on pressing matters at all. And I've only messaged my boss, Randall, once but at least it wasn't about work. It was an Instagram-worthy photo I'd casually staged. The shot is of my toes in the nearly white and oh-so-soft sand with the clear blue ocean in the background. I wanted to show him that I have taken his order to disengage from all stress seriously.

He'd texted back: *That's a start. Go to a luau. Really decompress.*

He means well, that I know. But he should also know that the last thing I'm going to do is dive deep into a tourist trap like a luau.

Coming to Maui wasn't exactly my idea. Randall insisted that I take this time off. He went so far as to book my plane ticket and hotel, telling me both were covered by the firm as part of what he euphemistically coined my rest and recovery benefits. No such benefits exist, of course. It's just one of the many ways he takes it upon himself to look after me. He's treated me like a daughter—or granddaughter, I should say, given his age—almost as soon as I started working at the law firm of Miller, Newell & Kahn six years ago. In return, I've come to think of him as a sort of surrogate grandfather.

This unusual bond is the result of the incident that happened the day I interviewed with the firm, fresh out of law school.

I wasn't a top contender for the entry-level job of first-year associate. Not with having graduated from an undistinguished school like Southwestern Law School without any internships under my belt. I'd sacrificed the vital experience of internships in favor of working double-shifts at a high-end Beverly Hills restaurant that paid surprisingly well, even if I did have to slap away one too many drunk hands of entitled rich men. I was also busy helping my mom with her house-cleaning service, Mobile Maids, the business she started out of necessity after my father passed away unexpectedly when I was thirteen years old. So, while I ended up with great "real world" experience, it wasn't the kind of background most law firms appreciated.

I'd applied for the position at Miller, Newell & Kahn, along with a dozen other firms I'd placed in the "no chance in hell" category, figuring I'd have nothing to lose. They were the only one in that category to call me in for an interview. The interview process at a firm like that is rigorous, to put it mildly. They had me in back-to-back meetings with all levels of staff, some as individual interviews and others as panel interviews, throughout most of the day. There was even a coffee break and lunch break interview. Each person was seemingly more intent than the last on tripping me up with a question on some obscure law or case study, making for an intense day. But I held my own—outwardly, at least. I was able to come up with credible answers, falling back on the studying that had left me with virtually no social life for the last seven years of undergraduate and law school combined. Inwardly, though, I was frazzled.

By the time I had my last interview with Randall Miller, senior partner of the firm, I barely held it together. Our time started innocuously enough, with him asking all the typical questions about my studies and what I thought I could contribute to the firm. He stared at my resume the whole time, having not made eye contact with me since the initial glance we shared when I took my seat in front of his impressive carved mahogany desk at the start of our interview.

His questions became more listless, and my answers got shorter. We were both flatlining and I knew this didn't bode well. But my nerves and exhaustion made it hard to push through, especially when I had every indication from all my other interviews that I wasn't the right fit. They never said those words, of course, but I'm realistic enough to understand that as a Latina, I was fighting an uphill battle in a firm like this that is at least 90 percent white.

"Well, Miss Ruiz," Randall said, clearly on his way to wrapping up the interview that had only lasted twelve minutes. "I want to thank you for coming in."

And there it was. The brush-off from the man who surely held the final word on my candidacy. I smiled ruefully and stood, extending my hand to him.

When he rose, he was clearly struggling. I had researched him before this interview and knew he'd had a long, successful career. He'd started this firm after seven years as an Assistant district attorney, making it into a highly respected, multi-faceted organization focused on the rigors of the law rather than gimmicks or loopholes. He was married with four children and six grandchildren. The picture of health for a man in his mid-seventies, he was known to play tennis at a private club four times a week. But the moment he reached for my hand, the color drained from his face and he staggered to his right. Before I could move, he went crashing down to the floor, trying and failing to hold onto the desk as he went, sending papers, books, and files down with him.

If he had blacked out, he'd already come to by the time I rushed around to his side of the desk.

"Mr. Miller, are you okay?" I asked, moving to my knees on the floor beside him.

He groaned but didn't reply otherwise. Instead, he blinked rapidly and shook his head, as if to reboot himself from some unexpected shutdown.

Just then, the door to his office swung open and the efficient secretary who had earlier escorted me into the interview gasped.

"I think he's okay," I said.

4

"I'll get Manny," she said, though she stood frozen in the doorway. "And call 911."

That got another grunt out of Mr. Miller, along with a wave of his hand, which I took to mean he was trying to stop her from taking these actions. But she disappeared before he could make himself understood.

"Can I help you up?" I asked. He was still propped awkwardly on his side where he had fallen.

He nodded vigorously, and I reached down, slipping my arm under his. With considerable effort—I'm five foot five with decent curves while still being on the slimmer side, while he's at least six foot three and over two hundred pounds—I got him to his knees. Even during this brief moment, I could sense his discomfort at needing help. Like most men, he seemed proud and unaccustomed to asking for help. But really, I wasn't doing much. Just trying to get him into a position where he could have more control. It didn't occur to me that it might not have been the best reaction since he should have been evaluated by a medical professional. I just acted on instinct. The same could be said for why I reached out to smooth back his hair. It had gone askew during his fall, and I sensed he'd want to appear as put together as possible.

"Randall, are you okay?"

Mr. Miller and I both looked up to find Manfred Kahn, the sole remaining living partner in the firm, rushing toward us. I had released my hold on Mr. Miller, but we were now both on our knees, our bodies close, and I could feel the energy in the room change. It was so tense that it was almost hard to breathe. Mr. Miller stiffened, and I knew without having to examine this reaction that he was horrified that Kahn was seeing him this way.

"I'm fine," he said, though with a catch in his voice. He was still shaken by what had happened.

"Candace has called 911," Kahn said.

"I don't need paramedics," he replied gruffly. He looked like he wanted to say more but struggled to get the words out.

It pained me to see him so vulnerable, so mortified by this moment.

"It was silly," I blurted out and all eyes turned to me. "I tripped over my own two feet when I got up to shake Mr. Miller's hand." I forced a laugh. "And *bam*, I went flying right into the desk and knocked everything over. Can you believe that? Just my nerves, I'm sure. Anyway, Mr. Miller was kind enough to help me clean up the mess I made. That's all."

"Is that right, Randall?" Kahn asked. "Because Candace was pretty sure you ... *fainted*." Kahn's expression wasn't exactly the picture of concern. There was something much more like *hope* in his eyes. That kind of attempt to prey upon someone's weakness always makes my stomach turn.

Again, without thinking, I burst out into laughter. "Oh goodness, no," I said. "Mr. Miller was just being far too kind to me. I'm sure I've lost all chance at the position here now. I'm so sorry about all this fuss." I stood and before I could reach out to offer Mr. Miller my hand, he grabbed the edge of his desk and pulled himself to his feet with only a barely audible grunt.

"It's no problem, Miss Ruiz," he said, meeting my eyes. "Thank you for coming in today."

I saw genuine gratitude in his gaze. But then he looked away, addressing his secretary.

"Candace, why don't you tidy this up? I have a match at the club in half an hour. I have to get going."

I'm usually good at keeping my emotions under wraps, but

I don't think I did a good job at hiding my disappointment at that moment.

"You're sure everything is okay?" Kahn asked a little too eagerly.

"Perfectly fine," Mr. Miller replied with finality.

I nodded to myself, gathered my attaché case and purse and said quick, polite goodbyes to everyone before showing myself out.

Two days later, I got an offer from human resources. A *good* offer. I was dumbfounded, but not dumb enough to turn it down. It was three months of twelve to fourteen-hour days, six days a week of working at the firm before I had occasion to see Mr. Miller again. It was at one of the semi-regular office happy hours on a Friday evening. They were always casual affairs, designed mostly to throw the grunts like me a bone for working so tirelessly. The upper-level staff rarely attended. Partners *never* attended.

That is until Mr. Miller showed up. I watched him make perfunctory greetings to some of the other newbies before he reached me.

"Miss Ruiz," he began, "a pleasure to see you again."

"And you, Mr. Miller. How have you been?"

He hesitated, his intelligent gray eyes examining me for a moment. "Just fine."

I understood in that response that we were not to acknowledge his incident. That was perfectly fine with me. It had been awkward and stressful enough when it happened. If he was ready to act like I'd never witnessed his moment of weakness, then so be it.

"Glad to hear it," I said.

"Listen, I understand you speak Spanish. Is that right?"

That was a curveball I wasn't expecting. "Yes, I do."

"Perfect. I'm assembling a team for a case. We're meeting tomorrow morning at nine. I'd like you to join us."

"M-me?" I stammered. Like an idiot. But really, how was I to react when the senior partner of the law firm I had only barely started working for recruited me for his case team? This was less expected than that curveball. This was a knuckleball (yes, I'm a baseball fan).

"See you tomorrow, Miss Ruiz," he replied, clearly amused.

"Yes, sir. See you then."

"Girl, you have just landed the golden ticket," Tyler murmured, having sidled up to me. Like me, he was a first-year associate. We started the same week and almost immediately bonded over late-night takeout eaten at our desks as we commiserated over our lack of a love life, both of us longing for a boyfriend to go home to. In our fantasies, these boyfriends of ours would be waiting for us with a home-cooked meal and ready to rub our temples.

"Do you think?" I asked.

"I don't think. I know. Take it for all it's worth."

"Uh-huh," I said, my eyes still glued to the back of Mr. Miller's silver-haired head as he moved across the room.

"Oh, and if he needs someone who speaks gay, bring me in!"

I'd laughed distractedly, still not believing what had happened.

IT TURNED out that he really did need my Spanish skills for the case, a class-action lawsuit involving minimum-wage custodial workers who were being cheated out of their rightful overtime pay. It was a rare pro bono case, making it all that much more meaningful to work on. I put in even longer hours, wanting both to do a good job and to prove myself.

We were several months into the case prep when one night everyone else happened to peel away, leaving me alone with Mr. Miller. It was then that my fatigue got to me and I wondered out loud whether the Dodgers were winning. We got to talking about baseball and I confessed that my father had taken me—in the nosebleed seats, of course—to as many games as he could when I was growing up. When he asked if my father still took me, I admitted he passed away when I was thirteen. It might have been that moment of vulnerability that led him to explain what had happened in his office on the day of my interview. He shared with me that a combination of the flu he'd been fighting and plain old low blood sugar had weakened him. He hadn't wanted to admit to this because Kahn had been actively working to oust him and would have used this episode, no matter how temporary or innocuous, to argue to the board that he was incapable of remaining at the helm. It was then that he formally thanked me for the kindness—and the cover—I had given him. He'd beaten back both the illness and Kahn in part due to my help.

We got to be on a first-name basis after that. There was an unspoken trust and comfort level between us that led to him becoming both a mentor and a friend. We started having lunch together twice a month where we'd talk work and he'd help me navigate the politics of the firm as well as answer questions about the cases I worked on. He had me and my mom over to his house for dinners and other social affairs. Our lives became intertwined.

I know there are whispers around the firm that say I've risen in the ranks due to his favoritism, but I do my best to ignore all that and instead remember the countless hours of work I've put in.

Which brings me back to my current chore of counting the hours.

Not many people would consider going off the grid for a week in one of the world's most beautiful destinations an imposition, but I'm just not a get away from it all type of girl.

So, now I've got five days to somehow pass here in Maui before I can get home and back to work.

2

AVA

I t turns out that three days is my max for pure
relaxation. I did it all in that time: sunrise yoga on the
sand, snorkeling, a hike on a dormant volcano, a whale-
watching boat tour, drinking mai tais and eating mahi-mahi
for dinner, a massage at sunset, stargazing on the deserted
beach in the still-warm night.

And all the while, I thought a lot about what "forced" me
to be here. It was a combination of two mistakes I made: one
personal and one professional.

The personal one was how rashly I broke up with my
boyfriend of almost two years. Bryce was an attorney at a
different firm, ten years older than me, and had already established himself professionally. We met at a California Lawyers
Association event. After flirting while waiting in the long bar
line, later that night, we went to bed together. There was a
degree of convenience I think we both subconsciously understood right from the start. We had the same type of
demanding career that we'd made our sole priority. But we
still had needs. It was easy, if not romantic, to be together. We

saw each other sparingly as each other's date for job-related functions or evenings when we allowed ourselves time away from work. Those dates usually consisted of Netflix and chill.

Though our relationship seriously lacked romance, I still had feelings for him. He was entirely supportive of my work ambitions, for one. And ... we both enjoyed fine wine. That counted as an area of commonality, I told myself, though it was a reach.

At the same time, a part of me understood that I was settling. We weren't *really* friends. We were work confidants rather than emotional confidants. At best, we were a support system for one another. A convenient pairing. What I was doing, whether I consciously understood it or not, was creating the illusion of a connection instead of truly investing in one. It was safer than ... truly letting down my guard. Still, I'd convinced myself that this was enough, that surely, we'd eventually take our relationship to the next step and could have a solid, if not entirely enviable, marriage one day.

But that all changed a few months ago when on Christmas Eve, I'd gone with him to his sister's house. I'd only met his sister once before and we'd never spent the holidays together, especially not Christmas. It was a holiday I usually reserved for celebrating with my mom, but I knew I'd been especially unavailable in the weeks beforehand and thought it would be a good way to give a little.

It was a casual family affair—something I realized too late when I showed up in a form-fitting emerald-green cocktail dress and black heels—focused on a big meal, eggnog, and watching the kids parade around in their Christmas pajamas. As dessert was being prepared, Bryce took my hand and led me out onto the balcony.

His sister lived in a gorgeous modern house nestled into

the hillside off of Mulholland Drive that offered stunning views of the city of Los Angeles spread out in glittering fashion. The temperature was in the sixties, so not too chilly, but I was glad for Bryce's embrace as we stared at the lights of the houses, buildings, and traffic below us. I inhaled the comforting scent of fireplace smoke.

"They say," Bryce said, "that Christmas is the most popular holiday for proposing."

It felt like the temperature dropped twenty degrees because I was suddenly frozen in place. Was he really going to propose? Here at his sister's house? I was still tucked under his arm, my body pressed against his side. This was an awkward way to pop the question.

Before I could respond, he laughed. "Don't worry, I'm under no illusion that marriage is something you want."

"Oh?" I managed to say, my heart sinking in disappointment. I pulled away from him and took a step closer to the railing, trying to sort out his lack of sensitivity.

"It's ridiculous, right?" he said, joining me. "I mean, I know you're not the kind of woman who gets caught up in those kinds of societal expectations. And I'm actually happy that's the way you are. You don't feel the need to follow these silly cultural norms of scoring a big ring meant to symbolize the value a man has for a woman. Or having a flashy ceremony like so many women feel the need to have so they can show off like they've won some prize."

"Well, I don't know that a *flashy* ceremony would be needed—"

"See? I was right. We have it figured out. We don't need to change a thing, do we? Especially, with us not even having time to get together more than once or twice a week. Can you imagine taking the time to plan a wedding? And then what?

You'd sidetrack your career for kids? We both know that's never going to happen."

He laughed again, shaking his head at the notion.

It hurt to have him speak so dismissively of my ability to have both a career and a family. And yet, I couldn't deny that I knew where he was coming from. I'd spent the last six years single-mindedly devoted to my work. I regularly spent twelve hours a day at the office, six days a week. What free time I had, I spent visiting with my mother. But that didn't mean that I wasn't capable of figuring out the right balance ... one day. His disregard for this, on top of his surprising definition of marriage being all about the superficial—a big ring and a flashy ceremony—rather than a commitment made out of love, woke me to the realization that we were living in two different worlds.

It also made me realize that there was no point in being with someone who felt that way.

"You have no idea who I am," I said, almost absent-mindedly.

"What?" he asked with a laugh. He clearly thought I was toying with him.

"You don't know me. You don't know what I really want," I said.

The look of condescending amusement he gave me was a combination of the alcohol he'd already had and the arrogance I'd always generously excused as confidence.

"Don't I?" he asked with a suggestive grin, completely ignoring the gravity of what I had said as he pulled me to him, an arm around my waist. He always took an inordinate amount of pride whenever he satisfied me in bed. I mean, the sex was good, but it wasn't spectacular. He got the job done and no more, really. And now he seemed to want to try to shift our talk into an area where he thought he had the ability to please me.

Despite the hunger in his eyes, however, there was zero chance he'd be having sex tonight. At least not with me. My own eyes were wide open now to just how wrong he and I were together. And yes, I'll admit that my ego was also bruised. What those things added up to was that I couldn't let this relationship go on.

Just as I was ready to pull away and let him down gently, he tightened his grip around my waist and leaned his body against me.

"It's been too long," he said, kissing my cheek and neck.

"You don't know what I want," I told him again, wanting to return to what I'd said earlier, wanting him to acknowledge what I really meant.

His hand fell to my ass. "I'll give you anything you want, baby."

I pulled on his tie so that he leaned even closer to me. My breasts pressed against his chest and I could feel him starting to respond to our bodies being so close together.

I bit my lip seductively and asked, "Anything?"

That got a stupefied nod out of him.

That's when I released my hold on his tie and took a step backward. "What I *want* is what you can't give me."

Now my entirely serious tone got his attention. But he was mostly just confused, apparently unable to fathom what I was really getting at.

"What is it that you want, Ava?" he asked flatly.

"I want it all," I said, my voice barely a whisper. "I want my career and I want a fairy-tale love story. And I want someone who understands that."

That only further confused him. Once he realized I had no

intention of either sleeping with him or staying in a relationship with him and he lashed out.

"You are not the fairy-tale princess type," he said with a scoff. "You actually have to give a little to be in a relationship, you know?"

I've long known I'm not perfect. I clearly don't know how to create a work—life balance. But I've never thought that made me incapable or unworthy of one day finding it.

"You're wrong," I said. "I told you. You don't know me."

He raised his hands in defeat. "How could I, Ava? How could I when you never let me into your life?"

That might have been a valid point. Actually, in hindsight, it *was* a valid point. I hadn't given everything to him that I could have. But at that moment, I wasn't ready to admit it. Instead, I just shook my head. Then, I went inside and gave my sincere regrets to his family, saying I was sorry to cut the evening short, but I'd promised to take my mother to mass.

They didn't know that my mother isn't religious and that there was no mass planned, of course. How could they? They didn't know her. In truth, I'd never even introduced Bryce to her.

But I did go straight to her house in Boyle Heights, confess everything to her, and let her make it all better with her homemade pozole soup and *Tajin* popcorn.

MY MOTHER, Rafaela, is the one I always turn to. She's the kind of mother and friend everyone should have. She's that to our whole neighborhood. Though she works tirelessly to run her own house-cleaning business, she always has time to lend an ear or offer some comfort food to anyone in need.

And she's who I called on my third night in Maui when I couldn't take the isolation and lack of work engagement anymore.

"*Mija?*"

She sounds groggy. Shit. I remember too late that I'm running three hours behind Los Angeles time.

"I'm sorry, Mama. Go back to sleep. I'll call you tomorrow," I tell her.

"No, it's okay."

I can hear the rustle of bedding as she's likely sitting up.

"I forgot about the time difference. You need your rest. Go back to sleep." I know she'll be up at four thirty in the morning, just like she has for as long as I can remember. She doesn't just run her business, she's hands-on, and that means she's scrubbing bathrooms and kitchens alongside her staff, as well as sorting out the accounting, HR, and marketing. Not that she would ever define her job duties in that way. Her company isn't big. It's a handful of women who each give their all to clean four to five homes a day.

When I was growing up, my mother was a housewife but would do the odd job of cleaning houses for some side money. When my father passed away, the occasional job turned into a hustling full-time for as many houses to clean as possible. I was only a teenager at the time, but I understood, without her having to admit it, that we were in trouble financially. She also barely held on emotionally. She and my father were the perfect couple, so clearly in love, so clearly meant for each other. Her devastation was so great that it didn't leave room for me to dwell in my own sadness. Not when I instinctively knew I was the only thing keeping her going. I grew up fast, knowing I had to step in and get us through the roughest time of our lives.

When we decided to make a real business out of the housecleaning service, I suggested we target customers in San Marino, the wealthy enclave of Pasadena. With hard-working, reliable employees that provided impeccable services, she created a niche for herself in the area. She's also earned intense loyalty from her staff by paying them well.

That kind of selflessness is on display now as she says, "I'm awake, Ava. Tell me about your vacation."

There's no use in arguing with her. I got my stubborn streak from her, after all.

"What can I say? It's beautiful."

"But?"

Of course, she can hear the lack of enthusiasm in my voice.

"But, I'm going stir-crazy. I think I have island fever."

Mama stifles a laugh. "You've been there for three days, *mija*. Enjoy your time off."

"But all I want to do is log on to my work email and check on a few things—"

"You said Randall forbade you from doing that."

I sigh. "I know. But what if everything is falling apart? Shouldn't I at least take a quick look?"

"You mean you want to see how they're resolving the issue that sent you away."

Opening my mouth to speak, I think better of it and let the silence spread out between us.

"It's going to be okay," Mama says. "Everyone makes mistakes. From what you told me it wasn't all that big of a deal."

"*I* don't make mistakes, that's the thing. You're right, it is something that can be handled, but the fact that it ever even happened is what I can't get over."

"No one is perfect, not even you."

"I should have been perfect at that deposition, though. I could have been."

"Don't you think this is more to do with Bryce than some silly mistake?"

"Mama, no." I shake my head in frustration.

The fact is, I hadn't seen Bryce since I left his sister's house on Christmas Eve. I'd wanted to call him to try to smooth over the way I ended things, but the fact that he never reached out to me made me hold back. It proved our relationship amounted to nothing more than wasted time.

But then I came face-to-face with him at a client deposition. He hadn't been the attorney on record but was filling in for an ill colleague. That threw me, but worse still was the way he acted as if we didn't know each other. We'd always been professional whenever we crossed paths for work, but that didn't keep us from being friendly or even slipping each other a knowing wink or a whispered flirt. At that deposition, though, he was ice cold. It disturbed me enough that I fumbled during the testimony. I put our side at a disadvantage because my head was elsewhere. The worst part was I only realized my mistake when I saw the condescending smirk on his face.

Even though I've never admitted the effect he had on me that day, both my mother and my boss sensed the truth. Randall, kindly suggested I was overworked and sent me here to Maui, insisting that a change of scenery and the chance to decompress would work wonders.

"Okay, my girl," Mama says. "But maybe really give this time a chance to help you ... re-set?"

Though she can't see me, I nod. "I'll try."

"Call me again later?"

"Yes, of course. Get some sleep, Mama."

We say our goodbyes, and I stare at the walls of my hotel room. I'm staying at the Ritz-Carlton. It's a lovely place with stunning ocean views, luxurious appointments, and a sense that it's a haven away from the world.

I should love it.

Instead, I'm counting the hours until I can leave.

3

FORD

My phone's alarm goes off and I groan.

Yes, I'm the one who set the alarm. Yes, I actually do want to get up, so I can catch some waves. But, it's early. Like, still-dark early.

And my head is pounding. I might have had one too many shots of tequila last night. It felt good at the time, though. That fuzzy, happy oblivion of drunkenness—it was exactly what I needed to forget that my time's running out and I have to face the thing I've been avoiding for almost a year.

The second alarm I had set to make sure I didn't sleep after turning off the first alarm goes off.

Silencing it, I force myself to sit up. The shades in my tiny beach hut are closed and the space is darkened, but I can hear the waves. Those aren't the waves I set my alarm for, though. They're too small, too tame. No, I need to get my ass up, down some coconut water (the hangover cure I swear by), get in my truck and head over to Honolua Bay. That's where the waves are, the ones that can get up to twenty feet in the winter months. Though it's late March and I'm probably being overly optimistic that those kinds of big swells will still come through.

Maybe I can afford five more minutes before going I rationalize as I lie back down and close my eyes.

But the sleep I'd hoped to catch doesn't come. Instead, my thoughts are occupied by the trip to Los Angeles I'm going to have to make in a week. I haven't been to the mainland in a long while. No reason to go over there, not when I've got such a sweet setup here. I live in the most beautiful place in the world, I surf every day, and I have a low-pressure job I love. The only reason to go to LA is because I *have* to.

I don't mind being in the city itself, though the traffic is a waste of precious time. What I do mind is being under my father's control while I'm there.

My father, Ford McAvoy—*Senior*, thank you very much— is the most arrogant, controlling prick I've ever known. I still shake my head anytime I try to envision him and my mom together. She's his opposite in every way: sweet, thoughtful, and generous with her time.

They were only supposed to be a quick vacation romance. She was working in one of the resorts on Oahu the summer before her junior year at UC Berkeley. He was celebrating passing the bar with a dozen of his fellow law school buddies. They had a fling and, oops, I was the fruit of their indiscretion. When she tracked him down to tell him she was pregnant, he offered financial responsibility but straight out told her he had no interest in taking on parental responsibilities, not when he was about to get his career started. She opted to stay in Hawai'i, eventually moving to Maui where she set up a music school and taught local kids.

She raised me on her own, though her parents visited us often. The two of us loved the island life, even though our status as *haoles*, or non-natives, presented challenges now and again. I was one of those kids who ran around barefoot everywhere, was dirty more often than not, and learned to swim before I could walk. Learning to surf came only a few years later. I loved the freedom of it all.

But when I was twelve, my father had a change of heart and insisted that I be sent over to meet him. He wanted to get to know me after all these years. My mother would only agree to have me visit for two weeks in the summer and I went kicking and screaming. After all, this was a stranger I was being forced to meet. That's not to say I wasn't curious about the man whose good looks I was beginning to favor. It was a confusing mix of emotions, combined with the surging hormones of my age, and I couldn't help but be a brat to him the whole time. There was part of me that wanted him to abandon me all over again, just so I wouldn't have to deal with figuring out what he meant to me. His absence had never really bothered me. I didn't know anything else. And I always had my mom, and then later, her long-time boyfriend, too. They were the only steady, supportive presence I had while growing up, and I'd convinced myself that they were all I needed.

On my last night at my father's place in Brentwood, a posh suburb of Los Angeles, he took me to the backyard for a project he said he'd been meaning to get to ever since I'd gotten there. It was a model airplane. He wanted us to make it together.

Those kinds of crafts weren't my thing. I was an outdoors kind of kid. Give me the beach, a pool, a dirt bike for exploring trails, or a skateboard for trying tricks—anything where I could move, be active. Sitting in one spot for hours on end to painstakingly piece together tiny parts was not my idea of fun. I wasn't shy about voicing this opinion, either.

"You *will* sit here, and you *will* work on this until we are done," he said in his insistent way. "Understood?"

I'd been back talking him the whole trip. Maybe I'd just exhausted myself from the effort of it or maybe I figured I'd offer him a parting gift since I'd be leaving, but for whatever reason, I decided to do as he said.

Then, the weirdest thing happened. After almost forty-five minutes of working in near silence, he started to talk to me. Like, really talk to me. It wasn't the barking of orders like it had been for the last two weeks. It wasn't the disappointed-in-me instructions to tuck in my shirt or wipe the dirt off my face. It was him telling me a little about himself. About who he had been when he was my age. I was shocked to learn that he had the same sense of adventure that I did. He told me tales of spending all day getting lost in Griffith Park with his buddies, of biking in the Santa Monica Mountains, even of trying to learn to surf at Zuma Beach.

I saw him anew for those few hours we worked together. I thought, maybe he wasn't so bad. But as we were finishing up the plane, his real motives for the bonding session came to light.

He put his hand on my shoulder and said, "It was after that summer when I was about to turn thirteen that my father had this sort of talk with me."

I'd looked up at him, a sense of impending doom filling me. I couldn't know exactly what he was about to say, but I was certain that I wasn't going to like it.

"What I'm saying, Ford," he continued, "is it's time for you to buckle down. Now is the time when it starts to matter what kind of grades you get in school. Now is the time to start learning how to get on in polite society instead of running around like a feral animal." He paused here, squeezing my shoulder hard enough that I winced. "Now is the time for you to come live with me so I can assure your path in life."

I remember shaking my head but being unable to utter a word.

"Listen, I know you're full of all these ... *feelings* about me not having been around. But that time before, I couldn't have been of any use to a young kid. I had a career to start. I needed to dedicate myself to becoming something. And before you give me lip about the fact that I work for my father's firm, understand that there is tradition in that. It's important to maintain a line of succession when your family has built something of value."

"I don't want to live with you," I said.

He considered me for a moment, obviously less than impressed with the stubborn look on my face. "Well, it's not really up to you, is it?"

"My mom won't let me live with you."

"This is for your own good. You may not realize that right now. But by coming to live with me, you'll get the best of everything. The best schools, the best—"

"I won't leave my mom," I insisted.

He sighed, clearly out of patience. Arguing with a child, even his own, was a waste of his time. "Do you really want me to go through a protracted custody battle with your mother? Do you understand the toll that would take on her financially? It could ruin that little music school she has."

"You'd do that?" I asked, mouth agape.

"It's time, Son. It's time that I impose some discipline in your life. You need the kind of order and structure that I had at your age. It changed everything for me. Whereas once I was wild, I soon had a sense of direction. It was invaluable because it led me to become the man I am today."

"The kind of man who knocks up a random girl and leaves her on her own with a baby, you mean?" I muttered.

His hand flew at me before I could flinch. The smack across my mouth stung, but I didn't care. I wasn't going to let him think I believed his bullshit.

"That's the kind of attitude we'll rid you of," he said. "Now, you'll go back to Maui, but only long enough for you to collect your things so you can return here."

"I won't."

He leaned down to make eye contact with me. "Understand one thing, young man. *You* will destroy your mother's life by refusing this."

I looked up at him, my eyes shining against my will.

"Tears are for the weak. Remember that." He turned then to move back into the house.

Before he could disappear inside, I took the completed airplane and dropped it to the ground. The crunch of it under my foot was incredibly satisfying. But the fury on his face as he whipped back around to see what I had done was even better.

I wanted him to know that I'd never stop resisting him, that he'd never *tame* me.

And yet, I followed his plan of moving to LA, but only so that my mother wouldn't be crushed by legal bills. I went to a private boys' school and spent the first six months defying every authority around me. After realizing I was the only one suffering because of this attitude, though, I gave up and fell in line.

I made friends with the popular kids. I got into playing baseball, which my father loved because he had played in school, too. I studied, finding that a little went a long way as I was exceptional at picking up and retaining information if I put even minimal effort into it. By becoming more like the son my father wanted me to be, I earned the freedom to go to Maui for the summer. Soon, my "good behavior" meant I spent every single school holiday with my mom. I learned to straddle the two worlds, but the whole time I was just biding my time until I could make my own decisions.

Or so I thought. When I was almost sixteen, something shifted. I actually started to crave my father's approval. I think it started when he took me to the office for the first time. He worked long hours, which I'd always considered a blessing since it meant we didn't have to spend all that much time together. But the day he had me sit in his big leather wingback chair, I felt a sense of wonder at the grand space and furniture. He spread legal texts in front of me, having me read case law and quizzing me. To the astonishment of both of us, I answered every question correctly. It was then that he declared I had a photographic memory. He was so delighted with this that it made me feel … special. I felt special to him for the first time in my life. When he started talking about me one day joining the firm to carry on the family practice, I was suddenly eager to please him. Another thing that happened for the first time in my life.

After that, I still went home to my mom whenever I could, but I also stepped up my studies. I had a mission. I wanted to burn through high school and college to get to law school. I wanted to be a part of my father's plan.

I got through all that schooling and took the bar. I worked at that stuffy law firm for almost four years before I snapped, walking away from it all and moving home to Maui. My mom's boyfriend lets me stay in this place. It's not much more than a shack, but it's on the beach and gives me a roof over my head in between bouts of surfing.

That was a year ago.

I've been content during this time. Just living in the moment. Just living for me. Just trying to get back to who I used to be … before I bought into my father's expectations.

But now I've got the trip to L.A. looming over my head.

There's only one thing that will take my mind off this sense of dread. I haul myself to my feet, stretch the kinks out of my body, and reach for coconut water. It's time to catch some waves, time to think about nothing but the sweet ride of the water.

4

AVA

I'm awake before sunrise. It's still relatively cool, so I put on my running gear and hope that the exercise will shake the restlessness I haven't been able to dispel since I got here.

By the time I make it to the Kapalua Coastal Trail, the sun has risen enough to ensure my run along the volcanic rock path is safe. The air smells sweet, and the water is the deepest blue. When the waves crash against the cliffside, the white-wash splashes up and glitters in the morning light. Even though I'd still rather be back at work, I do appreciate the beauty and tranquility of this spot.

After I've run the entire route, about four miles round trip, I stop and take advantage of a natural formation that works as a chair. I sit and stare out at the ocean for a long while. The regret I have for how impulsively I broke up with Bryce is something I can live with. I don't want him back. I just wish I had dealt with it better. It's the mistake I made at work that bothers me more. My instinct is to redouble my efforts, to work even harder. But there's a part of me that isn't sure that will get me what I need. Because I'm starting to understand that I need some kind of change in my life. I've finally begun to think I need a *real* life. One that is about more than work.

I just don't know if I'm even capable of opening myself up to that.

AFTER SHOWERING and grabbing a quick breakfast of local fruits and coffee, it's still only seven o'clock. That means another long day stretches out in front of me.

Before I can convince myself otherwise, I call for my rental car at the valet and set off in search of a store to buy a laptop, not even thinking of the fact that such stores wouldn't be open at this hour.

A working vacation is better than nothing, I rationalize as I fiddle with the GPS. I'm not all that far from the hotel when I realize I've started in the wrong direction. I have to go several miles more before I can find a spot to make a U-turn. Just as I get going on the road that will lead me to some kind of civilization, a chicken appears in front of me.

Yes, a chicken.

Tons of wild chickens roam all over the island, and everyone just lets them be. It's a little weird.

This particular chicken startles me so much that I slam on the brakes and swerve onto a dirt road, not wanting to hit it. Coming to a stop, I try to catch my breath. My adrenaline is pumping.

Over a chicken.

Laughing, I shake my head.

Once more, however, I need to find a spot to turn around. I slowly continue down the rust-colored dirt path. The road isn't wide enough to make an easy turn, so I keep going, hoping it will open up. On either side of the road, tall green grass cast golden by the morning sunlight, waves in the breeze. It feels like it's just me out here, and for a moment, I don't mind. I don't think about my mission to go find a laptop. I don't think about how much longer I *have* to stay on vacation. I don't think about the mistakes I made. Instead, I roll down my window and put my arm out, letting my fingers graze the tips of the grass as I go unhurriedly by.

It's a fleeting moment of peace because soon I've come to the end of the path. It overlooks the ocean from at least two stories above and is a breathtaking vista. I drag my eyes away from the expansive blue water and realize the area has opened up with plenty of room to make a U-turn, even with the handful of other cars parked here.

Deciding I'd better use this opportunity to get a better sense of where I'm going, I park the car, grab my cell phone, and step out. The salty air is humid as I watch the scattering of surfers down below. A few of them catch a long, rolling wave, but most hold back. It's hard to tell from here whether the waves would be considered "good." What I can see is that there are a lot of rocks, even a large outcropping, that must be avoided. It looks dangerous, leading me to think that the surfers must be well experienced if they're out there.

Turning to my phone, I quickly find that I have absolutely no service. I fiddle with it anyway, hoping that if I angle it one way or the other, I'll get a couple bars. Nothing. Desperate, I hold it up over my head and wave it around a little.

"If you add a little hula dance, it just might work."

I gasp at the suggestive words directed at me, turning to find a grinning man to my left. It takes me a second to realize how foolish I had probably looked as I contorted to try to find a signal on my phone and that this stranger is teasing me over it.

Check that.

This *gorgeous* stranger.

The man is tall with lean, sculpted muscles straining against his thin T-shirt, a chiseled jaw lightly covered by the scruff of a beard, and defined cheekbones. His skin is tan, his eyes are pale brown with gold flecks, and his medium-brown hair is on the shorter side and untamed. But it's his playful smile that does me in. And it's the upturn at one corner of his mouth that has me wanting to taste his lips.

There's an expression in Spanish that perfectly captures how positively delicious someone like him is: *Es un mango.*

He's a mango. A sweet, *juicy* fruit.

"I was just playing," he says, thankfully pulling me from my completely inappropriate thoughts. "Odds are good you won't be able to use that thing out here, though. You need help with something?"

Uh, yeah, I need help. I need help pulling my tongue up off the dirt and back into my mouth. Figuratively, at least. He is objectively one of the finest men I've ever seen. And he's left me speechless. I realize I must look like one of those hyper-dramatic actresses in a telenovela, at a loss for words when faced with a handsome stranger. I remind myself that I'm a thirty-year-old attorney and that I need to snap out of it.

"No, no thank you," I say, standing taller. "I'm fine."

"You sure about that? You really seemed to want to get that phone to work."

God, even his voice is sexy. It's deep, but with a hint of raspiness.

I can't remember the last time I was so intensely attracted to someone. It sure wasn't like this with Bryce. I mean, he checked all the boxes: handsome, smart, in great shape. But there was no real *heat* between us.

And even though this stranger is still eyeing me with amusement, waiting for me to answer and probably thinking I'm some sort of flaky weirdo, *heat* is exactly what I feel between us.

"I, um," I start. "I was on my way into town, actually. But one of those crazy chickens ran me off the road, and I turned down here sort of by accident."

He laughs, but it doesn't feel like it's at my expense. Not when his eyes are so warm, his expression so open. There's something both boyish and world-weary about him. The combination doesn't make sense, but it is incredibly compelling.

"Yeah, those chickens don't exactly follow the rules of the road. But that's a good thing for you, isn't it?"

A red flag goes up with that last comment. It makes me think he's about to give me some obnoxious come-on line about how that chicken running me off the road brought me to him and doesn't that make me a lucky little lady?

"How's that?" I ask, a challenge in my voice.

"If it weren't for that crazy chicken, you may have just blown on by and never seen one of the most beautiful parts of Maui," he says with a grin.

"Oh." I feel foolish for presuming ill intent from him.

"This is Honolua Bay. If you go down that way a bit more, you can find a rad jungle trail to the water. But it's pretty rocky and not that easy to get into the water. Once you do, though, if you swim out past the shallow, you'll find a snorkeling paradise."

"Is that what you're doing here?"

"Nah. I'm here to hopefully catch some waves." He glances

over my shoulder at the water, and I can tell he's anxious to be in it.

"Don't let me stop you."

His eyes drift back to mine. And then they slide downward, surveying me. Every inch of me.

The gauzy white slip dress I'd thrown over my ruby-red bikini falls short against my thighs. I've always thought that my legs, shaped by the quick, high-intensity runs I squeeze into my schedule whenever possible and accentuated by wedge sandals, are one of my best features. By the way this gorgeous stranger is eyeing me, he would seem to agree.

"Listen, uh, I'd invite you to join me in the water down there," he says, tearing his eyes from me, "but it's not the best place for a casual swim."

"That's okay. I'm sort of on a mission, anyway."

"Right. You said you were headed to town?"

"Yeah. I'm desperate to buy a laptop. I need to check in on a case."

"A case? That sounds like lawyer-speak. God, I hate lawyers," he says absently and I cringe. Thankfully, he doesn't notice, as his eyes have once more been drawn to the water below. "Uh, you're not a lawyer, are you?"

"A lawyer? Me? No. Um, nope." Why I felt the instinct to lie to him baffles me, but there it is.

"Oh, good." He graces me with that crooked grin once more. "Well, Hula Girl, good luck with your mission."

"Thanks." That one word trails off prematurely as I watch him pull his T-shirt off, revealing a chest that makes my mouth water. It's smooth, except for ridges of muscles. The exquisite definition I noticed earlier in his arms is matched on his torso and even down to his hips where his black and gray swim trunks are slung low enough to showcase a perfect V.

He turns to the bed of a Chevy pickup truck that has seen better days and pulls a surfboard from it.

I hesitate longer than I should before forcing one foot in front of the other toward my rental car.

"Oh, hey," he calls out.

I whip around to face him once more.

"There's a little place, a locals' place for food and drinks, called Makai's. I'll be there tonight after eight. Why don't you stop by? That is if the chickens don't run you off the road."

His smile is a tease. A flirt. An invitation.

It makes me melt like a teenager. I struggle not to show the effect he has on me.

Clearing my throat, I give him a noncommittal shrug. "Maybe."

He nods before securing the surfboard under his arm and making his way barefoot down a barely defined red-dirt trail.

Instead of going my own way, I edge closer to the cliffside, watching his descent. It's not an easy path, but he manages to glide down. Within minutes, he's reached the water's edge and has carefully climbed onto the rocky entry, finding just the right spot to drop his surfboard before diving in after it.

Now that I have the perspective of watching someone in particular, rather than random bobbing figures, I realize that the waves are big. Bigger than any I've ever seen in person. My gorgeous stranger soon mounts his board and rides a glassine wave with ease, though. He navigates the rocky shoreline as if by instinct, dropping off the board before he gets too close to danger. I spend the next twenty minutes transfixed by his grace in the water, enjoying what appears to be his natural talent for surfing.

But then he looks up and spots me. He's straddling his board, in a lull between waves. I can see his grin even from this distance, and I'm mortified to have been caught watching him. He, however, seems amused as he raises a hand and flashes the hang loose sign.

I finally turn away, wondering what I was doing staring at this surfer boy.

Time to focus once more on my mission.

5

FORD

Hula Girl.

The spur of the moment nickname, inspired by the way the stranger's hips twisted and swayed as she made a ridiculous attempt to find some bars on her phone, had amused me.

Telling her to add a hula dance to get a better signal was just me being me. I've never been good at listening to that inner voice. You know, the one that warns you to shut up before saying something inappropriate, or walk away from a contentious argument, or pass up a pretty girl.

But any amusement fell away the second she turned to me on that cliff at the top of Honolua Bay. In its place was something ... overpowering.

Talk about attraction. Man, there's no doubt in my mind that something pulled us together. It was like a magnetic force that I couldn't resist. Even if I wanted to.

How could I walk away from Hula Girl, anyway, when she was so obviously giving me the once over with those dark, sparkling eyes.

At the same time, I felt an underlying sense of danger in our mutual attraction. Because let's face it, when did that kind of heat between two people ever do anything but burn them?

And I almost let it go. I *almost* just wished her good luck and went on my way to catch some waves. But before I could move on, I went and invited her here, to Makai's. It's almost nine o'clock and I'm still alone, but the fact that she stayed and watched me catch waves makes me think she'll be here soon.

"Makai," I call out to the one-man owner-bartender-waiter. "One more, yeah?"

Makai gives me the dead-eye stare he's so good at and hauls himself to his feet. His place is one of those side-of-the-road kinds of establishments that if you blink, you'll miss it as you drive by. But it's worth stopping for the chill atmosphere, the cheap drinks, and the incredibly fresh poke. Plus, Makai doesn't care if I hang out with my buddies for hours on end or if I bring my acoustic guitar with me. He'd never admit it, but I think he likes having me around.

"No friends tonight, then?" he asks as he places a fresh shot glass of tequila in front of me.

"They had other plans," I reply.

"Your guitar have other plans, too?"

I laugh at the implication that I've got nothing to offer if I'm not bringing in my friends to spend money or my guitar to entertain him.

"Next time, Makai." Using my foot, I push out the chair opposite mine. "Join me."

"No can do."

"Why not?"

"Wouldn't be professional."

Again with the dead-eye stare. But there's just the slightest upturn at the corner of his mouth. I laugh again and shake my head.

I'm about to go at him over this weak excuse when the door opens and Hula Girl steps into the tiny place. Five groupings of tables for four guests each line one wall and a long countertop serving as a bar fills out the other wall. There are a couple of other regular customers, but Hula Girl's eyes go straight to mine.

And I feel that same thing again. That *pull*.

With her long, straight hair down and falling across her tawny, bare shoulders, she's a stunner. She's wearing a little strapless dress, the coral color contrasting with her dark eyes and thankfully showing off those legs once more. Don't get me wrong, I love—no, *adore*—every part of a woman's body, but I've always been a sucker for nice legs.

I force my eyes away from her lower half in time to see the second thoughts mapped out all over her pretty face. She probably envisioned this as a rowdy bar she could scope out before making it known that she had taken me up on my invitation. We're strangers to each other, after all. But this place is the exact opposite of that. There's nowhere to hide.

Before she can turn on her heel, I stand.

"Chickens stay out of your way this time?" I ask with a grin.

There's a moment of hesitation before she seems to decide to give me a chance. It's what I'd hoped would happen by bringing that up. When she smiles, I have final confirmation of what I'd suspected earlier: There is something irresistible about this girl. I know it by the way I'm suddenly desperate for her to stay, by the way I want her to get close enough to me so that I can tell whether she's wearing perfume, by the way I've lost sight of anyone else in this place. It's a strong reaction. I don't usually respond to women like this. I'm usually a take 'em or leave 'em kind of guy. I just don't tend to get invested in women, as some of my ex-girlfriends would likely say in a more accusatory way. But this thing with Hula Girl feels different.

"Glad you came," I tell her when she joins me at my table. "What's your drink? Me, I'm having tequila. It's the sipping kind. Good stuff. Not that trash you have to throw back in a hurry."

She eyes me for a minute. "I do like good tequila."

I gesture for her to take the chair I'd offered Makai. When she sits, I push my shot glass in front of her and ask Makai for another. He grumbles and waves at me dismissively but ambles over to fill my order once more.

"So," I say, "mission accomplished?"

She gives me a blank stare. "What?"

"You said this morning you were on a mission. To buy a laptop?"

"Oh, right." She shakes her head. "I decided that the chicken running me off the road was a sign reminding me to, you know, *be* on vacation, not work. So, I didn't end up going to town after all."

"I have the feeling that was the right decision."

"What makes you say that?"

"Nobody should be as wound tight as you were this morning."

When she laughs this time, it's more out of disbelief than humor. Like I said, I should probably know better when to hold back. It's just not in my nature, I guess.

"Well, that's an interesting way to welcome a girl. Call her uptight?"

Thankfully, she seems more amused than angry. And

better yet, Makai interrupts the moment by setting down another shot of tequila.

"Poke?" he asks gruffly.

Hula Girl looks confused.

"Are you hungry?" I ask.

"I, um—" she starts before Makai interrupts.

"I'll bring two."

She watches as he shuffles away.

"Don't worry about him," I say. "What he lacks in charm, he makes up for in poke."

Laughing, she asks, "What *is* poke?"

"Oh, my dear Hula Girl. Are you ever in for a treat if you've never had poke before. Makai's version will knock your"—I pause to look at her feet under the table—"sandals off. You'll be ruined for any other poke after this."

"I still don't know what you're talking about, Surfer Boy."

I like that she's given me a nickname in return. Makes me think we're off to a nice start. "It's fish. Some of the freshest tuna you'll ever have. It comes with rice and vegetables and an umami sauce that you'll crave for weeks afterward."

"You certainly know how to talk things up. First the tequila, now this?"

I shrug. "It's just about appreciating the simple things."

"Next, you'll tell me you're just living 'one wave at a time,' right?"

I laugh. "Pretty much."

"How old are you?"

The question throws me for a second. "Twenty-seven. And you?"

"Thirty."

"Cheers to that," I say, raising my glass.

She fights a smirk before knocking her glass against mine.

We both take a sip and I watch as she slowly closes her eyes, savoring the rich, sweet agave of the tequila.

"Good, right?"

When she looks at me again, her eyes have lost the wariness she had when she first arrived. While she might not be completely relaxed, she's definitely not wound as tight as she was this morning. Then she takes another sip and I know we're heading in the right direction.

"So, you appreciate the simple things," she starts, and I can hear a challenge in her voice.

I smile, up for whatever she might throw my way. "I do."

"That includes surfing, poke, and tequila."

"Exactly."

"And flirting with tourists?"

I raise my eyebrows, not sure how to respond.

She laughs. "It's okay if that's your game. I'm not bothered. I figured as much when you invited me out here."

"Figured what exactly?"

"That you've got a pretty good deal for yourself. I'm guessing it's not too hard to hook up with your pick of women."

"No use in arguing with you," I tell her, mostly to get a rise. I'm not above the odd one-night stand with a pretty tourist I might meet at one of the bars in town. But I've never invited anyone here. This is my local place for hanging with my buddies or just on my own.

"Didn't think so," she says with a self-satisfied nod.

I squint, appraising her. She carries herself with sophistication and self-assurance. I can tell that she's clever, that in her "real" life, she's probably someone to be reckoned with. All of which is why I decide to turn the tables on her and make light of her accusation that I'm some kind of player on the prowl.

"How do *I* know *you* didn't go to Honolua Bay looking for a local surfer to flirt with?"

"What?" When she laughs, her dark eyes sparkle with amusement. It's such a pretty sight.

"I've heard about you tourists. You know, the ladies who scope out us vulnerable islanders to keep you warm at night."

Now she's appraising me, her smile lingering. Then she picks up her glass and raises it up for a toast. "Cheers to that," she says.

Damn, if I'm not lost in her for a second. I love the way she just acknowledged this attraction we've got going. She's not going to bullshit me. She's not going to play any games. I tap my glass to hers and when we each raise our glasses to our lips, we keep eye contact. I can *feel* the heat between us. I've never wanted to be this close to an open flame before.

"So, you're on vacation here?" I ask.

She nods, playing it cool.

"I suppose you've done all the expected things? Luau and such?"

"Ah, no. I did a lot of the usual sightseeing, but that one just seems like a tourist trap," she says dismissively.

"There are some good things about luaus."

"Such as?"

"Well, if you went to one that truly focused on the tradition behind it, you'd see that it's a celebration of music and food. The authentic food is amazing. Like kalua pork that's been buried and roasted overnight in the beach, fresh poi—that's taro root—local purple sweet potatoes, and even poke. Most kids have one for their first birthday and then it keeps on going for other milestones. It's a really cool way to share stories and catch up with the community."

There's a new sense of appreciation in her eyes. I'm glad to have enlightened her. Hawai'i has become such a cliché for so many people that they lose sight of the basis for all those tourist things they've come to roll their eyes at.

"And I suppose you can enlighten me on what hula is really about, too?"

"Besides being hella sexy, you mean?"

She laughs. "Yes, besides your peculiar fixation on that point."

I laugh. "Well, it's definitely more than all the cheesy tourist versions would have you believe. There's Hula Kahiko, the ancient style, and Hula Auana, the modern style, that would be more familiar to you now. The first one was an homage to the gods and tells the stories of Hawai'i. But they say it was only danced by men. So, you can guess that I'm a bigger fan of the second one."

She laughs. "Somehow not surprised."

I give her a wink. "Exactly. So this modern version is less religious but still tells stories about Hawai'i. And it's got more westernized music and singing. And it's a bit more ... sensual. At least by my take."

She raises her eyebrows at this last bit but holds back any comment. I get lost in her sparkling brown eyes for a moment. There's a tease in her gaze. And something more alluring. I like it.

"So, are you vacationing on your own? No boyfriend?" I ask.

"Um, no. Not at the moment."

"I bet you won't be single for long."

"Why do you say that?"

"You're beautiful. You're smart. You're fun. I bet you get hit on all the time."

"No, not really."

"Because you close yourself off?" I ask, examining her.

"Yeah, I could see that. Some guys don't like to put in the effort to get past the don't-fuck-with-me vibe some girls project."

"I don't think I—"

"Doesn't bother me, Hula Girl. Shouldn't keep any real man from wanting to get past it."

"And you're a *real* man, I suppose?"

I know how to take an opening when I see one. I lean forward, level my eyes on her, and put on the intense expression I know women usually fall for. "You better believe it, honey."

She takes that in and smiles appreciatively at me. We stew for a minute in this magnetic thing we've got going until Makai interrupts to offer us a refill on our drinks and I readily accept. She doesn't seem to mind as we then drink quietly for a time, content to just be while we take sips. Eventually, her eyes drop from mine and she turns contemplative.

She murmurs something but I can't quite catch what she's saying.

"What's that?"

She looks startled by my query as if she hadn't meant to say anything out loud just now. "Oh. Um, my father. I was just thinking he would have appreciated this."

"Would have?"

Taking a deep breath, she nods. Her expression has morphed into something different. It's gone sad, regretful. "He's passed away."

"Oh, I'm so sorry."

"It was a long time ago."

I shake my head. "You don't have to say that."

"Say what?"

"Qualify that it was a long time ago. He was your father. You *lost* your father. That loss isn't made any easier by the fact that it was a long time ago."

Her eyes tear up, which wasn't what I'd intended. I meant to honor the place he would always have in her life, rather than let her think she needed to dismiss the subject altogether.

"Hey," I say, leaning over the table, "tell me about him. What was he like?"

"Um, you don't really want to—"

"I do. Tell me one thing, at least."

She takes a moment to think about my request and then a beautiful smile transforms her face. I can't help but mirror it in return.

"He was a *huge* baseball fan. He made me into one, too."

"Dodgers?"

"Of course," she replies with a laugh. Her eyes go distant as she seems to replay memories in her mind. "When I was really little, he'd sit me on his lap and we'd watch games on TV. Or sometimes, we'd just listen to Vin Scully make the call on the radio. But the best times were when he'd take me to the stadium—up in the nosebleed seats."

I nod. "But it wasn't about the seats, was it?"

Her eyes come into focus as she looks at me again. "No, it wasn't."

"It was about the shared experience."

"Exactly." There's a kind of relief in her voice now, as if me understanding this bond she had with her father gives her some kind of peace. "We always wanted the Dodgers to win, but even if they didn't, watching the game together was really about having that time that was just ours. Sometimes we talked about other things like school or which boy was picking on me on the playground. And other times, we didn't talk about anything other than baseball. But I always came away feeling better. Feeling more secure." She takes a deep breath. "I haven't been back to a game since he passed away. But I still love the sport. He left me that."

"Sounds like a really good dad, if you ask me."

She nods, and a wistful, sweet expression follows. "What about you?"

"Me? I love baseball. I played first base in high school. We were state champions, in fact."

"That's awesome. But I meant, do you have a good dad, too?"

I knew that was what she meant but had hoped to slip out of any talk of my father. I know I could find a way to avoid it, but for some reason, I opt to be brutally forthcoming.

"No, I grew up without a father," I tell her. "He knew about me, but he wasn't interested in being around. Him not being around was all I knew, so I didn't dwell on it too much. But, honestly, that didn't mean it wasn't hard."

That hangs in the air for a long second as I realize I've just said far too much. I want to change the subject, but she speaks before I have a chance.

"Well, I know one thing," she says.

"What's that?"

"You must have been raised by a strong woman."

I laugh. "I was, for sure. My mother is the best person I know."

"Mine is that for me. She's my best friend. There isn't anything I wouldn't do for her."

"Yeah, I know the feeling." I don't elaborate, but I get the sense that she understands that I truly mean this, especially when she tells me more.

"I was thirteen when my dad died," she says. "It was sudden. We were pretty much financially fucked."

I grimace, not at the profanity, but because of how much I identify with her financial straits. Everything always comes down to money.

"She was devastated by her grief," she continues. "I was, too, of course, but she needed me. So, I stepped in to help. Sort of by sheer force of will, I figured out what needed to happen for us to survive. I suppose I've been 'wound tight' ever since."

Though she laughs, the throwback to how I described her stings. "I didn't mean—" I start.

She holds up a hand. "It's okay. I get what you meant. I know I can seem closed off." She laughs ruefully. "My ex would agree with you wholeheartedly on that."

"Oh, jeez," I say, "I really didn't mean to be such a dick. Listen, I'm sorry I said any of that."

"Don't worry about it."

"But I am worrying about it. I sometimes don't know when to shut my mouth. I'm sorry about what I said."

She meets my eyes for a long, silent moment. And then I see a shift in her gaze. It's the moment where she's decided she's done talking about it because she says, "Maybe we can drop the heavy conversation? I'd love to just ... have fun."

Though I absolutely enjoyed our brief back and forth sharing session, I'm glad to do as she asks. "Of course. Whatever you want, Hula Girl."

She laughs. "I like the no-names thing, too. That sets the right tone."

"Two poke," Makai announces, dropping our bowls down on the table unceremoniously.

We share a look before laughing at Makai's interruption. When she smiles, her eyes brighten. That I have the power to make that happen gives me a thrill—and makes me want to do it again. And again.

What is it about her?

I can't say. All I know is that I'm glad she got lost this morning.

And that I found her.

6

AVA

The more tequila I have, the more I enjoy the fact that I don't know Surfer Boy's real name. As we eat and drink and chat, I realize the lack of a proper name is giving us permission to do what we really want: flirt until we can acceptably leave this place—together.

The poke was just as he described. I declared myself obsessed after the second bite and he was delighted. We've each had another serving of tequila. Make that two servings each. Makai, as Surfer Boy calls him, eventually just leaves the bottle on our table.

I drag my finger over the ornate bottle of Dos Artes Reserva Especial. "You're right. It's good. Smooth." Like your muscles, like your tanned skin, I almost add. He's just as gorgeous in this dim light as he was in the bright morning sunshine.

"Goes down easy," he says, his voice just a touch lowered for effect.

I'm surprised to feel myself blushing and the innuendo. I've never been shy about sex. That coquettish, girly thing of pretending I don't really like sex just isn't me. I definitely like sex. It's a shame that I've been so busy working the last few years that I haven't had nearly as much of it as I'd like, in fact. But the naked lust in Surfer Boy's eyes takes me aback. There's no doubt that we're in tune with how much we want each other.

"I'll have to get some of this in LA," I say.

"When do you head back?" he asks. He's leaning on his hand, elbow on the table, watching me languidly. Not that I think he has any other mode. He's relaxation personified. The prototypical surfer dude. I can't imagine *he's* ever been wound tight in his life.

"Three days, not counting the day I leave."

"What made you vacation on your own?"

"Nothing *made me* do anything," I say with a laugh. But that's a lie. The truth is that Randall made me come here. But I can't go into that because I've already lied and said I wasn't a lawyer. "I actually haven't had a real vacation in six years. This was overdue."

"Six years? What kind of job do you have that's kept you from vacationing for six years?"

Whoops. I scramble to think what I can tell him. I consider saying I'm the owner-operator of the house cleaning business that is actually my mother's. But I don't want to lie to him any more than I already have.

Instead, I swallow, and say, "Let's leave the 'real world' out of this ... thing we've got going here."

He watches me appreciatively. "I can do that. I happen to be really good at—how did you describe it? Living one wave at a time?"

I wince. "Sorry. That was a total oversimplification, wasn't it?"

"Nah. You're right, I'm just a surfer boy," he says with a laugh.

"No other ambition?"

"I've had my fill of ambition. But that's a whole other story. One that belongs in that real world we're ignoring."

That bit of information intrigues me. He's hinted that he is more than he appears to be but, like me, he doesn't want to talk about what all that entails.

"Look at us. Just a couple of mysterious strangers," I tease.

He squints just slightly at me. "I suppose you're right. But, at the same time, you don't feel like a stranger to me at all."

"I, uh." I stop, stumbling over my tongue as I realize he's right. He doesn't feel like a stranger to me either, no matter how I've danced around the truth. There's something about him that feels comforting, welcoming. So much so, that I told him about my father. I never talk about my father. "Well, tequila does seem to make people extra friendly."

With a knowing nod, he says, "Uh-huh," as if dismissing my weak effort to explain away our connection.

"So, you've lived here all your life?" I ask, trying to steer us into different, more banal territory. I'm not ready to accept, let alone admit, that he and I have anything more than a random hookup in the making.

"Pretty much. I'm considered a *local haole*."

"What does that mean."

"White boy," he says. "But one who has been accepted for the most part."

"Only for the most part?"

"Now, it's all good. When I was a kid, it wasn't always so easy. Can't blame locals for having some resentments after the way their culture and sovereignty were subjugated."

I raise my eyebrows. Not at the characterization of how

Hawaiians were mistreated, but at his vocabulary. My Surfer Boy doesn't seem so uncultured himself.

"But you're saying you took the brunt of some of those resentments?" I ask.

He shrugs. "There was a time where I really felt like an outcast, to be honest. I got run off from the beach, run off the road while riding my bike, threatened at school. Then I got in with some friends who were real locals. Good guys. That helped a lot."

"And how long have you been surfing?"

"All my life, basically. I grew up sort of wild, always on the hunt for adventure. Riding waves is the biggest, best adventure I could find."

"Those waves this morning looked really big. You must be good."

He hesitates, leveling his eyes on me in a way that is so sensual it makes me shift in my seat.

"I'd say I am."

I feel my cheeks burning again and I wish I could wave it away. He does something to me whether I like it or not.

Thing is, I suspect I do like the effect he has on me. *A lot.*

"You should come out with me to see for yourself," he adds.

"*With* you?" I ask, confused by the offer.

"Yeah, I can use a longboard and help get us up on a wave. We could ride it ... together."

I'm lost for a moment in his gold-flecked eyes, my mind caught on the way he said *ride*. And then I laugh, realizing I've been played. "God, that must work so well with the pretty tourists."

He looks offended and I wonder whether I've gotten

things all wrong. But then he smiles in that gorgeous crooked way of his, making me want to bite his bottom lip.

"What I really prefer," he says, leaning toward me over the table again, "are hula girls."

It's a good save and I let him have it. "I'm not sure I have the proper moves of a hula girl."

"Oh, I think you do." His gaze is pure sexual suggestion. "Why don't you test it out."

"Here?" I look around and focus on the fact that Makai is chatting with someone at the end of the bar but also glancing our way.

"Would you rather get out of here?"

"And go where?" Yes, I want to go to bed with him. I want it so much, in fact, that I'm aching for some kind—*any* kind—of touch by him. But I'm not above also wanting him to work a little harder before that happens.

"Uh," he says, hesitating. He's trying to read me, to see if I'm putting him off. "Just down the road, there's a little inlet to the beach. It's a full moon. We can test those hula moves by the water."

I make a show of considering this idea before gesturing at the tequila. "Take the bottle with us?"

He looks at me, squinting slightly with amusement and delight. "Hell, yeah," he says with a sexy grin.

7

AVA

The thing about island life is that it gets *really* dark at night. It's the kind of dark that I never experience in LA where light pollution makes this kind of stargazing impossible. Even with a full moon, I'm enamored by the blanket of stars in the sky.

Surfer Boy grabs my hand to keep me from wandering in the wrong direction as we cross the road. When he doesn't let me go once I've lowered my eyes to pay attention to where we're going, I don't mind. His hand is large, easily enclosing mine and feels good.

When he steers us off the road, toward the ocean, the rocky path makes me hesitate. He's already gone ahead, somehow navigating his way in flip-flops with ease. Turning back, he looks up at me. It's only three or four feet down, but it feels like more.

"This is it," he says, holding out his hand to me. "Come on, Hula Girl."

"I feel like I'm going to break my ankle on those rocks."

"It's fine. It's not as scary as it looks. I just did it, right? You can do it."

I take one tentative step and feel my foot roll. "Nope, not going to work."

"Come here, I'll help you."

He steps as close as he can to me while still standing on the sand. But it feels awkward.

Taking my hand, he looks me in the eye and says, "I got you."

Why I should trust him the way I do when he says this is beyond me. But in the end, I fall into him and he catches me, wrapping one arm around my waist and the other holding me tight just under my butt. As his grip loosens and my body slides downward against his, my mouth falls open as I register the heat of him against me. Once I'm on my feet, he doesn't pull away. Neither do I. Instead, we stand like that, our bodies touching, looking into each other's eyes, his arms still around my waist. My breathing has quickened just being this close to him. I swallow hard to try to contain myself.

But, god, he's just so *hot*.

He leans even closer to me, lowering his face to mine. I can smell the soap on his skin, the tequila on his lips. With his strong arms around me, the sound of the gentle tide, and the moonlight, it's an intoxicating moment. Just as I start to close my eyes in anticipation of his kiss, I see movement out of my peripheral vision that startles me.

"What was that?" I ask, pulling away.

Following my gaze, he smiles. "Turtles."

"What?" I wonder if I've had too many sips of that tequila.

"Come on." He takes my hand and pulls me toward the shoreline.

It's there that the movement I'd seen comes into focus as

several large sea turtles are slowly making their way into the water.

"I love these guys," Surfer Boy says, crouching down to get a better view.

I don't join him in that position but instead stand by his side, staring at the creatures that are at once reptilian and majestic. And then I feel his hand on my calf. It's a gentle brushing at first, as his palm moves cautiously over the outline of my muscle.

I never would have thought this part of my body would be an erogenous zone, but his touch is sparking little fires on my skin, especially when he trails his fingers along the back of my knee and then in between my lower thighs. Letting my hand fall to his hair, I suppress a whimper of pleasure as his hand glides upward. He's no longer gentle, though, as he squeezes my inner thigh with urgency before grazing his fingers against the increasingly needy spot between my legs. I close my eyes and surrender to his touch, to the way he teases me by tracing the strap of my thong and caresses my backside in a way that tells me he's having a hard time restraining himself. At the same time, he's pressing his lips to my thigh with slow, lingering, reverential kisses.

Just when I think my legs might give out, overwhelmed by the stimulation he's generating, he pulls away. Standing, he slides his hand along the side of my neck, his fingers in my hair, and takes my mouth in his. It's a commanding, confident move that makes me moan at the exact moment our parted lips meet and our tongues tangle, desperate to taste each other. He pulls my body to his with such unexpected force that my breath leaves me, and I have to break our kiss.

I look at him and he looks apologetic, as if he just can't help himself, that having me in his arms somehow isn't close enough. I can't lie—being desired this intensely is a total turn-on.

I reach up and grab him by the back of his head to pull him to me once more. Once more into a kiss so deep, so full of need and want, that I can't imagine how we'll ever satisfy each other. But I'm open to trying, that's for sure.

And so is he, by the feel of it. He's hard and pressing insistently against me.

"My place is just up the beach here," he murmurs as he plants kisses under my ear and along my neck.

I nod vigorously and suddenly he's got my hand in his again and is pulling me along the shore in strides suited to his long legs, but which makes me struggle to keep up.

"Wait," I say, and he stops abruptly. I take a deep breath and then hold out my free hand. "I need a drink after that."

Smiling, he releases my hand, so he can remove the top of the tequila bottle we took from the restaurant.

"Sorry, no glass," he says.

Raising the bottle, he tips it to my lips, easing the liquid into my mouth so that only a dribble spills onto my bottom lip. He doesn't let that get too far, though, as he leans down and presses his lips to mine, sucking gently at the spot where the alcohol escaped.

God, he's good.

"Where did you come from, Hula Girl?" he asks as if I'm the one to have weakened his knees and not the other way around.

I can only smile at him. After a quick swig for himself, he takes my hand once more and we're walking briskly over the cool sand.

There's nothing but beach from my viewpoint. It's water to our left and deepening vegetation and the road beyond that to our right. I can't imagine where his place could be. But after a few more minutes of walking, he pulls me to the right. Before I can ask where we're going, I see an opening in the trees and bushes. It's a little hut almost entirely tucked away from view. Glancing backward, I notice that the entry to the water here is particularly rocky, meaning that tourists probably don't frequent this beach and making for a perfect hideaway.

Reaching behind the overgrowth of bushes by the front door, Surfer Boy releases some unseen catch and the door edges open.

He turns to me with a grin, saying, "Shhh."

"Who am I going to tell?" I reply with a laugh, looking around at the barren beach.

When he flips a switch inside, I see that "his place" is no more than a one-room shack that looks like a strong breeze could knock it over. The lights aren't a central overhead unit but rather a string of small multi-colored globes, each wrapped with twine to look like fishing net. Those, along with the five or six surfboards leaning against the walls, give the hut a charming beach chic vibe. There are stacks of books on the floor, an acoustic guitar propped in a stand, and a skateboard next to it. The central feature of the space is the queen-sized bed, sparsely covered by a navy-blue sheet and a single pillow, telling me Surfer Boy really is all about the basics.

He scrambles to straighten out the sheet, then pats the end of the bed.

"Have a seat," he says. "I've got glasses for that tequila."

I watch as he goes to a countertop along one wall that seems to serve as his kitchen. Underneath is a mini-fridge and open shelving with a few boxes of crackers, cereal, assorted condiments, and a handful of plates, bowls, and glasses. On top is a hot plate and a coffee maker.

"So, this is where you take the ladies to wow 'em," I say as he hands me a tumbler too full of tequila.

Sitting next to me, he laughs and spreads his free arm out to showcase the place. "Impressed?"

"Is this really where you live? Or is this more like a crash pad?"

"I really live here, Hula Girl." He takes a big sip from his glass. "Now, about those moves you were going to show me—"

Laughing, I say, "Oh no. I'm going to have to finish this obscenely large glass of tequila before I'm up for that."

He knocks his glass against mine. "Cheers to that."

But before I can take a drink, he does that thing again where he slides his hand into the hair at the nape of my neck, pulling me confidently, possessively, into him for a kiss. Though his kiss is what I want, I've accidentally sloshed some tequila out of my glass and onto my leg. I'm ready to ignore it, but he looks down and sees the liquid slowly rolling over my upper thigh.

"Oh, honey," he murmurs with a mischievous gleam in his eye, "we can't let this go to waste."

Before I can respond, he's slid to his knees on the floor in front of me, casting aside his glass in favor of reaching out to hold my hips with his hands. He lowers his face to my lap, flicking his tongue against the spill of tequila and sending a shiver through me. Heat fills my body and my core tightens in anticipation. The way he licks, sucks, and nibbles at the tender skin of my thigh, slowly making his way inward and upward, has me panting for more.

I'm still sitting upright, still holding my glass, though. I want nothing more than to surrender to what he's doing to me. What he's *going* to do to me. It's a very bad idea, but I gulp down the tequila just so that I can put down the glass without spilling any more. And then I fall back onto his bed, just as he peels off my thong and pulls one of my legs over his shoulder.

It's such a vulnerable position to be in, especially with someone I just met. But I'm too turned on to be worried about that. Besides, I've felt oddly comfortable with him since this morning when he snuck up beside me to say that doing hula moves might get me a better signal on my phone. Despite the fact that he makes me salivate with desire, he also somehow manages to set me at ease. He's just so relaxed, taking everything at its own pace. That easy demeanor has a way of rubbing off on you.

Not that we're exactly in the calmest state at the moment.

It's impossible for me to be calm. It's impossible for me not to writhe against the firm strokes of his tongue as he alternates between teasing my clit and probing deep inside me. And when he greedily trails kisses along my entire slit before concentrating on the throbbing bud of my clit once more, I give in to the sensation of his warm tongue sweeping over me in motions that send me closer and closer to the edge. It's when he ever so gently nibbles before sucking hard on my clit that I lose it, my body racked with the most intense orgasm I can remember. It goes on and on as he doesn't let go until he's gotten everything he can out of me coming for him. I finally have to pull his hair as I go slack because I can't take it anymore.

"What have you done," I say with a laugh, covering my eyes with my hand. "I'm destroyed."

I can hear him retrieve his glass before taking a swallow. Then the bed shifts as he joins me. I let my hand fall away and open one eye, looking at him. He's on his side, still dressed, and very relaxed.

He does that sexy thing where he squints slightly and smiles his crooked grin. "You're not destroyed. You're *alive* and you are, without a doubt, the sexiest woman I've ever seen," he says.

"If that's what me flailing around while having an insanely incredible orgasm seems like to you, then I'm good with that."

"Flailing? Nah, those were the hula moves I was looking for."

I laugh and pull him to me. "I want more of you," I say and kiss him.

We kiss until we're so needy that we have to break apart to remove our clothes. He takes the initiative to grab a condom and after he's rolled it on and turns to me, his back against the flimsy headboard, I waste no time, climbing onto him while he's still sitting. But I don't rush the part where I guide him into me. I do that slowly, wanting us both to feel every inch of sensation. He's long and thick and fills me so completely that I never want to stop riding him this way, even if doing so means we're creating a rhythmic knocking noise as the bed pushes against the wall. Then he takes the words out of my mouth.

"Ahh," he moans, "fuck, you feel good."

He's got his eyes closed, savoring our connection. But when I pull my upper body away from him, so I can angle my hips even closer to his, he watches me through a lust-filled gaze, his mouth slightly open. I reach out and touch his bottom lip and he grabs my wrist, pulling me to him again so he can devour my mouth with his while deftly changing our position. On top of me now, he works his hips in a slow grind while toying with my nipple and has me building toward another orgasm. Raising himself on his arms, his muscles flexed, he watches me for that sign that I'm close.

"You're so fucking beautiful," he says. "Come for me, honey. I love having my face between your legs, but I want to watch you come this time."

His words and movements have the intended effect and soon I'm doing as he asks, completely shameless in my pleasure, crying out with each wave of ecstasy.

"Hell, yeah," he says approvingly as I slowly come back to myself.

I should be depleted after the heights he's brought me to, but all I want is for him to have his own mind-blowing experience. I raise my legs up, my knees against his ribs.

"It's your turn," I say. "However you want ..."

That's all the permission he needs to now do as I ask, plunging deep inside me, one hand on my ass and the other on my breast as he raises himself up on his knees for better leverage. He's pumping so hard that I can feel his balls slap against me and he's on the verge. But then he lowers his hand once more to my clit and I automatically try to move it away, certain I'll be too sensitive to allow his touch.

"No," I moan when he won't let me push him away.

"Yes," he counters. His touch is light, more a tease than anything else.

To my surprise, it generates that aching desire all over again and now I press his hand down where it is, wanting him there. Needing him there as he thrusts in and out of me from tip to root, his motion slower now but no less satisfying.

"Yes," I moan, my eyes half-closed as I build up once more.

As soon as I come, he returns to more forceful fucking and I go along for the ride, now the one watching as he comes with a deep, satisfied groan.

When he collapses on top of me, the weight of his body against mine feels so good that I wrap my arms and legs around him to keep him there. Slowly, we both regain our normal breathing and beyond that, I can hear the waves outside his door. It might be that the tequila is finally hitting me, but I don't think I've ever had a more thrilling, magical experience.

8

AVA

That thrill and magic is nowhere to be found when Surfer Boy gently wakes me in the morning with a kiss on my temple.

I groan and squeeze my eyes closed, not wanting any light to assault my hungover senses.

"Definitely too much tequila," I whisper hoarsely.

"I've got some coconut water right here for you," he says, amusement in his voice. "Sit up a little and drink it down. You'll be glad you did."

I do as he says, barely opening my eyes and wondering if he's doing this to get me to leave. He probably has to get on with his day and hadn't bargained on the tourist still in his bed.

"Good," he tells me when I've had the last of the coconut water. "Go back to sleep, honey. I'm going to catch some waves. I'll be back in a bit."

He presses a kiss to my lips and is gone before I can muster a response. I drift off to sleep once more, taking refuge in this stranger's bed whether he likes it or not.

THOUGH I CAN'T BE certain, it feels like I've been asleep for a couple hours when he wakes me again. This time, there's no tender kiss on my temple. This time, he presses his naked, damp, and salty-from-the-ocean body on top of me and I automatically open my legs to make room for him.

The pounding in my head has receded enough so that when I open my eyes, I don't cringe at the natural light coming in through the one window covered by a thin strip of fabric.

"Good morning," he says, grinning.

"Morning," I reply, feeling slightly less comfortable being this intimate with him without all that tequila to buffer things. The calculating lawyer in me realizes I may have gone overboard in my efforts to enjoy this vacation. I resolve to extricate myself from this scenario quickly.

"Don't do that," he says.

I raise my eyebrows, wondering for a moment if I had said my thoughts out loud. "Don't do what?"

"Retreat. Put up walls. I'm the same guy you were with last night."

That he could read me so well catches me by surprise and I laugh.

"What?" he asks, smiling and game for getting in on the joke.

But I'm not about to confirm to him that he's right in seeing my walls go up. Instead, I deflect, saying, "You're naked. Between my legs. I wouldn't call that retreating."

He tilts his head to acknowledge my point. But then adds the obvious observation. "There's a sheet between us."

I watch him for a beat. He's definitely the same guy from

last night. The same sexy, gorgeous, playful guy. It's a good reminder that I don't need to cut things too short.

"Don't let that stop you," I tell him.

His brown and amber eyes light up and I figure one more —one *last*—time with him couldn't hurt. In fact, I know it will feel just the opposite because when our bodies come together, it is a spectacular feeling.

THE BATHROOM of this little shack is tiny and purely functional, with a sink right next to the toilet.

And no shower.

There has to be a shower somewhere. Maybe one of those outdoor showers? I didn't notice one last night when we came in. But then again, I wasn't paying much attention to anything other than the man I was about to go to bed with.

Sighing, I clean up the best I can before noticing that my hair has that mussed up I-just-got-ravaged look. There's no use in trying to comb through the tangles with my fingers. Instead, I smooth my hair back as best as I can and tie it in a top-knot.

My dress is still somewhere on the floor in the other room. There's a robe on the back of the door and by the look of the faded Sheraton logo on the chest, it was appropriated quite a while ago. Still, it's clean and I slip it on.

Surfer Boy isn't there in the small space, but the front door is open and I can hear music. When I poke my head outside, I find him sitting in a beach chair, acoustic guitar in his hands as he plucks at the strings. Sitting there in just swim trunks and a bare chest, his hair tousled, he's a vacation fling fantasy come to life. I watch him without interrupting, enjoying the way he handles the instrument. There's something almost masterful in how he plays. He makes it look easy, even as I can see his fingers making complicated adjustments that belie that impression. The music itself has a sort of rock-swing vibe with an undeniable hook. I don't recognize the song but I feel like I should. It has the feel of something proven, something I must have heard on the radio.

He strums the last few notes and then lets the guitar go quiet. I applaud softly and he turns to me in surprise.

"Hey, you. Join me?" He cocks his head toward a second beach chair.

I sit next to him. "That really impressive. What was it?"

"Nothing really. Just something I like to play around with."

"You wrote that?"

He rests the guitar on his lap and gives me a noncommittal shrug. "How's your head?"

"Not too bad. That coconut water must really work."

"Glad to hear it." Retrieving a travel mug from the beverage holder of his beach chair, he holds it up. "Coffee? All I have is black, so hope you don't need it to be sweet."

"No," I say with a playful grin, "I don't *need* it sweet. But I don't mind some sweetness now and then."

"Shit," he says softly.

"What?"

"You're a romantic, aren't you, Hula Girl?"

Though his tone is light, I can't help but feel defensive. "Um, if I was a romantic, I wouldn't have gone home with you last night after a few drinks."

"What?" He puts on an incredulous expression. "I thought last night was incredibly romantic. Come on, the beach under a full moon?"

I start to reconsider. "Well—"

"And me between your legs? That's the very definition of romance."

I can't help but laugh. "You're right. It was just like a fairy-tale."

"Exactly. You're my Hula Princess and I'm your—"

"Surfer Prince? Wow, our relationship seems to have escalated quickly."

He smiles appreciatively at me and we go quiet as I sip his coffee and enjoy the morning ocean breeze.

"Seriously, though," he says, "I had a really good time."

"Me too."

He takes a deep breath and regards me, clearly hesitating with what he's going to say next.

I realize that I truly have overstayed my welcome now and he's trying to figure out how to get me out of here. Me sashaying out here in his robe as if I might never leave probably put him on edge.

"I'll get out of your way," I say and start to stand.

He grabs my hand. "I hate to cut this short—"

"It's no problem. I, um, I have things I need to do, too." I start toward the front door.

"It's just that I have to go to work in a bit," he calls after me and I stop.

"I understand. Really, I know all about work obligations."

I move inside and quickly grab my dress, taking it with me back into the bathroom, and dressing quickly. I don't have any makeup with me but that's the least of my worries. I stow my thong in my purse, stare at my reflection in the mirror for a second, and then take a deep breath. I just want to move on from this vacation fling. It was fun while it lasted, but it's clearly over now.

When I step out of the bathroom, he's leaning in the doorframe, taking up most of the space with his fantastic build. *God, he's gorgeous.*

"I'll walk you back to your car," he says.

As if he needs to pull out the gentleman card after he spent the night and morning ravaging me.

I smirk. "That's okay, Surfer Boy. You don't need to do that."

"Oh. So, you remember exactly how we got here last night? Don't think you'll need any help getting up at that little inlet?"

Oh, that.

Great, now we'll have to have an awkward walk of shame together.

"I guess I could use a little help with that," I say.

He nods, amused. Holding out his arm gallantly, he asks, "Shall we?"

I laugh softly but walk right by him, starting out on the sand.

"Hula Girl? That's the wrong way."

Great. I turn around and see him watching me, his arms crossed over his still bare, still ripped, chest. I suddenly feel so awkward. Where did all that easiness with him from last night with him go? It's likely the feeling that I've somehow allowed myself to read more into this little encounter than what it really was. It felt so good, so natural that I forgot I'm probably just one of the many, many, tourists he sleeps with.

The awkwardness slips away when we start trading notes on the view. The morning light is achingly beautiful. The air is in that delicious in-between state of still cool with an undercurrent of the humid heat sure to edge its way to domi-nance. Gentle waves ebb and flow. I walk on the dry side of the sand while he lets the water slosh over his flip-flops.

"See that spray of water out there?" he asks, pointing to some middle distance in the ocean.

I just catch the remnants of the spray he's spotted.

"Is that a whale?" I ask.

"Sure is. Oh, look a couple more that way."

"Where?" I put my hand over my eyes to create a shield from the sun, trying to find the other humpback whales.

He moves behind me, puts one arm around my waist and uses his other arm to create a line of sight. His body pressed into me like that causes flashbacks from this morning. From the way he pushed deep into me from behind. From the way he held me tightly to him, one arm around my hips and the other cupping my breast.

"I see them," I say, forcing my thoughts away from the way his confident hands had touched me all over earlier.

"Amazing, aren't they?"

Slowly, he pulls away from me, but not before I feel him drag his lips over the shell of my ear. The heat of him sets me on fire. He's made me feel something I haven't felt in as long as I can remember: insatiable. I have not-so-fleeting thoughts of him taking me one more time right here on the sand.

"I really wish I didn't have to get to work," he murmurs.

That he's feeling the same reluctance to part sends a tingle through me. I turn to face him but he's got his eyes in the opposite direction, looking at the rocky inlet we had climbed down last night.

I take it as my cue to keep moving and when he follows after me, his fingers brush mine, our tips lacing. It's sweet. And intimate. More intimate than a one-night stand should feel.

He navigates his way up the rocks and holds his hand out to me, helping me up the precarious path.

"Makai's is just down the way," he says, nodding at the road.

Everything looks different in the light of day. I don't really recognize where I am and am glad he's willing to walk me all the way back to my car. It's parked right where I left it the night before, thankfully.

"Listen," he says as we stop in front of the rental, "my name's Ford. I'd love to know your name."

"Ford," I repeat. I like it. I like knowing him as something other than Surfer Boy. Even if there's no need to know it now, not when we're saying goodbye. "My name's Ava."

He smiles widely. "That's beautiful. Suits you."

The compliment makes my heart swell. Like seriously, it feels too big for a moment. I have to silently admonish myself for taking any of this too seriously. We are in the process of saying goodbye forever, after all. "Thank you," I tell him softly.

"Could I get your number, Ava?"

"Um." I hesitate. As much as I'm drawn to him, I fear that if we push this thing beyond our one-nighter, it'll get weird. I mean, what if our connection last night and this morning was based mostly on the fact that we knew we were never going to see each other again? Shouldn't we just end it here?

But then he does something that makes me laugh. He pulls his cell phone from his pocket in preparation for getting my number. It's a flip phone. It's so unsophisticated that it looks like a child's toy.

"What is that?" I ask.

"No laughing," he replies. "This is called 'simplifying your life.' I don't need it for anything other than making phone calls. Everything else is a worthless distraction."

"You don't text anyone? Or need to check your email? Read the news? Watch videos?"

"I've lived that way before, obsessively glued to my phone. But it didn't really *add* anything to my life. It was more of a constant drain on my focus. I'm happier without all that."

I shake my head in wonder. "I can't even imagine. Being here without any connection to work has had me going through withdrawals."

"Seems like you've enjoyed yourself recently without ever once checking that thing."

I open my mouth to reply but then stop. He's right. During this brief time with him, I haven't once picked up my phone. I was, for once, living in the moment.

"Anyway, I know you'll be here for a few more days. I'd love to see you again. Take you for a ride on a longboard, like I said."

"Is this part of your MO with the tourists?" I ask with a smirk. "Go back for seconds when time allows?"

He squints at me in that way of his. "You're really invested in this idea, aren't you?"

"What idea?"

"That you're just another one of the many women I take to bed?"

"Well—"

"If it turns you on to think that, then, by all means, be my guest. But I'll tell you the truth—I've never invited anyone to Makai's. And I've never taken anyone to my place. And no, I've never gone 'for seconds' in the way you're talking about. I just ... I like you, Ava. I know this is temporary. That you'll go back to your life in a few days, but I still think it's worth enjoying more time together. What do you say?"

Looking up at him, I see the sincerity in his eyes. He's gorgeous, sexy, and decent. How can I say no to seeing him again? "Um, yeah, I'd like that, too."

We exchange numbers. "I'll give you a call, okay?" he says.

I nod and when he tips my chin up so he can kiss me goodbye, I melt into him, my hands going to his bare chest. It feels like the kind of kiss you'd see in a movie where the couple is desperately clinging to each other at a train station, or better yet, on the wet sand as the water rushes up on them. It doesn't feel like a goodbye kiss. It's more like confirmation. Confirmation that we've got some irresistible force keeping us connected.

As our kiss grows deeper, more heated, I drop my hand from his chest to his hip. The exquisite muscle in a V shape leading into his low-slung board shorts is exposed just enough for me to trace it.

"Fuck," he moans as he pulls away. "I gotta go. But I don't want to go."

I drape my arms around his neck and press my body against his so that we're both aware of the way he's reacted to our kiss.

"I know exactly how you feel," I tell him softly.

He laughs and kisses me again, quickly this time and nipping at my bottom lip as he pulls away. "You're something, Hula Girl."

I sigh in pleasure and contentment. "Go do your thing, Surfer Boy."

He walks backward for several steps, keeping his eyes locked on mine. Finally, he smiles and shakes his head before turning away.

I don't know if he'll really call or if that was just his way of ending this on a polite note. As I touch my kiss-bruised lips, I feel absurdly giddy, excited for the possibility of what might happen.

And suddenly, my vacation seems too short.

9

FORD

I try not to wince as I listen to the cacophony of noises coming out of the eight student musicians in front of me. They're trying their best, I know that. But still, it's not coming together. They're all playing at their own tempo, throwing each other off. The funniest thing is that by the way they are giving each other the side-eye, I can tell that they think it's someone else's fault, not their own.

I let them battle it out, hoping they'll find the rhythm and balance on their own. When I was a kid learning instruments in this very same place—my mom's music school—I always made the biggest leaps when I was given some freedom to explore on my own.

This is my day job, the thing that pulled me away from Ava so that I had to walk awkwardly home sporting a boner when all I wanted to do was climb with her into the backseat of her rental car with her.

Jesus, what a time we had. She's beyond sexy. Clever and witty, too. I wonder what it might be like to really know her.

And yet, I know there's no chance of that. The logistics are just not in our favor. She lives in Los Angeles. I live here. There's no point in seeing her again, no point in indulging in this ... whatever this thing is. Yes, she's beautiful and I'd love to take her to bed again. And again. And again.

But the problem is, I already know it's not just sexual attraction with her. This would all be much simpler if that were the case. Instead, I'm itching to talk to her again, to hear more about her life. And that is *not* what you do with a one-night stand. And that's exactly why I shouldn't have told her I'd call her.

Sighing, I close my eyes tight and try to focus on my kids. They're a ragtag bunch of eight and nine-year-olds. The instruments they're playing range from the acoustic guitar to the trumpet. They've been working on this modified version of Beethoven's "Ode to Joy" piece for eight weeks. The culmination of that hard work is meant to take place tonight with a recital for parents, friends, and the local community. They've all been excited about this moment, so it especially pains me that they're so obviously off.

Me being so distracted by thoughts of Ava probably doesn't help.

Standing, I focus on Eli, the boy on clarinet. He's an interesting character, often overcompensating for his insecurities by acting much older than he is. His parents got him into learning an instrument so that he could build a real sense of confidence. But so far, it has only triggered him more. He can't hide behind a witty comment while playing. I've given him a little extra attention and developed something of a bond.

"Hey, bud," I say. He looks at me even as he keeps playing.

They all keep playing, so sweetly determined. "Sit up straight. Head up, too." He does as I say, but as is his bad habit, he's got the instrument almost clutched against his chest. I gently pull it about forty-five degrees away from him. The clarity of his efforts improves immediately and he smiles around the mouthpiece. "There you go."

I then give each of the other students some individual attention and see a change for the better overall. Settling back into my chair, I have them start from the top.

As they play, a stray thought comes to mind. Should tell Ava I'll be in Los Angeles in a week? Maybe we can get together out there?

But that would require telling her a whole lot more about me. And that isn't what this thing with her is. This thing is just a vacation romance.

Romance.

No, not even that. This is just pure chemistry unleashed. She and I are very good at fucking. That's all.

And yet.

And yet, I can't stop thinking about her. Not just for her smoking hot body, either. I can't stop thinking about the look of sadness in her eyes when she told me about her father. About how I could relate so strongly to the fear in her eyes when she said his death left her family in a terrible financial bind and how, at an age far too young, she took on responsibilities she shouldn't have had to.

More than any of that, I can't stop thinking about why she *let* me see that. I pegged her right from the start as building up protective walls. Hell, she even admitted to that. So, why did she expose herself that way?

It shouldn't matter. Getting to know her better isn't an

option. Or at least, it isn't a smart option. There's no point in investing any more time in this passing connection. Because that's what it is, just a fleeting moment. After this, she'll go home to LA and tell all her girlfriends about the surfer she slept with while on vacation. And I'll go back to my normal pursuit of riding waves.

I've got to shake her from my thoughts. Not just because of the task at hand with these kids, but because I need to start mentally preparing for my own trip to Los Angeles.

My time has run out. I've been disconnected from all my obligations for as long as I can manage. Now, I'll have to face the music, as it were.

Time for me to announce my intentions at the firm I left behind. Either I end my leave of absence and return fully committed or I resign and give up my shares and any future opportunity I might have to be a part of the family business.

It's a big decision. But I know what I'm going to do. This leave has been the best thing I've ever done. Coming home to Maui, being close again with my mother while being a help to her with her music school, has been incredibly satisfying. Living this stripped-back life, without all the nonsense material things I had come to think I needed, has been enlightening. The choice between this life and my old life is a no-brainer.

What's held me back from doing anything until I'm absolutely forced to is my grandfather.

Well, *grandfather* is too familiar of a term for him, I'd have to say. I've never called him that, nor used the term *grandpa*. He's always been Palmer to me. Palmer McAvoy started his firm when he was just in his twenties and built it into something highly regarded, known as much for its cut-throat tactics as its exceptional record of cases won. From what I can tell, he has an innate ability to pick the right legal challenges. Every decision on that front goes through him and he isn't shy about vetoing taking on a client if it doesn't suit his criteria.

He would have vetoed my father bringing me over if the decision had been under his purview. From what I could sort out through overheard arguments, he thought Senior should have left well enough alone, that I wasn't *really* his son, not after living so many years apart. He presumed that I'd never be more than some kind of island heathen and he never bothered to hide his distaste for me.

It wasn't hard to steer clear of him for the first few years that I was with my father, but when I studied for and registered an insanely high score on the LSAT—Law School Admission Test—he sat up and took notice. Not only took notice but began to insist that I report to him in his large corner office on a weekly basis so he could coach me on matters of the law. I went to these meetings with open hostility. Until that one time when I was able to stump him on some arcane point of legalese I recalled. Gotta thank that photographic memory for some things. He'd sputtered and called me a liar and a cheat before calming down long enough to realize the potential I had. The potential to enrich him further in the law firm, that is.

After that, he did everything he could to spoil me. He bought me a BMW as a gift for getting into Yale. When I graduated ahead of schedule in just three years and went right into Yale Law, he bought me a condo. When I earned magna cum laude and made plans to move home to join the firm, he set up a shares system that was tied to my performance. The more revenue I was directly responsible for, the more shares were transferred to me. It was meant to last six years and be nearly impossible to get more than an inconsequential number of shares overall but I maxed out the scheme in the first two years.

And like the greedy sucker I had too easily become, I welcomed it with open arms. All those things, plus the black American Express card that he paid for. I took it all because even though I'd established a relationship with my father, I could see how Palmer paying attention to me gnawed at him. It was easy enough to see that Senior's relationship with his father was just as dysfunctional as ours was. As much as I had done a one eighty and craved his approval, I also couldn't stop from wanting to torture him a little. After all, he had abandoned me until it suited him otherwise. Those scars may have been covered over by tough tissue, but they never really went away.

It wasn't until I'd been fully immersed in this life of petty retributions, professional successes, and material gains for almost four years that I was forced to snap out of it.

I'd gone back to the office late one night, intent on researching a case I couldn't stop thinking about when I heard my father's voice. The door to his office at the far end of the floor, one of the only offices not exposed by glass walls, was mostly closed, but I caught glimpses of him as he paced while speaking on the phone.

Normally, I'd ignore him and go about my business. But something about the opportunity to hear what he was so focused on at this late hour made me stay put.

"That's all part of it," he said soothingly. I had no idea who was on the other line. But his argument soon became clear. "I'm telling you, I've got Junior on my side. With his shares combined with mine, the old man's position here will be completely debilitated. No more kowtowing to his every little whim."

It was so callous, so cold. And so like my father. I shouldn't have been surprised that he would be conspiring to push his own father out of the firm. But I was. I stood there gobsmacked and torn. I didn't want to be a pawn in this family drama. And yet, I had no loyalty to the grandfather who only ever saw fit to use me for his own gains. If my father wanted me to join forces with him to take over the firm, that would just give me more power.

Wouldn't it?

"In due time," my father had continued on the phone. "Once things have settled here after we take over, I'll find a way to get Junior lost in the stacks. He won't have a *real* controlling interest, after all. We'll just stroke that ever-expanding ego of his, and he'll go along with it, I'm sure." Senior laughed then with a kind of pleasure I'd never been privy to.

If it wasn't so personal, it would have seemed cartoonishly evil.

But it wasn't just a moment of feeling hurt by the attempted manipulation, it was much bigger than that. It triggered a long-overdue reckoning. It was the realization that I had spent years abandoning my better instincts, years casting aside what I really valued in life, all in a vain effort to win my father's approval. To win his respect. To gain his love. None of which ever happened.

I actually laughed when I understood this.

And then, I quietly retraced my steps out of the office, went back to my overpriced Brentwood townhouse to pack a few things, and headed straight for the airport. I flew to Maui on the first available flight and spent the next several weeks ignoring all emails and calls while I tried to figure out a plan. I finally reached out to the firm's Human Resources department and informed them that I was taking a leave of absence. I left no forwarding contact information.

Instead, I settled in at my mom's place before her boyfriend suggested I take over his old surf shack. Staying there with no television, no computer, no internet, has been a dream. It's brought me back to a true sense of self.

This life has been all about surfing, the music school, time with my mom, and a kind of serenity I hadn't realized I'd been aching for.

That didn't stop my father from trying to get an answer from me about returning, though. He guessed that I was back in Maui and hounded my mom, sending her bullshit registered letters to try to scare her into admitting I was here. He forgot that she'd seen that side of him before and therefore couldn't be intimidated.

I'd been banking on my memory of a loophole in the contract I'd signed with the firm to guarantee me up to a full year of leave due to being a shareholder. But that time has just about run out. I now either have to return to work or formally resign.

The thing is, my quick disappearing act might have postponed my father's plan to force my grandfather out, but I'd bet he's only been biding his time. Giving him the chance to do that to his own father is my only hesitation in formally resigning. So, I still have to figure out how to manage this situation.

I let out a breath and drag my hand through my hair. After a moment's hesitation, I pull my cell phone from my pocket and step outside. Punching in the number I've already memorized, I wait for three and a half rings before it's answered.

"Is that you, Surfer Boy?"

Ava's voice makes me smile. And I realize I did the right thing after all, by asking for her number.

A musical experience. That's what Ford said in his invitation over the phone. He said, "Would you be up for joining me tonight for a musical experience?"

I didn't think twice before saying yes. I didn't even think about the odd wording. Not until now when I've arrived at the address he's given me and realize my assumption that I'd be up for another sexy night with Surfer Boy is completely wrong.

I'm standing on the outskirts of a parking lot that's been made into a makeshift area for a children's musical performance. I've overdressed in a little red dress suitable for a nightclub, which makes me want to turn around and leave, but Ford catches my arm before I can make a move. Wearing navy blue shorts and an Aloha shirt with faded blue floral patterns, he's dressed up by island standards. Still, there's no hiding the strength in his tan arms or the way he radiates sex.

"I'm so glad you made it," he says. "My kids will love having a stranger here to watch them."

I raise an eyebrow. "*Your* kids?"

"My students," he replies with a laugh. "My music students. My mom owns the music school, and I help her where I can. Tonight is a performance of a piece the kids have been working hard on."

"Oh," I say, trying to come to grips with my expectations coming nowhere close to reality. But it settles on me that reality is actually quite attractive. The reality is that Ford isn't just some surfer dude who randomly beds tourists. He's someone who works with kids to get the best out of them. That isn't just admirable—it's sexy as hell.

"Is this your girlfriend?"

We both turn to see a boy about eight years old standing with us, his wide eyes ping-ponging between us. He holds a clarinet at his side.

"No," we both answer.

Ridiculously, I'm disappointed in his disavowal of a relationship. Of course, I have no claim on him of that nature. We both know this connection of ours is purely a heat of the moment one that has an expiration date set to match my plane ticket home. Still, his quick reply stings a little.

Then the little boy grins and shakes his head with unwarranted confidence. "That means I have a chance, then."

I laugh, shocked and amused.

"Eli," Ford says with the sternness of a taskmaster, "go get on stage."

The little Casanova holds up his hands with mock innocence. "I'm just saying, if you can't close the deal, maybe I can."

"Down, tiger. You should know that Ava here is actually my princess."

"Princess?"

"Yes, she's a *hula* princess. And she's mine."

I fight back a laugh, tickled by Ford's sudden show of possessiveness.

"What's that make you? A prince?"

Ford makes an elaborate show of doffing his imaginary hat before bowing slightly. "You may call me Surfer Prince."

Eli laughs. "Yeah, right. In your dreams, Ford."

"Go make us proud on stage there," Ford said.

Looking over at the parking spot that had been designated as the "stage," Eli puffs out his cheeks dubiously. Then he looks back at Ford and all his earlier bravado is lost as he suddenly looks like the young boy he is.

"Forty-five degrees?" Eli asks, holding his clarinet out in front of his chest.

Ford adjusts his hands slightly before nodding. "Forty-five degrees, bud. You got this."

The kid seems to absorb the vote of confidence before nodding. "Yeah, I got it."

"Break a leg," I tell him.

"Thanks, princess."

Ford and I share what I imagine to be a "proud parent" type look before he gets pulled away by another performer.

"I saved you a great seat," he says as he moves away. "Front row."

I smile. "*VIP*. Thank you."

"Well, you are royalty, after all," he says with a wink.

The show doesn't begin right away, but I dutifully sit in the plastic folding chair up front. Looking around, I realize that everyone here knows each other. They must be parents and friends, but also others that are from the area. The support they're offering is sweet.

The community vibe spurs memories of the neighborhood I grew up in. It's where my mother still lives. It's very working class, but also the type of place where everyone knows everyone—for better or worse. My favorite time growing up was when three blocks were shut down for a summer street party. Everyone put out folding tables and canopies, offering their favorite dishes. It was basically a giant potluck, with kids running freely in the street, someone's nephew doing a DJ stint at one end, and the old timers listening to Vicente Fernández on an ancient boom box at the other end. By the end of the night, the kids were still going strong well past their bedtimes while the adults were tipsy and dancing like no one was watching. But the overwhelming feeling was that everyone was just happy to be there, to be in the moment sharing a silent understanding of connectedness.

That's what this feels like, at least a little bit. I relax into my chair and savor this unexpected experience. Once more, I'm finding that Ford isn't who I supposed he would be. There's more depth to him than I presumed at first glance.

I see him speaking with an older woman who wears a long graying braid over one shoulder. She's just as involved in the preparations for the performance as he is and I have to assume that she is his mother, though they don't look very much alike.

When the performance starts, I give Eli an encouraging thumbs up. When he blows me a kiss in return I laugh loudly and have to cover my mouth while I watch Ford admonishing him. I can't say the kids have a prodigy-level of talent, but there are glimmers that suggest that with more work, they'll find their rhythm, especially as by the end of the piece they've managed to come together to all play the same notes.

The crowd rewards them with a standing ovation afterward and the kids beam.

"THAT WAS REALLY GREAT," I tell Ford once he's found his way to me after twenty minutes of talking with students and parents.

He shrugs. "They'll get there. Might have been premature to have a performance, but I think they got a kick out of it."

"More than that. You could see their confidence rise by the end. It was really amazing to see them fight their way through and finish so strong."

"That's how I learned—just by doing it."

"How long have you been teaching?"

He takes a deep breath and releases it slowly. "Just under a year."

"And before that? What kind of work did you do?"

"That's real-world stuff. Are we going to go there, Hula Girl?"

Damn. What made me slip like that? He's thrown me in more ways than one, that's for sure. I do want to know more about him, but, at the same time, I know it's better to keep things as they are. To just play this all for fun. As much as I like him, there's no chance for a future.

"No, I don't suppose so," I tell him.

He nods. "So, you're dressed to go out. I think I owe you a drink. Maybe even a dance?"

I smirk. "Are you trying to get me to do a hula?"

"Always. I love watching those hips move," he says with a wicked grin.

"But I never actually did any hula moves."

"Believe me, I've seen your hips do some beautiful things."
He leans toward me, his lips grazing my ear as he says, "Like
when you had your legs wrapped around my neck. Fuck,
you're delicious."

"Ford," I whisper, my face burning with a mixture of desire
and embarrassment.

"I like the way you say my name," he says before kissing
the side of my neck.

A shiver runs through me. I want him to feel the same
kind of tingle, so I tell him softly, "Make me scream it later?"

He eyes me, his smile crooked and sexy. "Hell, yeah."

"Ford, introduce me to your friend."

Our reaction at the intrusion into our dirty talk is comical.
We both take a big step away from each other and look
guiltily at the woman with the gray braid who has approached
us.

"Oh, sure," Ford says. "Um, Mom, this is my friend Ava.
Ava, this is my mom, Rebecca."

I shake her hand. "It's nice to meet you. The children were
a delight."

"Thank you. We'll get there. And how do you two know
each other?"

"Just casually," I say.

"Do you live here, then, Ava?"

"No, I'm actually on vacation." This admission seems to
trigger something in Ford's mother. Her mouth tightens and
her eyes go hard.

"Okay, Mom," Ford says, "we actually have to get going."
"But—"

He turns to her so that I can't see either of their expressions. But I can hear him say, "I've got it covered. You have nothing to worry about."

After a moment, she nods and we say our goodbyes. Ford takes my hand and pulls me away without any explanation and I decide none is needed. Not with the temporary thing we have going on.

11

FORD

I can barely keep my eyes on the road. I've got Ava sitting next to me in my truck as we head toward Lahaina with the plan that we'll get a taste of the nightlife there. But she's got her legs crossed and her dress has inched up along those beautiful thighs of hers. And I've still got her challenge to make her scream my name in my head.

Truth is, I've never liked my name. Not when I know I'm named after my absentee dad. My mom once confessed she'd named me for him as a sort of passive-aggressive move since he hadn't wanted anything to do with us. She wanted him to remember that not only did he have a son, but that we share a name. From what I can tell, it was the only spiteful thing she's ever done and I can't blame her. She also made a point to tell me many times throughout my life that I'd do better things with my name than he ever would. She reasoned that I had the kindness and compassion that he lacked. That had been true for a time. And then I went and proved her wrong by trying to be exactly like him.

That regrettable period is over, though. Thankfully, my

mom welcomed me back without hesitation and we've been able to rebuild our connection. I could see her watching me with Ava earlier, see the fear in her eyes. I hadn't intended on introducing her to Ava because it would be all too obvious to her that she's a vacation fling, making her worry that I'd somehow replicate her mistake all those years ago. I didn't give her time to see that Ava is, unlike my father, a good person. I just cut it off with the reassurance that I was taking all necessary precautions.

Not that Ava doesn't tempt me to play a lot more recklessly. Especially now, as she leans toward me and slides her fingers into the hair at the nape of my neck, giving me a show of her breasts down the front of her dress when I glance toward her.

"You're going to make me run off the road," I say, only half-joking.

"Maybe you should pull over."

I laugh but she doesn't. Looking at her, there's a flirt in her eyes that has my dick rising to the occasion.

"Don't tempt me. I'll do it."

"Really?" she asks with an amused laugh as if she had been joking about pulling over.

"I've wanted to rip that dress off you since the second I saw you in it, honey."

Her hand falls from my hair to my thigh. "No need to rip it off. It pushes up really easily."

"Fuck," I groan and she laughs again.

The sky is in that twilight phase of going dark but night hasn't truly fallen. Still, there's a turnout ahead that's partially draped in overgrown trees and brush, making for a perfect spot to get us a little privacy. I swing the truck off the road and onto the dirt, not caring when branches slap at the windows as we pull to a stop.

As if synchronized, we both unlatch our seat belts and turn to each other, our mouths crashing together hungrily. This desire is insatiable. I want to consume every part of her. In one swift movement, I pull the lever to slide my seat back and grab her around the waist, sliding her to my side so that she's straddling me.

Pulling down the top of her dress, I find that she's braless. I take one of her small brown nipples into my mouth, sucking and biting as she rocks her hips against mine. She's pressing herself against my painfully hard dick, free in her pursuit of pleasure as she throws her head back.

"That's it," I tell her. "Ride me just like that until you come." I squeeze her tits and then cover them with kisses and bites that alternate between gentle and firm.

"Ford," she moans as she gets closer.

I drop my hands to her hips, guiding her in a faster rhythm. I want to be in her. I want to push my cock deep inside her warm, throbbing pussy. But I want to watch her come first.

"Louder," I tell her and her eyes lock onto mine. She's so close. Her breath is jagged. Her cheeks are pink. Her hips are thrashing against mine.

"Wait," she says and reaches down to unbutton my shorts.

I pull her hands away and press her to me once more. "Don't worry. I'm going to fuck you so hard. But right now, I need you to let go and come for me."

She must take me seriously because she wraps her arms around my neck, her face falls forward, and her whole body tenses. "Ford," she breathes as she comes.

Okay, so it's not her screaming my name, but damn if it doesn't feel fantastic.

"Ava," I tell her softly, "you beautiful thing." I stroke her long, shiny hair over and over until she's recovered.

When she wiggles her way off my lap and over to her side of the truck, my eyebrows come together in disappointment. That lasts mere seconds, though, as she's soon leaning over the center console so she can undo my fly and rub my swollen, slick cock with both hands. She replaces her hands with her mouth, and her hot, firm tongue sends my eyes rolling to the back of my head. I can feel her working my dick deep into her throat, taking as much of me in as she can in a rhythm that is sheer perfection.

My balls tighten and she must know how close I am because she changes her technique. I'm insanely grateful that she wants to prolong this. Using a combination of her hand and her mouth, she creates a different kind of pressure and suction that has my toes curling. Her moans of pleasure are matched by my own, especially when I slip my hand down and grab her ass. Her skin, bared by a thong, is smooth and tight but shapely enough so that I can get a good handful. I squeeze her with increasing need as I watch her head bob up and down. Pulling a few strands of loose hair away from her face, I watch her take me in her eager mouth and I'm suddenly at the point of no return.

"You're going to make me come, honey. It's too good. I can't—"

Her free hand covers my lips and stops me from speaking just as she starts sucking me off faster. And then I'm pushing myself hard against the seat, coming into her unrelenting mouth, groaning deeply. She takes every last drop, only stopping when there's nothing more. I'm completely depleted and completely sated.

"Jesus," I say on an exhale.

She's moved up enough so that her face is pressed to my chest and I wrap my arms around her.

"You didn't scream my name," she says, a tease in her voice.

"*Ava!*" I shout, drawing it out so that my voice goes hoarse to embody the searing, animalistic heights of desire she just brought me to.

Startled to laughter, she looks up at me with that pretty smile of hers. I lean down and kiss her, not caring that she's got my taste in her mouth. All I want is to show this woman that there's nowhere I'd rather be at this moment than with her.

WHEN WE GET to the liveliest bar on Front Street in Lahaina, Ava goes straight to the restrooms, while I grab us drinks and a table.

I'm still buzzing from that blowjob in the truck. And I'm wondering how on earth I managed to hook up with this sexy stranger.

Someone slaps me hard on the shoulder, shaking me from my lingering lust-filled haze. I turn to find my buddies, Pika and Hiro, standing there.

"Hey guys," I say as they help themselves to the tall chairs at the table. That leaves one more for Ava.

"You shouldn't have," Pika says, picking up the Negra Modelo I had ordered for Ava. His name means "rock" in Hawaiian and perfectly fits his short, stocky frame.

I snatch the bottle from his hand before he can get it to his lips. "Not for you, jackass."

Hiro laughs as Pika makes a show of looking around the small bar for my mystery guest.

Like most bars on Front Street, the heart of Lahaina, it's just starting to fill up and the music isn't quite at peak levels yet. The mostly tourist crowd that frequents this place won't get going until closer to ten o'clock. And by "get going," I mean, filling the tables and bar stools, and drinking sickly sweet mai tais until they've accumulated one too many of those little paper umbrellas that garnish the drink. I had thought this would give Ava and me a chance to hang out before it got rowdy, but now I've got these two guys breaking things up.

Don't get me wrong, they are my friends. As luck would have it—or rather, not so much luck, but the fact that we live on a very small island—these guys are the same ones I told Ava about. They are the locals who gave me a chance when I struggled to fit in as a kid. I grew up with them before I moved to the mainland. We used to run around our part of Maui looking for adventure together. We lost touch when I went to live with my father and only reconnected out on Honolua Bay when I returned. When we got up to speed on each other's lives, it was clear we'd gone in different directions. They're high school drop-outs and work odd jobs like construction, handy-man work, or tour-guide stuff. I not only finished high school a year early but went to an Ivy League school and became a successful attorney. Our divergent paths might have made regaining a friendship too difficult, but before too long, we understood that just like when we were kids, our love of surfing outweighed any other difference. They gave me a few weeks of hell for being a traitor for leaving before deciding I was okay after all, and we've become surf and drinking buddies. We only ever come to one of these Front Street bars when we're looking for some female company.

Thing is, I've got that part covered tonight. And she's heading my way now, looking apprehensively at the guys sitting with me. I hold out my hand, wanting to make sure she knows I'm not trying to ditch her.

Pika and Hiro both turn to see who I'm gesturing to and I see their appreciative expressions as they eye her up and down.

"Knock it off, you creeps," I growl.

"What?" Hiro asks, suddenly all gentlemanly innocence.

"Who's your fine lady friend," Pika asks, not pretending to be anything other than the letch that he is.

Ava takes the offer of my hand as she joins us. I should let her go, let her sit at the empty chair. But I don't want to stop feeling the heat of her skin on mine. She meets my eyes and for a moment, it feels like everything else fades away. I'm lost in her gaze. And I don't want to be found.

"Well?" Pika asks, breaking the spell.

"I'll introduce you, then you can go get your own table," I say brusquely. "Ava, meet Hiroto and Pika."

Ava laughs at my rude introduction. "It's okay. I don't mind if your friends want to stay."

"See?" Pika says. His demeanor is ridiculously triumphant as if Ava had just granted him permission to ogle her rather than simply saying she would tolerate them interrupting us. But he soon finds cockiness isn't something she'll tolerate.

"As long as you keep your eyes up here," she says, gesturing to her own eyes.

Pika's eyes snap up and away from her chest and he freezes.

"Damn, she called you out," I say with a laugh.

"We're good," she says. "Right?"

"Uh, yeah. For sure," Pika says.

"You can call me Hiro," Hiroto says, extending his hand. He's of Japanese descent, tall and obscenely handsome. He's never had trouble with women, though he has no interest in settling down.

Ava smiles and takes his hand before sitting to my right. When I slide the beer over to her, my fingers brush against hers. I can almost hear the crackle of electricity that passes between us in that moment.

"No tequila tonight?" she asks with a smirk. "Probably for the best."

I can't help but flash back to last night when I licked the spilled tequila from her inner thigh. Shifting, I marvel at how easily she can turn me on.

"Ah, so this isn't your first date, then?" Hiro inquires.

I meet Ava's eyes, unsure what I should tell these guys about the no strings thing we've got going.

"*Date*," she offers, "is probably too formal a word. We just met yesterday. And we're hanging out a bit before I go back to LA."

Pika clutches at his heart dramatically. "Oh, that's tragic."

"What is?" Ava asks with a laugh.

"You're just here on vacation?"

"I am. I leave the day after tomorrow."

"And then what? A long-distance romance?" Hiro asks.

I punch him in the arm. Hard.

"Fuck, man," he whines and rubs his bicep.

I should feel bad for that. But I'd rather cut him off with a painful punch than let Ava feel like this was some sort of setup, as if I planned for my friends to be here to play up the romance angle between us.

Ava takes a long pull on her beer and I see her eyes bouncing from me to Hiro and then to Pika. When her eyes circle back to me, she quirks an eyebrow.

I shrug and shake my head a little, trying to dismiss the incident and any suspicion it might have raised.

"So, what do you do over there in LA, Ava?" Hiro asks, helpfully changing the topic.

"Um," she starts, clearly uncomfortable.

"We're not talking about all that real world stuff, guys," I say quickly. "Ava's here for a true vacation from everything."

"That go both ways?" Pika asks.

"What?" I ask.

"Does she know about you? And your traitorous history of—"

"Fuck off," I say slowly, emphatically.

Pika had been grinning with his intention of telling her all about how I used to be a local but became a traitor by leaving. Now his smile slowly fades with his confusion over me shutting him down.

Ava leans forward and pats his hand. "Yes, it goes both ways. No real world stuff from either of us. Just the here and now."

He gets momentarily lost in her gaze before looking down at her hand on his. We all watch as she slowly moves it away from him. I realize that there really is something magnetic about her. Something that not just I feel. She's beautiful but there's more to her. You just want to be near her.

"Oh, shit!" Hiro says and drops his head into his hands with elbows on the table.

"Hannah?" Pika and I both ask, craning our necks to see around the bar.

"Who's Hannah?" Ava asks.

"Shh!" all three of us guys say.

I spot Hannah's platinum-blonde head outside of the open-air bar as she moves down the sidewalk with a crowd.

"She's gone," I declare. "You're okay."

Ava laughs. "Let me guess," she says. "Bad breakup?"

"It would be if she'd accept that we're broken up!" Hiro says.

"What? How does that work?"

"She's kind of psycho, Ava," I tell her. "Hiro's broken up with her four times, and she just keeps ignoring him or acting like they're on a break."

"Is she so bad?" Ava asks.

"She was sweet at first," Hiro says. "But then the *Fatal Attraction* stuff started."

"She killed your bunny?" Ava keeps a straight face as she references one of the famous scenes from the movie about an affair gone seriously bad.

The only reason I saw it as a twelve year old is because Hiro's dad had a VHS copy of it and we'd heard there was nudity. Turned out there wasn't enough of that to make it worth our while, but we watched until the end hoping to see more. Instead, we got a scene where the family bunny had been boiled to death by the psycho would-be mistress. That kind of thing leaves an impression on a kid. But it's not a movie I would have thought Ava would know. Turns out she's full of surprises.

"No, no dead bunnies. Yet," Hiro says.

After a beat, we all break out laughing at the absurdity.

"No, she just has a habit of showing up almost anywhere I

am—work, surfing, bars. She's even slipped into bed with me in the middle of the night. And every time, she acts like it's perfectly normal. No matter how I try to get her to see that we're broken up."

"Breakups can be tricky," Ava sympathizes.

"I had a girl break up with me once," Pika says, "because I made fun of the trash TV she watched. I should have known her love of the *Kardashians* and *Vanderpump Rules* was a red flag."

We all laugh.

"I had a girl break up with me because I brought her the wrong drink," Hiro says. "I thought I was being all gentleman-like by getting her an iced tea."

"What was wrong with that?" Ava asks.

"Apparently she hates iced tea. And said I should have known that. That me bringing her a drink she hates meant that I didn't know the first thing about her," he says with a shake of his head.

"How long were you together?"

"Two and a half glorious weeks."

Ava laughs. "Yeah, I'd say that's asking a bit much. The guy I was with last, we were together for two *years*. But he had no idea what I wanted."

This confession intrigues me and I lean forward to ask her, "And what do you want?"

She hesitates, clearly regretting saying anything. But she must dismiss her reservations given the fact that we're not meant to see each other again. It's always easier to be forthcoming with people you don't know well.

"I want," she says slowly, "to have my career *and* a fairy-tale romance."

Before my buddies can make some smartass remark, I ask, "Why can't you have that?"

"I can," she says. "Just not with my ex. Because I realized last Christmas that *he* didn't think I was capable of that."

"Is that what he said?" Hiro asks.

A wave of emotion passes over her face, but she quickly shrugs it off. "Pretty much. He basically said I'm not marriage material. And so, I walked away."

"Whoa," Pika says. "Like a badass." He holds up an imaginary drink since he still doesn't have one and toasts her.

She can't mask the hint of sadness in her face. Still, she gamely raises her now almost empty bottle to toast with him.

"It was actually a good thing," she continues. "It made me realize I'm not willing to settle for anything less. Women are always told they don't have to compromise, that they can have it all. I'm willing to test that proposition, to put myself first and stay true to what I really want."

I sit back in wonder at this statement. She's a rare creature. Someone to admire, especially as I'm still trying to come to terms with how to stay true to myself after losing my way for so many years.

"Yeah, well, your boy Ford knows all about walking away from things," Pika says with a laugh.

I ignore him, giving Ava my full attention. "You deserve nothing less," I tell her.

She watches me for a moment, searching my face, I'd guess, for some hint that I'm mocking her. But there's nothing but earnestness in my expression. Despite the fact that I don't really know her, I can't deny this overwhelming desire for her happiness.

When she smiles, her eyes sparkle. That flash of sadness has disappeared. "Right?" she says with a laugh.

I lean in and kiss her.

I kiss her like she's my girlfriend.

Like she's the one.

Because at this moment, that's what our connection feels like. I don't stop to think that our time is slipping away. It feels too good to pretend that's not the case. Especially when she kisses me back with the same intensity.

"Okay," Hiro says loudly. "We'll take a hint. Let's go, Pika."

Pulling away from Ava just enough to give the guys a nod goodbye, I then whisper to her, "Let's get out of here, Hula Girl."

12

Once we're back in Ford's truck, I suggest we go to my hotel and he readily agrees. While he drives he tells me about growing up with Pika and Hiro. I listen, enjoying the stories of misadventures he shares as I play with the hair at the nape of his neck. We're both relaxed and the twenty-minute ride passes by easily.

"Go ahead and use the valet," I tell him as he approaches the entrance to the Ritz-Carlton. "I'll have the cost charged to my room."

He gives me a wink. "It's okay. I do have a little money."

"I just meant—"

Pulling my hand up to his mouth, he kisses the back of my fingers. "No worries. It's all good."

The valet opens my door before I can respond. I hadn't meant to offend him. I just assumed he's not exactly rolling in dough, not with the spare way he lives, and so I didn't want him to feel obligated to take on the cost of parking himself.

He meets me at the entrance to the hotel where a doorman greets us with an *aloha*.

"Are you hungry?" I ask as I lead him to my suite.

"Starved," he replies.

When I glance at him, I see that he's not talking about food. He's got lust in his eyes. I feel a spark of the same desire. My heartbeat quickens and a rush of warmth travels through my core and settles between my legs.

We come to my suite and I slide the key card into the slot at the door and he follows me inside.

"Nice room," he says.

The suite has a separate living area with views of the ocean along with a balcony. The floors are hardwood, and there's both a comfortable couch and a separate small dining table. It's an insanely expensive room, and not the kind of indulgence I'd spend my own money on. I'm suddenly hyperconscious of how this makes me look.

I turn to face him. "I, uh, normally wouldn't pay for a place like this," I say. "I—"

"I'm not judging you, Hula Girl," he says with a crooked smile.

"It's just, I didn't grow up with this kind of ... luxury."

He leans in and kisses me. "A self-made woman," he says in between more kisses. "I'm impressed."

My discomfort at appearing like a wealthy tourist taking advantage of a local fades away when he holds my face in his hands. He kisses away any other thoughts. We fall naturally into a rhythm, our tongues doing a synchronized dance.

Earlier, he had promised to fuck me hard, but that doesn't seem to be his plan now. Not with the way he's taking his time in kissing me.

Just kissing me.

Kissing me until I've completely surrendered to every little nuance of the way his lips and tongue command my own. I've had glimpses of this kind of sensuality from him before, but this is the first time it's been sustained. This doesn't have the same raw intensity as our first time at his place or even earlier in his truck. Those times had been all about need. We'd aggressively taken from each other in the heat of the moment.

It's different now. Purposeful, as if he wants to enjoy and prolong every second.

There's something that both thrills and terrifies me about that.

I pull away from him, trying to get a handle on what I'm feeling.

As if he can see my struggle, he uses fingers under my chin to lift my eyes to meet his. "Don't get lost in that head of yours, honey," he says.

I attempt a playful arch of an eyebrow. "No?"

"No. Because I want every bit of you right now."

He emphasizes this by grabbing my ass in a firm squeeze. This gets us back to the surface-level sexual gratification I'm more comfortable with. But when he twists me around quickly and pulls my hair away from my neck, planting slow kisses on the sensitive skin there, we're back into slow sensual mode.

I soon find, however, that this is the kind of speed I can get lost in. He's taking his time, yes, but he's doing it in such a way that he's building layer upon layer of arousal in me. Trailing his mouth over the back and side of my neck, his lips and tongue graze against me gently at first. But then he kisses become hungrier, more possessive. He uses his teeth with each kiss as if wanting to consume me. He slips the straps of my dress and bra off one shoulder, and I try to turn to him, anxious for the heat of his mouth on mine but he's not done devouring me yet. Grabbing a fistful of my hair, he pulls my head back with enough force for me to let out a gasp as he winds his greedy kisses over my shoulder, neck, and ear, sucking and biting my skin along the way. In a tease, he uses his other hand to briefly squeeze my breasts at the same time that he quickly brushes his lips against mine. He's got all the control and I'm completely in his thrall, melting into him as he shows me just how well he can make me his.

And then he pulls away, leaving me panting and desperate for his touch once more.

"Bedroom?" he says.

I'm ridiculously eager to lead him to the other room.

The bedroom has the same hardwood floors and stunning views of the ocean. There's a king-size bed with sumptuous white bedding and forest-green accent pillows, a fine chest of drawers, and a settee. The lamps on either side of the bed provide soft lighting.

He sits on the side of the bed and gives me a crooked grin. "Nice view."

I'm standing in front of him with the windows behind me. I glance over my shoulder and see that the whitewash of waves is just visible under the waning full moon.

"Not that," he says.

I turn back and see that he's leaning on his hands, watching me appreciatively.

"Oh," I say softly.

I realize this is my cue to undress for him. Though my dress could fit in at a club, it's actually made of soft jersey cotton and is easy to pull off over my head. I hadn't brought sexy matching panties and bra sets on this trip, but at least what I'm wearing is decent enough. The black cotton thong and black satin demi-bra on my otherwise naked body seems to please him, though, because he sits up.

"Yes, I *really* like the view," he says.

"This?" I ask with mock innocence as I turn a slow circle for him.

"Hell, yeah," he says in a moan and pulls me to him so I'm standing in between his legs.

Using the back of his hand, he strokes the swell of my breasts and I shiver. His touch is gentle and slow, as if reveling in the smoothness of my skin. He uses his other hand to pull, first one strap and then the other off my shoulder. Leaning forward, he presses his mouth to the spot between my breasts at the same time that he reaches around and unclasps my bra. I let him pull it away from me completely and hear it drop to the floor.

He alternates between lavishing his mouth and tongue and teeth on one nipple and then the other, stirring a tightening in my core. I loosely wrap my arms around his neck and relax under his touch, taking his lead of just being in the moment and letting my arousal build without forcing the next move.

Finally, when I'm just about at the point where I can't take it any longer, he pulls away. "Come here," he says, his voice raspy with desire. He pats the bed next to him and then quickly unbuttons his shirt just enough to pull it off over his head.

Now I'm the one enjoying the view, looking at his bare, chiseled chest. His pecs and abs are fitness model level of defined. I want to trace every sexy ridge with my tongue, but he has other ideas. He gently pushes me onto my back, kissing me deeply before pulling away so he can again look at my body. His gaze wanders slowly from my eyes downward, lingering on my breasts, hips, and legs. Then, he trails his hands over the same path, moving reverentially. He's so deliberate in his touches, taking in every part of me, just like he said he wanted to do.

I realize what this feels like: worship. He's worshipping my body. Worshipping *me*.·

"Ford," I whisper, reaching for him.

"You're so fucking beautiful," he says.

I smile. "So, do something about it." I want to unleash that animalistic passion we've had for each other up until now. Up until he decided that this time would be different. That this time would be about making love. It somehow still feels too intimate to have sex this way. We shouldn't be connecting like this. We're nothing more than a vacation hookup ... aren't we?

He rubs his cock over his shorts. "Believe me, I will. I'm so hard for you right now."

But instead of ripping off my thong, he gently slides it off my hips and down my legs so that I'm completely exposed. He runs his hand up my inner thigh and lets his fingers dip into my folds, making me whimper as he finds me slick with desire. I arch against his hand, aching for more. My clit is swollen and so sensitive to his touch. When he reaches up with his other hand to pinch my nipple, I catch my breath. It wouldn't take much more for me to come.

He can sense as much because he murmurs, "Jesus."

"I need you," I tell him, pulling at his shorts, "inside me."

He nods and slides off the bed. In one swift movement, he manages to push down both his shorts and his boxer briefs, exposing his very hard cock. It looks too big for me to have ever taken in my mouth the way I did earlier. I want to reach out and stroke the glistening head of him, but he moves out of my grasp as he grabs a condom. When he climbs back onto the bed, he's lost his patient deliberation because he moves immediately between my legs, sliding deep into me. We both moan at the sensation as he fills me completely.

I raise my knees as he grinds his hips slowly against me. His mouth finds mine and he sucks on my tongue. I grab his tight ass, feeling the muscles contract and relax as he finds his rhythm with pushing into me. It's the kind of connection that is so electrifying that I'm almost instantly on the verge of coming, but yet, I want it to go on and on. I want to feel the weight of his body on mine and the hardness of him as he masterfully works his way in and out of me.

When I press my toes against the mattress, I get just the right leverage in pushing back against him, just the right pressure on my clit. My breathing quickens as my orgasm builds. I pull away from his kiss and bite his earlobe.

"Yes," I whisper, "just like that. Don't stop."

He keeps going and I can hear in his breath that he's getting closer too. But all in a rush, I come first, squeezing my legs around his waist as he continues to pump deep in me. I cry out in pleasure, unable to stop smiling as he then does the same. Not quite simultaneous orgasms, but so close.

WHEN I WAKE, the first thing I register is Ford's arm heavy against my waist. His warm body is pressed to mine from behind, his breathing steady and deep as he sleeps.

We'd lingered in bed after making love, content to hold each other for a long while before rousing ourselves for a quick shower and then a late-night dinner of room service while wearing the hotel robes. Afterward, we'd cuddled on the sofa, trading control over Spotify as we shared with each othe

the music we each love. He's definitely got that laid-back surfer thing going with his bands, too, as he's partial to Mumford & Sons, Bon Iver, Florence + the Machine, The Lumineers, Lord Huron, and X Ambassadors. I like all those bands, too, but to broaden his horizons, I introduced him to my favorite band from Mexico, Zoé. After that, I selected songs by La Ley, a Chilean band, then Spanish artist Ana Torroja, and finally Juanes, a Columbian group. At some point, I fell asleep, curled up against his chest. He later got us both to bed.

But I didn't end up sleeping well, my mind preoccupied with the way we had made love. Like real, tender love. It was both satisfying and unsettling. Unsettling because I'm not supposed to feel this connected to him. He's supposed to be my vacation fling.

Finally, I got up just before five in the morning, pulled on a robe and went out onto the balcony. The sky was starting to turn a paler shade of blue and I could hear birds making their morning sounds. I was staring at the ocean in the near distance when Ford came up behind me, wrapping his arms around my torso as he leaned down and kissed the side of my neck.

Neither of us said anything as he then untied my robe and slipped it off my body. A quick glance assured me no one else was out on their balcony this early in the morning. As a still cool morning breeze rushed over my exposed body, I shivered. But I didn't make any move to cover up or stop him from squeezing my breasts and pushing his hardness against me. Instead, I pushed my ass right back into him and then braced my hands on the iron railing while he tore open a condom packet. He took me like that, standing out in the open, each of us stifling our moans, even when he finally made good on the promise he'd made in his truck and fucked me so hard that my legs shook.

Afterward, he pulled me back to bed and I fell asleep quickly.

I've made up for the time I lay awake during the night apparently because it's now ten thirty. I can't remember the last time I slept this late. I've spent so many years sacrificing sleep in favor of studying and working that I've trained myself to survive on five hours a night. Now, I take a deep breath and release it, feeling refreshed.

Ford stirs and pulls me closer to him.

"Good morning, honey," he murmurs into my hair.

Turning to face him, I tuck my head under his chin and take comfort in the way we naturally fit together.

"You okay?" he asks, stroking back my hair.

I'm not. I'm feeling oddly emotional with the thought that I'll be leaving tomorrow. I don't want this to end.

But I can't say that.

"Yeah, just waking up," I say, but I don't dare look at him.

"Let's go grab breakfast from your fancy buffet," he says. "Then it's time to get you in the water."

We had made plans last night to do as he had suggested before to get us both on a longboard so he can help me ride a wave. I'd forgotten that we still have this time. He doesn't have to go to work. We have all day and one more night.

Looking up at him, I smile and smooth back his bedhead. "I can't wait," I tell him.

WE'RE SITTING at a table in the hotel restaurant overlooking the spectacular view of the deep blue ocean just beyond dozens of elegant palm trees, our plates overloaded with omelets made to order, bacon, breakfast potatoes, rustic sourdough bread so fresh it melts in your mouth, and local fruit. We're eating slowly and watching each other with knowing small smiles. It feels like we both have visions of our time together running through our minds, including that first night at his place, in his truck, and on the balcony.

God, he makes me feel giddy.

"Gotta say," he starts, "that was the best sunrise I've ever seen."

"Oh, is that why you got up at that hour, condom at the ready?"

He laughs. "I got up to see where you'd gone, honey. And when I found you on the balcony, the sunlight that was barely coming up gave me a perfect view of the outline of your gorgeous body through your robe. That quickly gave ... *rise* to other ideas."

That sends a shiver of desire through me but before I can respond otherwise, my cell phone buzzes with an incoming call and we both look at it.

It's sitting face-up on the table and Bryce's photo glows on the screen. It's the photo I had put there over a year ago, the professional portrait his law firm had arranged for marketing and press release purposes. He looks stiff in his Windsor-knotted blue and gold tie, starched pale-blue dress shirt, and navy suit. But he also looks handsome and intelligent. The truth is, by outward appearances, he's a catch. He just wasn't the one for me.

"You need to get that?" Ford asks.

"Um, no." I press the button on the side of the phone to send it to voicemail. "So—" I stop when my phone rings once more. Bryce again.

Ford squints at me in that way of his. "Go ahead. It's okay."

The back-to-back calls actually concerns me and so I answer, wondering if there's an issue with the case I need to deal with.

"Hello?" I say softly, turning in my seat so my profile is to Ford.

"Hey, there you are. I've been hoping to run into you, but you've disappeared," Bryce says.

"Um, I'm not sure what you mean?"

"You haven't answered my emails."

"Oh. I'm just behind, I guess. I'll catch up to them in a few days."

"When can I see you?"

"Why would you want that?" I ask cautiously as if Ford would care that I'm talking to my ex-boyfriend.

"You want me to say it? I will. I miss seeing you, Ava."

I furrow my brow at this, confused by his sudden desire to see me. We haven't spoken about "us" since Christmas, almost four months ago. And we haven't seen each other since he bested me in that deposition. I can't imagine why he's claiming he misses me now. Unless something is going on with the case. My gut tells me he's trying to manipulate something out of me to gain a legal advantage. The bastard.

"Listen, I'm out of pocket. I don't have anything in front of me, but I really think I should review all matters before we talk again. I don't want this to turn into a conflict of interest."

"There's my girl," he says with a laugh. "You always come to it." He sighs. "All right. I'll see you at the ABA event, anyway, won't I?"

He's talking about an American Bar Association event I know is on my calendar but it's something I haven't thought about since before I got to Maui.

"I don't know about that," I say.

"Yeah, right. There's nothing that would stop you from a nice dose of networking and we both know it. See you in the bar line, maybe?"

"Goodbye, Bryce." I disconnect the call and slowly turn back to face Ford, though I don't meet his eyes. I can feel him watching me, waiting for some kind of explanation.

"Real-world stuff?" he finally asks.

"Yeah."

"Work or personal?" He pauses. "Or both?"

I take a sip of my orange juice, taking my time. "Used to be personal. Now it's just work," I admit.

He nods. "The guy who has no idea what you want?"

"That'd be him." I try to make my voice light, dismissive.

"His loss, Ava. Truly."

I meet his eyes and see such warmth and kindness there. He's really unlike anyone I've ever met.

And there I go again, feeling way too many *feelings* with this guy. I blink away the emotion and stare down at my plate, focusing on the scoop of fresh mango I had taken from the buffet. I spear one piece with my fork and hold it up, watching a tiny trickle of juice run free.

"*Es un mango,*" I say softly, amusing myself with the recollection of what I had thought when I first saw him.

"*Si, y eres tan dulce y deliciosa,*" he replies, telling me I am just as sweet and delicious as a mango.

My mouth falls open in shock. "You speak Spanish?"

He shakes his head. "I've got a very rudimentary vocabulary."

Now I'm compelled to tell him the same thing he said that first night were together on the beach, "Where did you come from?"

Squinting at me ever so slightly, he smiles and shakes his head a little. "All I know is I'm right where I want to be."

My mouth drops open and then I laugh out of sheer delight. He has a phenomenal way of making me feel like I am something special.

And then he leans forward and takes the piece of mango into his mouth from the fork I'm still holding up. As he slowly savors it, he watches me with unmasked desire and I feel the same for him all over again. That, along with the realization once more that there isn't enough time left.

13

FORD

"**F**ord!"

Well, she finally did it. She screamed my name.

But not because I'm giving her a mind-blowing orgasm. No, she's screaming my name because she's overcome by the utter freedom and joy that comes with riding her first wave. I'm behind her on the longboard, helping balance the board while she soaks it all in. She's wide-eyed, a huge smile plastered on her face. The wave dies out and she turns to me, nearly toppling us both off into the water.

I grab her waist and manage to keep us up.

"Again, again, again!" she says with the unbridled excitement of a child.

Laughing, I kiss her quickly before pulling her down so I can paddle us out into position again.

There's nothing like that first wave. I had told Ava that it would be unreal to her. But she didn't really know what to expect. Seeing her experience that sensation of, for a very brief time, being one with the water was incredible. Sharing the gift of surfing is the best thing you can do. It opens up a connection that is hard to describe. Only once you've been in the water this way can you understand what it is. There is no other world when you're surfing. There are no worries about your job, bills, or other life demands. There is only the water. And when you're in it, it's all you need. It fulfills everything you feel you could ever want. Coming out of it is the hardest thing to do.

I can't believe how many years I sacrificed away from this kind of peace. It's why I now get up early, even with a hangover, to get in some waves every chance I can. I'll never stop wanting to make up for that lost time.

And now I've got Ava feeling a sliver of this sensation, too. It's amazing to share this with her, to know that she gets it.

We manage to catch a dozen more small waves, and with each one, Ava is just as thrilled by the ride. Her energy is contagious, making me smile just as broadly as she does.

When we take a rest during a long lull in waves, I lie flat on my back on the board and she climbs on top of me, fitting her body along mine. We kiss as the board moves gently with the ebb and flow of the water. When she rests her head on my chest, I wrap my arms around her in complete contentment. Connected this way and with the water beneath us, I don't think there's a more perfect feeling in the world.

IT ISN'T until we're back on the sand, drying off, that I think again of that phone call she had. She had suddenly snapped into corporate lingo that sounded very familiar. It made me wonder if she was a lawyer. But she's already told me she isn't. Still, it was a reminder that she'll be heading home. And her home includes the kind of working life I'm determined to keep my distance from.

"What do you want to do with the rest of your last day?" I ask, hoping my voice doesn't betray the tinge of sadness I feel. This thing with her hit me so unexpectedly, so fiercely, that I don't know how to manage the sense of loss I feel with knowing she's leaving tomorrow.

"Ooh, is it my pick?" she asks with a laugh.

"Yeah, you choose. I'll spring for a fancy dinner if you want."

"Hmm, tempting. But I think what I really want is more of what we already had."

"Hot sex?" I ask hopefully.

She smirks. "Yes, that. But also, I want to go back to Makai's. And I want to hear you play guitar."

"Cheap date," I say approvingly and she playfully slaps my arm. I grab her and pull her to me so she's sitting between my legs, her back to my chest. Wrapping my arms around her, I hold her and kiss her temple. "Perfect date," I amend.

This time, she relaxes and looks back and up at me for a kiss, which I gladly give her.

OUR TIME PLAYS out as Ava requested and we have a blast with each other. She's fun and witty and such a pleasure to be with. I'm so tempted to tell her I'll be in LA soon, to tell her we should get together there. But that would turn this carefree night into something different. It would mean we'd get into what that real world looks like. What she and I have right now is pure. It's simple. We'd lose all the easiness we have in this moment. Why mess with this perfection? I do, however, have thoughts of tracking her down in LA once I've dealt with my business there. I need to focus on that first before I can give her the attention she deserves.

On this last night, we indulge in another bottle of "our" tequila at Makai's, snatching it on our way out the door so we can drink it while sitting on the cold sand down by the water.

"Tell me something," she says, leaning her shoulder in a way that tells me she's tipsy.

"What's that, Hula Girl?"

"Is that place of yours legal?"

I follow her eyes to my partially hidden beach shack. "No, not exactly. Make you feel like an outlaw?"

She sputters out a laugh.

"You tell me something," I say and nudge her back.

"Okay."

"When are you going to actually do a hula dance for me?"

"Oh!" she says excitedly and struggles to her feet. "Yes, let me see if I can figure this out."

"Just pretend you're trying to get a signal on your phone."

"Ha-ha," she says with a smirk. "Okay. Don't laugh."

"I won't."

She stamps her foot in the sand when she sees my smile. "I mean it!"

"I won't, I promise. I'll probably be dealing with a raging hard-on, not laughing, anyway."

"Ford," she says.

It's meant to be an admonishment, but it comes out slow and sexy. God, I love the way she says my name.

"Go ahead."

For some reason, she clears her throat. It's not as if she's about to sing, but I guess this helps her re-set. Raising her arms and angling her hands and fingers delicately, she starts to sway. Her hips move from one side to the other in tandem with her arm movements. It's not even close to the real thing, but damn if it isn't the sexiest dance I've ever seen.

I watch her appreciatively for another thirty seconds before she drops her arms and laughs.

"Ta-da," she declares with a curtsey.

Getting up, I join her at the shoreline, pulling her into my arms. "That was fucking amazing," I tell her.

"I'm sure it wasn't."

"You know what?"

"What?"

I cup her face in my hands and look down at her. "I *like* you. I like you so much."

Her eyes sparkle as she touches one of my hands. "I like you, too."

"What are we going to do about it?"

"Hot sex?"

That's the obvious answer. The not so obvious answer I was looking for has to do with what we're going to do once she goes home. But I know why she didn't go there. On the surface of things, there's no way we can survive outside the little bubble of her vacation. I'm committed to rebuilding my life here in Maui and she's obviously got her life waiting for her in Los Angeles. There's no choice but to just go our separate ways.

Unless ….

Unless I can see her again in LA But again, I don't want to get into that right now. Right now is about living in the moment.

"Definitely hot sex," I say, nodding so emphatically that she laughs. "But first, how about a little nighttime swim?"

She looks dubiously at the dark water. "I didn't bring my bathing suit."

Pulling off my T-shirt, I quickly go for my shorts next. "That's what skinny-dipping is for, honey. Come on!"

There's only a brief hesitation before she's stepping out of her dress to join me. Though I have the feeling she's not normally this impulsive, I'm not complaining. Definitely not when I get to see her naked under the moonlight like this. Definitely not as she runs with me into the water. We both dunk our heads and come up smiling even though the water is cooler than one might expect. Still, it feels good against my bare skin. And it does amazing things to Ava's bare skin, as her body glistens under the moonlight and her nipples harden.

We don't go too far out, swimming just deep enough so that I can stand with the water coming to mid-chest level, but it's a bit much for my petite Hula Girl and she needs to hold on to me. Again, not complaining about that as I wrap my arms around her and pull her close.

"This is amazing," she says.

"Look at you. Jesus, you're beautiful," I tell her.

"Ford." She looks away from me but she's smiling.

"Ava," I reply with mock seriousness and she laughs the way I had intended and looks at me again. "You sure as hell aren't wound tight anymore, are you?"

"You make that impossible." She kisses me quickly. "In the very best way."

Cupping her cheek in my hand, I lean in and take her mouth with mine, kissing her with slow deliberation. Lingering in the softness and saltiness of her lips as the water moves gently all around us, finding its way between our bodies even as we're pressed together. In return, she slides her hand into the hair at the back of my head, wraps her other arm around my neck, and tightens her legs around my waist. As we kiss, small waves lift us up and then lower us in a smooth, hypnotic rhythm.

This.

I'm transfixed by *this* moment. By *this* woman. It's unreal and yet absolute perfection. I don't want it to end.

When she pulls away from our kiss and buries her face into my neck, I wonder if she's having the same thoughts. Then she looks up at the sky and takes in a deep breath.

"It really is paradise," she murmurs.

I follow her gaze and see the blanket of stars shining against the dark sky. "It is," I agree. "I'm so glad that you opened yourself up to the spirit of this place. It has a way of making you reevaluate your priorities."

Cocking her head, she looks at me. "Yeah?"

"There's something called *mana*—your life energy. Where you focus your *mana* is so important to what you get in return. If you focus it on moments like this, on enjoying and respecting nature, on living a life of meaningfulness in work, then it all comes back to you in the form of a kind of balance that's hard to find elsewhere."

She's quiet as she takes that in. I can see in her expression that she's considering what that means for someone who lives in a big city like LA, and perhaps wondering if I'm telling her she's not directing her *mana* in a positive way. I don't want that. I don't want her to feel like I'm judging her. I was just trying to point out how quickly she was able to benefit from the way of life here because she opened herself up to it.

Rather than lecture her on that, though, I try to make light of it. "And that's why they have yoga and meditation classes everywhere on the mainland, right?"

"Sadly, I prefer sprints on the treadmill."

"Hell, yeah," I say. "That's why you have such fantastic legs." I run my hands from her incredibly squeezable ass along her thighs.

"Maybe we should ..."

She tilts her head toward the shore.

"Yeah, let's."

We body surf the mild waves in and Ava quickly pulls on her dress. The thin material sticks to her wet skin, outlining her sexy figure and making my mouth water with need. I hurry to get my shorts on, to contain my dick, which has been hard and ready for more since she stripped down earlier to get into the water.

"Come on, Surfer Boy," she says in a teasing sing-song as she walks backward.

I rush toward her, sweeping her up in one smooth movement so that she's got her arms and legs wrapped around me again. I keep walking, not missing a beat as I carry her toward my place, kissing her as we go.

She lets out a yelp of delight when I swing her around in a circle. "Oh my god," she says. "You make me feel like I'm light as air." She grabs my forearms, leaning back slightly at the waist, her wet air whipping around and her smile big as she laughs. It's a pure, uninhibited laugh that matches the moment of perfection I'd felt with her in the water.

That's when I know I'm going to miss her.

That's when I know that after I figure things out with my father, I'm going to see her again.

WE END up staying the night at my place which means she has

to leave me earlier than I'd like since she had to get back to the hotel to pack her things. We do a repeat of me walking her to the inlet that gets her back to where her car is at Makai's. The walk is quiet, but we hold hands as we go. It's incredible how quickly we've gotten not just familiar, but intimate with each other. I may not know her whole story, but there's a part of me that connects with her in such a basic, primal way that it's astonishing we're about to say goodbye.

"Damn," I murmur.

"What?"

"There so much more I want to show you. So much more of the island you haven't seen."

"You showed me a whole lot," she says, and leans in for a kiss.

"I'd have loved to take you to Nakalele Point. It would give you some of that romance I know you crave."

"Oh yeah? What's it like?"

"It's just north from here, maybe less than ten miles. You look for mile marker thirty-eight-point-five."

"That's very specific," she says with a laugh.

"That's the best spot, anyway," I tell her, "to see the geyser. In the morning, the water sprays up and the sun shines through perfectly to make a rainbow."

"Ooh, that does sound romantic."

"The best part is that there's also a volcanic rock formation with a natural cutout in the shape of a heart."

She squeezes my hand and I see a smile of delight on her face at the prospect. Yep, that would have been a great place to take her. Anything to get that kind of sweet, carefree expression out of her.

Leaning her head on my shoulder for a second, she then looks up at me and says, "You're a romantic, too, Surfer Boy."

I shrug that off. I'm not about to admit that I can't recall the last time I felt the urge to do such things with a woman. That it's only with *her* that I've considered being that way.

Soon enough we've arrived at her car. We both hesitate.

"Well," she says, being the brave one to speak first, "thanks for making my vacation so wonderful."

"It was my honor," I tell her. "Really, I'm just happy that chicken ran you off the road. Worked out in my favor."

She laughs. "I'd say to text me some time, but I know it's virtually impossible with your relic of a phone."

"It's not impossible." I think we both know I'm referring to more than texting. I'd love for us to walk away from this believing that somehow, this isn't really the end.

"Would you mind—would it be okay if I took a selfie of us?" she asks.

"Here," I say, holding out my hand for her phone, "I'll do it."

When she gives me her phone, I deftly find my way to the camera option. She turns sideways, holding me with both arms around the waist and looking up at the phone. Adjusting it so that the blue water and willowy palm trees can be seen behind us, I take several photos.

"Can you even receive photos on that old-fashioned thing you call a phone?" she asks with a laugh.

"No. And I've never been so tempted to buy a smartphone."

"I'll mail you a copy. Send it to the music school?"

"That would be great." Again, silence falls between us. "Ava, safe travels. And hey, maybe I'll get over to the mainland and—"

"I appreciate it, but you don't have to say that."

"No, I mean it. I would like—"

"I'd like it, too. But we can be honest that the odds probably aren't in our favor, right?"

"Well, I guess that's a pretty pragmatic attitude."

She smirks. "Pragmatism is usually my default. Just ... not so much these past few days."

"Lucky for me," I tell her and she laughs with a small shrug.

"And me."

Smiling, I beckon for her to come in for a hug. She's petite, but I like the way she fits against me. I hold her longer than a simple hug should last, but finally give her a kiss and let her go. I should tell her that the odds are definitely in our favor because I'll be in LA soon, but with not knowing exactly how my time there will go, I don't want to make promises. I'd rather reach out to her once I'm there and know exactly when I have the time to see her. Besides that, if I pushed the idea of seeing her over there, she'd probably pull those walls of hers up and retreat, worrying that her vacation fling is obsessive.

"Take care," she says, pulling away and getting into her rental car.

"You too."

And that's it. She drives off with just a little wave of her hand out the window as she goes.

I'll be damned if I ever meet someone like her again.

14

AVA

"This is not like you, *mija*," my mother says. "I thought you couldn't wait to get home from vacation and back to work?"

I've come here to her house straight from the airport, having spent the five-hour plane ride doing nothing but thinking of Ford while staring at our photo together, like some lovesick teenager. This ache in my chest is so unfamiliar. I thought I could have a little fun with a gorgeous surfer and leave it all behind. I was wrong. He turned out to be more than a vacation fling. God, he was so much more. Why did he have to be so smart and charming and intuitively supportive of me? Why did he have to be, not just a bit of fun, but perfect would-be relationship material?

"Well?"

Mama has been waiting for a reply while I've been lost in lamenting what will never be. I sit up straight in my kitchen table chair. "I am excited to get back to work," I say, but my attempt at normalcy falls flat even to my ears.

LARA WARD COSIO

Mama looks at me with her famous all-knowing expression.

"Okay," I say, quickly dropping all pretense. I can never keep from telling Mama everything. It's how we both survived after my dad passed away. We'd talk about everything we were feeling, fearing, and hoping. "I met a guy over there and he was just so ... perfect."

"Perfect, but ...?"

I sigh, continuing to channel my teenage self. "He's perfect in the context of where he is, you know what I mean?"

She laughs. "No, not exactly."

"It was a vacation fling. It was fun and romantic and ... not real. He's a surfer and a music teacher. He lives in this little shack right on the beach with hardly any possessions. He doesn't even have a proper phone."

"But he makes you happy?"

"He did. But it's hopeless. Maybe that's why it was so easy to give in to the moment," I muse.

"What do you mean?"

"You remember how Bryce told me I'm basically incapable of letting people in? That I'm to blame for him not knowing me."

"Oh, I remember," Mama says with a look of annoyance she doesn't try to hide. She had never cared for him and that final Christmas night was proof to her that her instincts were right.

"I think there was some truth in that," I admit. "No, really. I've been in self-protection mode ever since Papa passed. I don't stop for anyone. I don't let anyone in."

Mama considers this brutal truth for a moment before nodding. "Yes, I've seen that. But I've also never seen you with someone who deserves all you have to offer. Maybe there's a part of you who knows that, too, and that's why you've kept your distance."

"Could be."

"But, this surfer? Did you feel differently with him?"

"I did. But that's probably only because I knew all along that it was never going to last. So, that made it easier to let down my guard."

"I suppose that's possible."

I nod, trying to convince myself that's all it was.

"How exactly did you let down your guard?" Mama prods, obviously sensing I have more to say.

"I talked to him about Papa," I say. "You know I *never* talk about him."

"Only with people you feel safe with."

"Wait, what does that mean?"

"Haven't you spoken of him with your boss?"

I suck in a breath at that, remembering how I had confided in Randall about my father being a big baseball fan and that he had passed away. But that was *years* ago.

"Oh, Mama. How do you remember things like that?" I ask softly.

She strokes my hair back behind my ear in the same soothing way she's done for as long as I can remember. "It's just what a mother does, *mija*."

I reach out and put my arms around her, giving her a big hug. She squeezes me in return and I feel a measure of relief, the ache in my chest lessening just a bit.

"Now," she says as she pulls away, "*una quesadilla?*"

There's a sparkle of amusement in her eyes. She's always trying to feed me and the offer of a quesadilla comes so often that it's become a joke.

But this time I'm actually hungry. "*Si, por favor*, Mama," I tell her.

My acceptance of food makes her ridiculously happy. She claps her hands together and grins, going to the fridge to grab the *queso Oaxaca*.

"I have fresh chile, too," she adds, gesturing to the *molcajete* on the counter where she had just ground up roasted tomatillos and peppers among other goodies for spicy salsa in anticipation of me dropping in. She knows me so well.

"You're the best, Mama."

She waves away the compliment. "Just remember that *you* deserve the best."

That's a point she's made to me throughout my life. It's such a shame that someone you know and love can tell you this truth for years before you finally come to understand it. It was only on that balcony with Bryce at Christmas I realized that I do deserve the best in this world. But no one will hand it to me. I have to make it happen in love, just as I have with work.

15

FORD

The murmurs slowly fade to complete silence as I walk through the McAvoy & Partners law firm situated high in a tower building of downtown Los Angeles.

I know the reaction isn't just because I'm conspicuously underdressed in jeans and a weathered gray T-shirt, but rather because none of these people have seen me in almost a year.

I won't be staying long. The plan is to give my father a heads up that I'm in town and will be wrapping up some loose ends in conjunction with resigning.

"Mr. McAvoy," Doris, my father's long-time secretary, says as I approach his office.

She's a true gatekeeper, having earned a reputation for being able to make access decisions on his behalf. With the way she's assessing me over her bifocals, I have the feeling she's ready to say I can wait to be seen. But I'm not here to play games.

"Doris," I reply and keep moving past her to the office door.

I knock twice and open it.

"You can't—" she starts.

I move into the office and close the door behind me before she can finish her attempt to stop me.

My father is at his desk, suit coat off and sleeves rolled up. He's examining papers while on a conference call and shows no surprise when he glances my way. He only holds up his hand to me, a silent gesture to wait.

There goes my momentum. Forcing a deep breath, I turn away and tune out the back and forth coming from his speakerphone and instead look out the window at the creep and crawl of bumper to bumper cars forty-six floors below us on the street.

My thoughts drift, as they have so often in the last few days, to Ava. I've picked up my antiquated flip phone a dozen times with the intention of calling her. But each time, I put it down, telling myself that it's not the right time. Still, that doesn't stop me from reliving every sexy moment of what we had in Maui. And it doesn't stop me thinking what our reunion will look like once I'm done with this part of my trip. Thinking of her has tempered the mood I'd started with when I came here.

I'd come in hot, ready to rip the Band-Aid off and tell my father that I was going to officially resign. That I knew this meant I'd have to sell off my shares. And that I'd be severing all ties with the man I had once worked so hard to impress. What I also knew would come from this was his disdain. There's no doubt in my mind that he'd judge me as weak. He'd declare I wasn't up to fulfilling the responsibilities he so magnanimously bestowed upon me. That, or he'd say he had waited too long to bring me over. That my mother had softened me up too much to ever recover.

And I'll tell him he never knew the first thing about me and he still doesn't. Not even after all this time of me jumping through hoops just so that he might be interested in actually getting to know me. I'll tell him that I have regained the kind of peace and happiness he'll never know because he's too afraid to even examine who he is, let alone who his son is. I'll tell him he can take his job and his shares and shove it up his ass. That if he wants his legacy to be that he drove away his only son *and* screwed over his own father all for some power trip, he can have at it. Because I am done.

I'm having this imaginary fight in my head while he keeps blathering on. I realize I'm wasting time.

"How about you wrap that up?" I say and then turn to look at him.

His steely stare finds my eyes.

"Jesus, just tell them you have them boxed in based on Lemmond versus Hewstan." I guess I had been listening well enough to his call after all. The subject matter had brought to mind, in that photographic way I have, a particularly relevant case.

After a beat, Senior tells the gaggle of lawyers on his call that he's going to investigate the case I mentioned and get back to them.

Finally, it's just the two of us.

"You don't have to research it," I tell him. "I can recite it for you right now."

Leaning back into his chair, he raises his arms and puts his hands behind his head. "No, I'll have one of the associates pull it up for me."

"Well, you're welcome in any case."

I can't help the snark. This is the first time I've seen him in almost a year. The first time I've spoken to him since I over-heard him plotting ways to marginalize both me and my grandfather. As much peace as I've found by being away, I'm just now understanding that I've only buried all my anger at him, not let it go. It's a toxic mix of my latent abandonment issues, disappointment in myself for stooping to his level, and the deep, seething frustration that's come from finally accepting that he has no desire for a real relationship with me. It was all only ever a transactional one for him. It was about what *I* could do for *him*. How I could make him look like a good father who supported my ambitions. He wasn't up to the task of being a father twenty-seven years ago when I was born, he wasn't capable of it when he had me move in with him when I was twelve, and he's definitely not up to it now. It would require too much effort from him. It would require him not being a fucking narcissist.

Yeah, you could say I'm angry.

"You look … *tan*," he says instead of taking my hint to thank me. "I suppose wasting your legal talents in pursuit of the next wave is worth it to you?"

"Really?" I groan. "Listen—"

He drops his arms and leans forward, elbows on his desk. "No, I want *you* to listen. You owe me that after the latitude I've given you this past year. I can pretty well guess that you're done contributing to this firm. It was very clever of you to remember the lax leave of absence policy we had for share-holders. Thanks for that. As you know, I've corrected it."

"Right. So, I'll—"

"Resign and sell your shares at base level, yes, I know. And then you'll—what? Live out your days being a beach bum? Where is your pride?"

"It's back where it should have been before you forced me into your empty world."

He shakes his head in frustration. "The 'empty world' that gave you a top-notch education and placed you in a highly esteemed law firm? That's what you're disparaging?"

"There's no point in trying to get you to understand that we don't have the same values."

"Really?" he asks with a laugh. "Seems to me we were lock-step in pursuing wins on cases and big payouts for a while there."

"That was my mistake. I'll own it. And now I want out."

"You'll be back. You'll eventually tire of that lazy Maui life. Your mind is too ambitious to go unchallenged."

I grin before laughing. "You won't ever get it."

He lets that hang in the air for a minute before standing. "Listen, you're about to get a very nice payout with those shares. But I need you to do something for me first."

"Oh, boy. What are you plotting now?"

He looks at me quizzically. He never did know I heard his conversation that night I left for Maui.

"I need you to hold off on your resignation and shares sale until after the board meeting."

Of course, his main priority wouldn't be trying to reconcile with me. It would be trying to protect his company. I scoff and mutter, "You want me to lie to the board?"

"What I want, what I *require*, is for you to see the big picture and not rock the boat at this sensitive time. The board doesn't need to know about your official departure at this moment. It's about protecting the firm. That's always my overriding concern."

"No shit," I mutter. I really can't control that mouth of mine sometimes.

"Don't be such a child about this. You're going to make enough off those shares to allow you to waste your days surfing for quite a few years. Just play the game for a few more days."

I make a show of thinking about this, but the request to extend my stay is exactly what I need. It will buy me time to research an idea I have for what I might do with my shares other than sell them to him.

"All right. I'll stay, but only as long as I have to," I say grudgingly. "Then I'm out of here for good."

My father looks pleased with himself. He really has no vision of anything other than his own worldview.

"I'll have Doris send you the itinerary for the board meeting," he says. "And dust off your old office."

"Fantastic," I say flatly and start to turn away.

"Oh, and I'll need you to attend the ABA event tonight. It's important to make a show of solidarity."

"Ah, no. That's not part of the deal." I have no desire to be put on display at an American Bar Association event, pretending to be the prodigal son returning home to the nest solely to boost his image.

"Remember, *Son*, that you're not in a position to pick and choose. You have less than a week where you need to abide by my rules. Then you'll get your goddamn early retirement, complete with a golden parachute you have done nothing to deserve."

I could argue with him about this point. I could cite all the cases I helped the firm win, all the revenue I've brought in, all the new clients I've attracted with my reputation for a photographic mind and the ability to connect the finer points of the law. But I just don't care.

Instead, I tell him honestly, "I don't have the right clothes for something like that."

"There's a suit in your office."

When he sees my surprise, he adds, "You didn't think I wouldn't know when you were finally coming back, did you?"

I hold back a shiver at the thought that he's had spies checking on me since I've been away. I should have known he wouldn't have just let me be.

"Doris will arrange for a haircut and a shave, too," he says as I turn away. "Appearances matter, Ford. At least for this week, I need you to look the part you used to play so well."

Yes, that's all it is, I tell myself. It's only a part I'm playing until I'm truly free.

16

AVA

It's the kind of lawyers' event I'm normally thrilled to be a part of. Sure, the presentations can be dry, but the networking during the cocktail hour has always been my thing. I usually relish reconnecting with work colleagues or making new acquaintances, determined to further opportunities to advance my career in any way I could.

But not tonight.

Tonight, I'm here physically, but still distracted otherwise. I've been back to work for two full days now, gotten completely caught up on my emails and cases, and should be in the swing of things. But I'm still off. My thoughts stray so often to Ford that it takes effort to redirect my attention. I'll find myself revisiting our time together, indulging in replaying those moments where lust overtook us.

"He's here tonight."

Startled by the voice in my ear, I turn to see Tyler, my friend and co-worker. He's even more of a social butterfly at these things than I am. We'd gone our separate ways a while ago as he mingled and I stood off to the side, being unusually reserved.

"Who's here? Bryce? Yeah, I know. I saw him earlier. And I'm keeping my distance," I say.

"No, not him. I'm talking about McAvoy Junior," he says, his eyes dancing with excitement.

I laugh. "And who is that?"

"Girl, you really have no idea of the gossip in our world, do you?" He makes a show of looking around. "Where did he go? He was here a minute ago."

"Who? You're going to have to educate me."

He sighs. "McAvoy Junior is the absolute hottest lawyer in LA. I mean, hot as in he's drop-dead gorgeous *and* he's brilliant at the law. His dad, McAvoy Senior, isn't too bad himself, I must say," he says with a salacious grin.

"Ooh, so your odds are doubled!"

"Don't I wish. No, neither play for my team. Anyway, they call Junior *Boy Wonder* because he skipped a grade in high school and finished college in three years. A real brain. But word is he absolutely loathes that nickname."

"Okay," I say slowly, bemused.

"Anyway, he made a big splash working for his dad for a few years. He's supposed to have this really amazing memory for case law. But then he disappeared about a year ago. The official line was that he was taking a leave of absence. But there were plenty of people who said he had it out with Senior. Anyway, this whole room is positively *buzzing* because he's back."

"People are easily amused, is what you're telling me."

He laughs. "That is true. But just wait until you feast your eyes upon this hunk of a man, Ava. He's *unreal*."

"Well, I may not get a chance to experience this amazing

hunk of a man because I'm going to go soon. I'm just not feeling it tonight."

Tyler shakes his head in disappointment. I'm usually up for a little fun banter with him, but I just don't have it in me at the moment.

"I can't believe you haven't shaken vacation mode yet," he says. "Okay, I'm going to see if I can find him real quick. Don't leave. I promise it will be worth it."

I shake my head, smiling at his dedication to this mission. "Okay, I'll stay for a little bit."

I watch him rush away, his head swiveling from side to side as he hunts for his prey in the sea of suits and cocktail dresses. I'm wearing one of my favorite day-to-night dresses for the occasion along with heels. Without the blazer I pair it with for work, my arms are bare and the scoop neck somehow becomes more suggestive. The way it hugs my curves and exposes my legs above the knee has gotten me a few lingering looks. Me being me, I shut down any interest by pulling up my walls and moving on quickly. I have no desire to get involved with another lawyer, not after the disappointment that was Bryce.

Speaking of whom ... here he comes, making a beeline for me. I have no choice but to stand still and await him, as I've already made accidental eye contact.

"Ava," he says, his slightly gravelly voice revealing that he's had a few cocktails already.

He leans in and I give him my cheek to kiss, but at the last second, he plants his lips against mine sloppily. I pull away and wipe at my mouth, glaring at him.

"Oops," he says.

"Not cute," I tell him and he shrugs. "Neither was that

move you tried with my client while I was away. Good thing my firm had it covered and you didn't succeed."

He had tried to approach my client directly, without involving me or my firm. That's a big no-no and he should know better. Other than pure hubris, I don't know why he tried it.

"Where were you, anyway?" he asks.

"On vacation."

He laughs. "No, seriously. Was it that conference in Boston?"

"No, I was actually on vacation. I completely disconnected."

Eyeing me skeptically for a moment, he finally nods sagely. "Yeah, sure. Okay, if you don't want to share, I guess I can live with the mystery."

"You need to recuse yourself from this case," I tell him, preferring to get back to business. That's the only relationship we have left, at least in my mind.

"What? Why would I do that?"

"You were only supposed to be temporarily filling in for Polanski when he was out sick. Why are you sticking with this? Just to mess with me?"

He smiles and steps closer to me. "I'd love to *mess* with you again, it's true."

"Ugh." I put my hand on his chest and push him back. "Your whiskey breath is not charming."

"Ah, give me a chance," he says, reaching out for me.

I step back just as I feel someone else's hand circle my waist from my right side.

"There you are, honey."

What I see makes me catch my breath.

It's Ford.

My Ford.

Only, he doesn't look the same. His normally tousled hair has been trimmed and is tamed into a neat style. His scruffy face has been cleanly shaven. And his usual board shorts have been replaced by a finely tailored gray suit, light-blue dress shirt, and no tie. He smells the same, though. God, he smells so good. It's some sort of sandalwood, salty, beachy scent.

Before I can ask what he's doing here, he offers his hand to Bryce, saying, "I don't think we've met. I'm Ava's fiancé."

I open my mouth to dispute this surreal notion but stop when I feel Ford's fingers squeezing my waist.

"Fiancé?" Bryce repeats dubiously. His eyes fall to my left hand. My *bare* left hand.

"The ring is getting sized," Ford explains smoothly. "We should have it back in no time, shouldn't we, Ava?"

"Um, well," I mumble, trying to sort out just what the hell is happening.

"Wait a second," Bryce says. "Let me get this straight, Ava. *You*, of all people, are getting married? And it's to the *Boy Wonder*, Ford McAvoy?" He laughs, clearly finding the whole thing preposterous.

That's exactly what it is. Still, I'm irritated that's what *he* thinks.

Before I get a chance to say anything, Ford leans in close to Bryce, telling him with absolute confidence, "Ain't nothing *boy* about me, old man. Now, why don't you go ahead and get yourself *another* drink? You'll need it for when it really hits you that Ava walked away from your ass."

My hand flies to my mouth as I fail to suppress a laugh at the expression on Bryce's face. He's shocked and angry at being talked to this way.

"Real mature," Bryce sneers.

I catch Ford winking at Bryce before he turns us away and toward an empty cocktail table.

"Kiss me," Ford says.

"What? No. I don't even know what is—"

"Fine. Then, I'm going to kiss you. And it's going to be a *real* kiss. Slow, deep, and leaving you wanting more. Both because I want to—so fucking much—and because your ex is still watching us."

"Oh," I say on a sigh, powerless to refuse him when he puts it like that. I raise myself to my tiptoes as he gathers me to him.

When he kisses me, I lose all sense of anything else. My body melts into his, just the way it had during our few days together in Maui—no doubt a perfect display of our desire and attraction to each other.

When we slowly, oh so slowly, pull apart, he caresses my cheek with his hand and stares into my eyes.

"I was desperate to see you again, but I never thought I'd find you *here*, Hula Girl," he says softly, a smile tugging at the corner of his mouth.

"Where did you come from?" I ask and he laughs. Before he can attempt some kind charming reply, I continue, "No, I mean it." I pull fully away from him, needing the distance to try to comprehend what's going on. "I really want an answer. Because I'm so confused. And honestly, I think I'm a little mad at you, too."

"Mad at me? Why?"

I shake my head, trying to formulate all the reasons. In the end, I simply say, "Because you lied to me."

"Uh, no, I didn't."

"You're not just some surfer dude. You're a lawyer. You don't live in Maui. You live here. You played some really jacked up game over there, pretending to be something you're not."

"No, you've got it all wrong."

"Ford McAvoy? That's your full name?" I realize with some embarrassment that I never got his last name.

He nods. "And you're Ava ...?"

"Ruiz," I say dismissively. "That's not the point. The point is that my friend Tyler told me who you are about fifteen minutes ago."

He cocks an eyebrow at me. "What did he say?"

"That you're well known as a brilliant *lawyer*. That you've been away. And now you're back." I pause. "He also said that you're gorgeous, which I won't argue with."

That gets a laugh out of him. "Your friend Tyler doesn't know the whole story, Ava. No one does. I left the law about a year ago when I moved *home* to Maui. I do live there. I really do teach music at my mom's school. And I spend all my time otherwise surfing."

I still can't sort out what all this means. "Then—then, why are you *here*?"

"I wish I could say I planned this as some elaborate way to get in touch with you, but it's trickier than that. I have some business to wrap up."

Looking past him, I try to process all of this. "Wait a second." I look back at him. "You knew that whole time that you'd be in LA and you didn't plan on seeing me, did you?"

"I, uh—"

"I think our engagement is over."

Laughing, he holds up his hands in a pleading gesture. "No, listen. The only reason I didn't make plans to see you is because this stuff I have to deal with, this work stuff, it's complicated. But I swear, I was going to reach out to you as soon as I had a handle on it."

"Yeah, right," I scoff.

"It's true. I just didn't want to make promises when I knew I had this work thing to sort out."

"And you couldn't tell me about that? As if little old me wouldn't understand? I have my J.D., just like you."

"Well, I didn't know you were a lawyer back in Maui, did I? You said you weren't one."

"Because you said you hated lawyers," I snap back. "Why would I admit to being one?"

He bites his lip and looks at me like he wants to devour me next.

"What?" I ask impatiently.

Squinting at me in that way he does, he says, "It's our first fight." Leaning closer, his lips graze the shell of my ear. "It's fucking turning me on."

Despite the shiver of arousal running through me, I pull away. "Ford, what is happening?"

"Honey, I don't know for sure. But I really want to figure it out. With you."

That's enough for me to stop resisting and let him pull me to him again. He looks so fine in that suit, but all I want to do is tear it off him.

And then I catch a glimpse of something that makes me freeze. I see Bryce walking back toward us. This time, he's with an older gentleman who looks a lot like Ford.

17

FORD

I'd been at this insufferable event at the Millennium
Biltmore hotel for just over half an hour when I spotted
my Hula Girl. I was so happy to see her that I forgot to
be shocked for a moment. But there she was, across the main
foyer, standing on her own and looking distracted. And beautiful. So incredibly beautiful in her body-hugging black cocktail dress, her lips painted kiss-me-red, and her hair shiny and
falling down her back.

Besides happiness and attraction, the next thing I felt was
amusement. Shaking my head, I realized there was only one
reason she would be here. Turns out she is the thing I have
grown to despise: a lawyer. At least it explains the suspicions
I'd had those few times the real world came out in our
conversations.

But I sure as hell never expected to run into her. I don't
remember ever meeting her when I lived here, either. She
must practice a different kind of law. Still, she's hard to
ignore.

And so, I watched the person I recognized as having

phoned her back-to-back when we were having breakfast at her hotel approach her. Even from my distance, I could see he was on his way to being drunk. Their body language made it clear that she wanted nothing to do with him. I was inordinately relieved by that.

When he kept ignoring her obvious signals to back off, I strode right over and inserted myself. Claiming to be her fiancé was a bit much, but I didn't think it through. I remembered that she said this guy hadn't thought she was marriage material, and so it seemed a perfect way to stick it to him. For him to realize he'd make a big mistake by letting her go.

But there is more to consider with this spur-of-the-moment game than I originally thought. I know that now that my father and Bryce are headed our way.

"Ford," Senior says, "Bryce here was just telling me how *surprised* he was to learn of your engagement."

Shit. I recognize the steely look in Senior's eyes. It's the same look I came to know all too well as a rebellious twelve year old. With just the hardening of his gaze, he can convey a stern warning that's basically him saying, "You'd better not test me. Because there will be consequences if you do." I'm less concerned for myself than I am for Ava. She has no idea how cut-throat he can be. This has just gone from harmless screwing around with Ava's ex to opening her up to Senior's wrath.

If I admit that it was all a joke now, Senior would be furious. *Appearances matter* might as well be his mantra. That's why I'm here in the suit he bought for me, after all. Trying to project the image that I've returned to the fold, that I'm an active part of McAvoy & Partners again. All to appease my father for as long as it takes to get past the board meeting.

Well, that and also to buy myself the time I need to leave on my own terms.

So, if I piss him off now by admitting to this fake fiancé ruse, it's very likely that he'd be angry enough to *want* to fire me. But he can't. Not before the board meeting. And so, if he can't go after me, he might just go after Ava to get at me. The last thing I want is for her to get caught up in the war I've got going on with my dad. In that split second, I decide the best thing to do is let the clock run out on this game I'm playing. The only question is whether Ava will shut it down or go along with me.

"Well," I say with a forced laugh, as I try to steer this whole thing in a different direction. "I guess Bryce can't be blamed for being a little jealous. He is Ava's ex-boyfriend, after all."

"Is that right?" Senior eyes Bryce with new distaste.

Outing Bryce as a jealous ex was a good move. My father does not like losers, which is exactly how he'll view Bryce now. And it will remind Ava of the gentle payback this gives her.

"Well, I really just wanted to give you both my congratulations," Bryce says, fumbling but sober enough to know that he does not want to get on Senior's bad side.

"Oh, we appreciate the congratulations," I say and wrap my arm around Ava, squeezing her shoulder and hoping she understands this is the best way to go.

"Congratulations for what?"

An elderly man has joined us. He's tall with silver hair and has a dignified manner. I recognize him as being a fixture in our circle for years, but before I greet him, my father speaks.

"Ah, Randall," he says, "how are you?"

The two shake hands and exchange pleasantries before

Bryce puffs out his chest and makes a show of greeting Randall like they're old pals.

But I sense some discord between the two. And when Randall looks at Ava, there's a tenderness in his eyes that makes me suspect he's got a soft spot for her. I like the idea that he's protective of her.

"You remember my son, Ford?" my father asks Randall.

"Can't say that I do," Randall replies, smiling and holding out his hand genially.

I'm surprised that Randall doesn't remember me because he's been at my father's house before for various dinners and parties. We've met more than once. I suppose it has been a while since one of those meetings, though.

"Well, that's odd," Bryce says. "What with he and Ava being *engaged*."

All eyes turn to Ava, and I hold my breath.

"We wanted to keep it a secret?" Ava explains, her voice coming out as more of a question than a statement.

"And now the proverbial cat's out of the bag," my father says with a chuckle. "Anyway, we were planning on making the dinner party at my house in a few days into a sort of surprise engagement announcement. Isn't that right, Ford?"

I grit my teeth before quickly forcing a smile. Senior has gone all-in on this thing. He wants to appear to have known all along about this pseudo engagement rather than cause a minor scandal with word getting out that he didn't know that his own son was planning on getting married. There's no turning back now. Telling the truth would be messier than just going with the lie.

"Well, now that it's out," I say, "maybe we can forego all the spectacle of a party."

"I wouldn't hear of it," my father says smugly. He may not

know the whole story of this "engagement" but he knows he's got me in an awkward spot. And he's enjoying it.

"And I'm going to make sure my schedule is clear so that I can attend," Randall says, his eyes fixed on Ava. There's a flicker of something wild in his expression, something he takes pains to get control over and dismiss.

"Great," she says meekly.

"I'd love to attend if you have room," Bryce says.

Thankfully, my father seems to have a good read on Bryce and says dismissively, "Why don't you call my secretary, Doris, and see what she thinks. She's handling all the details."

"I'll do that. First thing tomorrow."

I roll my eyes at Bryce's eagerness.

"We have to get going," Ava says, surprising me. "We have that thing, babe, right?"

"Uh, yes. That thing. Gotta get to it," I reply.

We say hasty goodbyes and she pulls me urgently away. She doesn't stop until we're past the pre-function area outside of the cocktail reception and down the grand marble staircase. It's then that she turns to me and crosses her arms over her chest, leveling a hard stare at me.

I hold up my hands in a "don't shoot me" gesture. I don't even know where to start with this. It all got out of control so quickly that I'm still trying to process what we're dealing with. I do know one thing: she's hot as hell when she's mad. I can practically see the smoke rising off her.

"Don't you dare look at me like that right now," she says, tossing her long hair back over her shoulder.

"Like what?" I can't help but laugh.

"Like you want to fuck me right here."

"Jesus," I say, pulling her to me by her waist, "I so do want to fuck you right now. You've had me turned on since I saw you across the room."

She puts her hand on my chest and presses but I don't let her push me away. "We need to get out of here."

"Yes, we do," I reply, dropping my voice an octave.

Exasperated, she says, "Not for that. So we can *talk*."

"Talk?" My mind is still on the idea of finding some nook in the lobby where I can have her to myself.

"Yes. Talk about how you just screwed up my life."

"Oh, that."

"Yes, that." She pulls away from my grasp. "Now, let's go."

Swallowing, I nod and follow after her.

18

AVA

I can feel the weight of Ford's expectation as I storm out of the hotel and down the street, but I don't say a word. I don't explain to him that we're going to my place. I don't explain to him that I live on Spring Street, near enough to walk. I don't explain to him that I'm grappling with how unreasonably betrayed I feel by all the half-truths he told me in Maui.

I'm in my own head, compiling the things that just don't add up when I realize he's no longer by my side. Glancing back, I see that he's a half-step behind me. With his eyes on my behind.

I come to an abrupt stop and he nearly runs into me. Turning to face him, I see his crooked smile.

There are plenty of people moving in both directions on the sidewalk. They're likely heading home after work, or meeting friends for a drink, or ducking into shops like The Last Bookstore, which happens to be catty-corner to the building where I live. There's been a huge effort to revitalize downtown Los Angeles into a place where young professionals like myself want to live. To a certain extent, it's worked. It can be a lively place, especially during the week. But on weekends, it still becomes a veritable ghost town. I've never minded, as the only reason I bought the place I live in is to be close to the office where I spend six days a week. The quiet on the one day I take off is usually of no concern since I'm more often than not at my mother's house, spending the day with her to check over her business' bookkeeping, catch up on neighborhood gossip, and eat the kind of made-with-love food only she can make.

Now, however, I'm conspicuously aware of the people rushing past us with impatience. That crooked smile on Ford's face makes me lose my own patience.

"You think this is all a joke, don't you?" I ask.

"What?"

"Do you even realize the damage you've done to my professional reputation? Do you even care?"

"Wait a second," he says, his expression going serious.

Before he can continue, I tell him, "No, of course you don't. All you care about is watching my ass walk down the street. God, I don't even know why I'm still talking to you right now."

Looking away from him, I eye the door to my building. It's only two storefronts down the block, just past the hipster barbershop. But Ford doesn't know that. I could just send him on his way right now, wait until he's out of sight, and then go up to my loft. That would be one way to fix all this—shut down this insane attraction we have to each other and truly go our separate ways. I can tell Randall that I was playing along with Ford's silly practical joke, that none of it was true, that I barely know him. I wouldn't even be lying if I did that. And then I could get back to my normal life. I could get Ford out of my system and go back to my usual routine of working my ass off rather than letting him ogle it.

"I *do* care," he says.

I reluctantly meet his eyes.

"Please, can we go somewhere to talk? I'll buy you dinner. Anywhere you want."

He's dropped the sex fiend act and looks contrite. The fact that his hair has reverted back to its usual unruly state and he's undone the top two buttons of his dress shirt have nothing to do with the fact that my anger is dissipating. Or at least, that's what I tell myself.

Okay, so I'm not really ready to shut this down. I want answers. I want to know what the hell just happened. And I wouldn't mind being in close proximity to the heat of his body while I do so.

Also, I'm hungry. Those events always skimp on food, only offering a paltry passed hors d'oeuvre or two before the wait staff disappears. My first thought is to take him to the little place nearby that offers a limited menu of mouth-watering tacos on house-made tortillas. They serve everything from steak to chicharron to tinga tacos. But it's their spicy specialty taco with four kinds of roasted peppers that always draws me in. Unfortunately, they don't have a liquor license and after skipping out on the cocktail reception before I could even get a glass of wine, combined with all this craziness with Ford, I really need a drink.

"I know a place," I say, thinking of my second-choice Mexican restaurant. "Let's go."

This time, when I start walking, he keeps pace with me.

"Thank you for giving me a chance," Ford says once we've been seated.

We got lucky, skating by a party of seven to secure the last open table for two. The restaurant is alive with the chatter of a full house, the mood upbeat and a contrast to our awkward unintentional date.

"Listen," I say, "I can't even start to talk until I have a drink and some food. I'm too hungry and I'm too irritated."

He nods and smoothly flags down our waiter, who had until this point been too occupied with other tables to even greet us.

I don't wait for the waiter to explain the specials. Instead, I ask for an Old Fashioned and an order of shrimp and avocado tostadas. Ford joins me with the same drink and asks the waiter for his recommendation, taking him up on the carne asada entrée.

Taking my earlier warning literally, Ford is silent while we wait for our drinks. He looks around the restaurant, surveying the one long aqua wall, the other brick wall, and the ceiling that's painted terra cotta between wood beams. In turn, I watch him, trying to decipher what he's all about.

Tyler was, of course, right. Ford is drop-dead gorgeous. There's nothing quite like a man who can rock both a business suit and a bathing suit. The way he cleans up is a sin. I can only imagine the impression he must make when he meets a client or shows up in court. I'd thought he was self-assured and entirely comfortable in his own skin in Maui, but seeing how easily he took down Bryce was a whole other level of confidence. It was both him standing up for himself and for me. And it was the sexiest thing I've ever seen.

He didn't need to leap to my defense that way. Hell, he didn't even need to come over to me in the first place. Now that I think of my interaction with Bryce before that, I can imagine what it might have looked like to an outsider. Bryce was crossing the line. He was also drunk. But I could have handled him.

Still, having Ford swoop in was—once I got past my shock at seeing him—incredibly flattering. It was one thing to have his attention when it was just the two of us in Maui, and yet another when he was making a claim over me to my ex. A very compelling thing, especially when I never thought I'd see him again.

And now we're having dinner together.

Our waiter delivers our drinks and my order since it's technically an appetizer. Ford takes the arrival of the food and drinks as his cue to speak.

"I'm sorry, Ava," he starts. "I don't know why I said I was your fiancé." He pauses as if he's fighting to keep from continuing. In the end, he can't contain himself. "It's just, that asshole of an ex needed to be shut down. I mean, I know guys like that. I know they think they're owed the world. And, he's clearly an idiot if he gave you up, so I was just pointing out the obvious to help him along in understanding his mistake."

I watch him for a minute, trying and failing to hang on to my anger with him. I can't help but smile. He's just so earnest. And sweet. Not to mention gorgeous.

Picking up my tumbler, I hold it out to him. "Cheers to that," I say.

"Hell, yeah," he replies, knocking my glass with his.

19

We drain our first drink, share her appetizer, and order a second cocktail before conversation turns from purposefully surface-level banter to confronting the circumstances we're in now.

"So, Mr. McAvoy," she says, the Old Fashioned having taken the edge off her anger at me, "what is this all about? Why are you in LA?"

Taking a deep breath, I let it out as I consider where to start.

"And what is the deal with your father?" she continues. "I thought you didn't even know him? That he wanted nothing to do with you when you were growing up? But that wasn't exactly the truth, was it?"

Looks like I was premature in thinking her anger had cooled off.

"I didn't lie to you about him," I say. "I just ... didn't exactly tell you the whole truth."

She nods as if this confirms something for her. As if she somehow knew all along that I wasn't to be trusted. That rubs me the wrong way because I never set out to deceive her. I wasn't running some kind of *con* on her. We both knew what we wanted from each other back in Maui. And we gave it to each other *so well*. To now turn that around and view our time together as something more calculating is a bit of revisionism.

"Okay, come on, Ava—we weren't exactly focused on baring our *souls* to each other. We were focused on more *physical* things, weren't we?"

Frozen by my words for a second, she suddenly breaks out into a big smile before laughing. "Oh, I see. Thanks for that, Surfer Boy."

"I'm not saying it wasn't a fantastic time. I'm just saying, it wasn't the time to tell you my life story."

"Well, now that you've got me mixed up in this fake fiancée charade, I think you'd better go ahead and *bare your soul* to me."

I want to do so many things with her, but baring my soul isn't one of them. The minute I saw her at that event, I wanted to give in to the intense attraction we'd had as strangers in Maui. I wanted to pull her out of there and explore her body in ways I hadn't yet. I wanted to disappear into that connection we have and leave behind all the bullshit I'm dealing with in my real world.

That instinct is probably why I've been drooling over her nonstop. Well, that, and because she's undeniably beautiful and sexy. And I can practically still taste her. I want more of her. So much more.

"Well?"

I snap out of my daze and see the impatience on her face. Opening my mouth to speak, but still not sure what to say, I'm given a reprieve when the waiter brings my entrée. The plate is basically a deconstructed taco with all the ingredients beautifully spread out, including thinly sliced beef with tomatillo broth, beans, grilled red onions, crispy bacon, avocado, radishes and cilantro with tortillas and salsa on the side.

It makes the half order of shrimp tostadas Ava ate seem paltry in comparison and I push my plate to the middle of the table.

"Share it with me," I say.

"Speak," she insists.

"Eat, and I will."

She eyes me warily before taking a tortilla and piling it full. Lust returns as I watch her take a bite and see a trickle of juice escape the corner of her mouth. I want to lean over the table and kiss and suck it off her. Just then, her eyes meet mine and she must recognize what's going on in my head because for the briefest second, I see her own desire. That thing we found in Maui has definitely survived. It wasn't a fluke. It wasn't fleeting. If I get this along with the other real world stuff, then I'm all in.

And then she takes her napkin and slowly wipes her mouth, forcing me to snap out of it once more.

"Uh," I start, knowing she's still waiting for me to speak. "Okay, so the thing I told you about him not wanting to be there for me is true. He and my mom had a vacation fling. When she realized she was pregnant, she tracked him down, and he immediately said he'd give her some money but he had no desire to be a father. So, it's true that I didn't have one."

There's sympathy in her eyes. But that's not what I want from her, especially because I wasn't some kind of victim in all of this.

"But when I was twelve, that all changed. Senior, as some of us call him, had a change of heart and sent for me," I tell her. "He insisted I visit him over here, and I went kicking and screaming. I was so full of anger over it all that I was a real jerk to him."

"Sounds totally understandable to me," she says softly.

"I don't actually regret that. I regret what happened next." In between eating, I proceed to tell her everything that happened after that first visit, including the way my dad blackmailed me into moving in with him and the way I eventually flipped and wanted to be just like him, if that meant that I'd finally earn his love.

"So, it's pretty pathetic," I say. "I became a complete asshole, just like him. I was ruthlessly ambitious just like him. I was materialistic just like him. And you know what the best part is?"

She shakes her head.

"It never mattered. None of it. Not me speeding through school, not my natural ability for the law, not any of the billable hours I brought in. In the end, he still wanted to push me aside. I overheard him speaking to someone on the phone about how he'd sideline me by using my 'ever expanding ego' against me. That's when I realized nothing I could do would really matter to him, that everything I'd done was all in vain. The only thing I had really accomplished was to become a shell of myself." I pause, thinking of that pivotal moment. Shaking my head, I laugh. "It was a cruel fucking epiphany, that's for sure. But it made me completely change my life. That's the day I walked out and went home to Maui."

"You walked away from practicing completely?"

I nod. "Thing is, I may be a good lawyer, but it isn't my passion. And now, it's tied to all the ways that I compromised myself. I may have been young when I left Maui, but I had absorbed the lifestyle there. It may seem lazy to outsiders, but it's about *balance*. It's about knowing that work has its place, but so does the rest of your life and it shouldn't be ignored all for the sake of materialism. I lost sight of that when I came here. Instead, I became ambitious and intensely focused on winning—cases, appeals, shares, a better car, more fucking materialistic *things*. Yeah, I got all that stuff, but I lost what is really important to me. I lost the *aloha spirit*."

"Which is what, exactly?"

"It's the alignment of the mind and the heart, the coordination of which brings each person to reflect on the basic life forces of kindness, unity, pleasantness, humility, and patience. In turn, each person is expected to think and express good feelings to others. That brings about a kind of mutual regard and caring without any obligation in return. And when you are surrounded with everyone living in this way, it's, well, it's the best kind of peace and freedom you could ask for. That's the way of life in Hawai'i." I take a second to breathe because I've spit all this out so quickly.

"That's beautiful," she says softly.

"That's what I've been working to regain since I went back. I just didn't realize how much I needed it and how much it meant to me until I went without it for too long. So, even if I did want to practice again, I can't see doing it at that level. It's draining. It's soul-sucking."

Seeing the look on her face, I realize I've insulted her.

"I don't mean that's how it is for you," I tell her. "I'm sure your motives and rewards are much higher than mine ever were. But I can't separate it all anymore. Being a lawyer is the epitome of everything I *don't* want. All I want is to have a life that is meaningful to *me*. I love living one wave at a time," I say and she winces, obviously recognizing it as the way she had demeaned me when we first met. "I love seeing my mom every day. I love teaching music and being around those kids. I *need* to live the aloha spirit."

She takes a moment to digest this before saying, "Okay, but you're here now because …?"

"My leave of absence is up. I need to either resume my position at the firm or resign."

"And you're going to resign?"

"Yes."

I see a flicker of disappointment in her eyes. Maybe the idea of me as a high-powered lawyer was more enticing to her than what I am now, just a surfer boy. That bothers me way more than it should given the fact that she and I were never meant to be. This reaction makes me realize I've been holding out hope for something more with her since before she ever left Maui. There's no choice now but to shrug it off.

"Where did you go to school?" she asks, changing the topic.

I'm game to steer this into a getting-to-know-you session. "High school?"

"Sure, we'll start there."

"Brentwood Preparatory Academy."

She nods. "That's a fine private school. Where did you go for undergrad?"

"Yale. What about you?"

She laughs and shakes her head. "Cal State LA. What law school did you go to?"

"Yale again."

"That's quite a pedigree for a surfer boy."

I laugh. "Where did you go to law school?"

"Southwestern."

The universities she attended aren't exactly on the same

level as Ivy League Yale, but she shows no embarrassment in that. I bet she's had a lot of experience at batting away condescending remarks about such things and rising to the occasion rather than letting anyone tell her she's somehow inferior. Like she told me earlier, she has her JD just like I do. That is, we both have law degrees. It's not necessarily a matter of where you earned it, but how well you absorbed the teachings. Seems to me she knows exactly what she's doing with that degree. Especially because she's currently in cross-examination mode.

"And you've only ever worked at your father's firm?" she continues.

"Yes. What about you?"

"Yes, just the one firm. But I have the feeling you've parlayed your years there into something impressive."

"Well, I do have shares," I admit.

Her eyes go wide. I can see she understands the value in holding shares in a firm like McAvoy & Partners. And it's a safe bet that she's never had the opportunity for the same thing at her firm.

"So, you're set, then," she says.

"Not exactly."

"What do you mean?"

"Per the bylaws of the firm, I'm required to sell them to Senior when I resign. Thing is, that will then give him a controlling interest in the firm."

"And ... you don't want that?"

"Let's just say, I'm not eager to give him that kind of power."

"But the only way to avoid that is to stay and continue to practice, right?"

"That's what I'm going to sort out. If there's a way where I can resign and keep my shares out of his control, well, that'd be a fantastic fuck you on my way out the door."

She bites her lip as she considers me. It's a sexy move, but I'm about to find out that it was just a distraction from what she was really thinking.

"Counsel," she says, "can we review your recent testimony where you claimed all you wanted was to live a life of *aloha spirit*? Where might petty retribution come into this?"

I smile in capitulation to her point. "Yeah, I know it seems petty. But I just need to see if I have any options. My father is a man who has lived his life getting everything he's ever wanted. Keeping these shares out of his control is the only thing that will really make him ... realize what he's lost when I go."

"I'm sure—"

"It's fine," I interrupt. I don't want her to try to comfort me by saying she's sure my father really does love me, that he just has a hard time showing it. I've tried that tact with myself many times, only to be disappointed by reality. There's a point in life when a man has to let go of trying to win his father's love and just accept that it's a losing proposition.

Ava sits back and after a moment of watching me, nods slightly, apparently seeing that there's no use in pursuing this. "So, where does this fake engagement thing come into all of this?" she asks.

"Well, I got sort of stuck with that," I admit, "when your ex was there trying to suggest that I was full of shit. Then my dad played along—"

"Yeah, why did he do that?"

"My guess is that he didn't know if it was true or not. In his mind, it easily could have been since we haven't spoken in a year. So, rather than appear to be unaware that his *beloved* son was engaged, he just went with it."

"Wow," she says. "He really doesn't know anything about you, does he? And he'd rather pretend he does just for appearances?"

I shrug. It's nothing new to me. But Ava pegging my relationship with him so quickly is a reminder of just how perceptive she is.

"If your Bryce hadn't been there trying to provoke the whole thing, this never would have had to happen," I say, mostly to avoid telling her she's dead on about my nonexistent connection with my father.

"He's not *my* Bryce."

"Yes, well, I'm just telling you how we got here."

"Ford, we're not going to let this go on," she says. "You're going to tell him that this isn't real, right?"

"Uh, yeah," I say, hesitating. "Yeah, I'll do that."

"Why *wouldn't* you want that?"

"I just need to stay on his good side for a little while longer so I can research an idea I have on giving up my shares."

"And us being 'engaged' keeps you on his good side?"

I shrug. "I think it would, especially as long as I don't make him look like a fool for going along with this. He's big on appearances. Since he's already turned his dinner party into an engagement party, it would only piss him off to back out of it right now. If we go along with this—temporarily—he gets to play the gracious host to this event, to look like he's *so proud* of me. Then he can pretend to be understanding of me wanting to officially leave the firm. He'll twist it into this phony thing that it's me striking out on my own." I don't add that this will also keep *her* on his good side. I still don't want her worrying about that possibility.

She looks dubious. "You're presuming a whole lot, aren't you?"

"I've studied him more than I've studied any law book. I know him."

"Okay, I get where you're coming from," she says. "I just can't go along with it."

My heart sinks. It's all so ridiculous that I would have even thought to push through with this thing, that I have to admonish myself for being disappointed that she wouldn't be game for it. Why should she put herself out for me, anyway? It seems like her affection for me has waned with this whole conversation. That fire we had has started to fade with the real world stuff coming to the forefront.

"I have my own career to think of, Ford," she continues. "The older man who you met, Randall Miller? He's my boss. But he's not just my boss, he's like family to me. He gave me a chance at a top-tier law firm when no one else would. He's my mentor, my friend. And I won't lie to him about all this. I also won't keep this up at the expense of my professional reputation. From what Tyler told me, you coming back has the LA legal world talking. Now, I'm going to be part of that. I'm already at a double-disadvantage with being Latina. I won't play along with your game and lose respect and credibility among my peers for it. I've worked too hard to get where I am to suddenly be dismissed because of my 'frivolous' love life."

Jesus. She's right. This "sudden engagement" could be interpreted as her being too easily prone to emotion. At least, I know that's what a lot of her rivals would latch onto. I'm such an asshole. Just as selfish and callous as my father. I thought I'd shed that skin. Turns out it's way too easy to put it back on.

"I don't want that," I tell her. "Really, I don't want to pull you into something that will drag you down. I ... I didn't realize all the ramifications. I'm sorry."

She watches me for a long moment before nodding.

"I'll figure out some way to get out of this. You don't need to do anything. It's on me."

After a moment of hesitation, she opens her mouth to reply but stops when someone approaches our table.

"So, it is true. My, have stranger things ever come to pass?" the man asks.

I recognize him as Manfred Kahn, partner along with Randall at Ava's firm. He's always rubbed me the wrong way and I can tell from the way that Ava recoils at his sudden presence and eager eyes that she feels the same way.

"Hi Manny," she says stiffly. "Whatever do you mean?"

He waves his hand between me and Ava. "I heard the big news just as I was leaving the ABA event that you are engaged to Ford McAvoy's Boy Wonder," he says with a self-satisfied grin. "That's one way to get a leg up, right?"

I'm about to leave my seat and flatten this guy when Ava speaks, "Really, Manny, how many times do you need to be talked to by HR before you realize you can't say things like that to me?"

I laugh, enjoying the pinched look on his face.

"Anyway, I really couldn't believe the news," he says, his voice dripping with mock disbelief. "I mean, everyone knows you're married to your job. You're too busy climbing up that ladder in your high heels, pulling twelve-hour days, six days a week to have a love life."

She smiles tightly. "I am dedicated to my job, that's true. Even in heels."

He ignores this, saying, "And I really couldn't believe that Randall—your backer—was just as shocked by all this as everyone else. Who knew you were prone to such flights of fancy?"

Now I have a real sense of the uphill battle for career respectability Ava had just described to me. One of the partners in her own firm has laid out all the reasons why this "engagement" is a bad idea. It will make her look shallow and not worthy of being taken seriously. At least by men like him. And he's a pretty important one for her job.

Fuck. What have I done? Before I can sort out how to fix this, she puts up a defense I wasn't expecting.

"You're just angling for an invitation to our engagement party, aren't you," she says, cleverly changing the focus.

"Well, that's the other thing, dear," he says, "I had already been invited to Ford's dinner party. It was never billed as an *engagement* party."

"Can you fault us for wanting to keep the happy news to ourselves for a time?" she asks, batting her eyelashes in a way that I intuitively know is not who she really is.

This pretense she's putting on gets ignored as Manny tells her, "Oh, don't get me wrong. I'll be delighted to attend your engagement party. In fact, I'll spread the word that Ava Ruiz is part of a new power couple. Good for you, really, since old Randall won't be in his position forever. It's smart that you have a backup plan, isn't it?"

She levels a withering gaze at him. "Thanks so much for your congratulations, Manny. We really appreciate it." The smile that comes to her face is so phony, it makes me laugh.

"Right. Sure," he says. He nods at me before slinking away.

"What a creep," I say, surely loud enough for him to hear before he's gone too far.

Ava leans toward me across the table. "Okay, this engagement thing of ours is on. I'm in. We'll pretend to be engaged at that party, tell everyone we're going to have a long engagement and then go our separate ways. After a while, we'll quietly let it be known it didn't work out. But in the meantime, you and I can both use this to get what we want."

I laugh at the wonderful absurdity of all of this. On impulse, I slide my hand into the hair at the nape of her neck and seal her words with a lingering kiss.

I'm relieved when she kisses me back with the same level of passion.

20

AVA

The first thing I do after pulling away from Ford's kiss is order another drink. I've already had one too many, which is likely why I've just agreed to this fake fiancée charade. Well, that combined with Manny provoking me. He and I have never been friends. Our animosity started the same day as my interview when he was sure I was covering for Randall. I'm almost certain it was because he didn't like that a young woman with no power suddenly had the tools to best him in his attempt to expose Randall's weakened state. We've had words over the years, but he's always been at a loss for how to push me out. I won't deny that Randall has a lot to do with that. But so does the fact that I absolutely pull my weight in that firm. My so-called reputation for being married to my job should prove that, if nothing else.

"So … congratulations to us?" Ford asks when our third round of drinks are served.

I laugh. "You mean on our engagement?"

He nods. "I really gotta get you a ring."

The thought throws me. I wonder just how invested we're going to get with this thing. "No, you don't."

"It's all anyone cares about when you say you're engaged. We'll find something for you."

"This is so weird."

His expression is warm, accepting. "It is." After taking a sip of his drink, he says, "Thank you for doing this. I know it's not ideal. But I really appreciate it."

"Well, I'll probably regret it later, but for now, you're welcome."

Laughing, he watches me for a moment. "I really hope you don't regret spending more time with me, Ava. Especially because I'm so looking forward to getting to know you better."

That makes my head swim. Or maybe it's the alcohol I've overindulged in. Either way, I do know that letting someone in, letting someone really *know* me, isn't something I do easily. Doing so as a pretense for our fake engagement sounds even more unpleasant than it normally would.

As if sensing the thoughts going on in my head, Ford takes my hand over the table and draws his fingertips across the sensitive skin on the inside of my wrist.

"It's okay," he says softly. "We'll figure this out together."

His assurance inspires totally unwarranted confidence in me given what we're going to do. Still, I take comfort in it and smile back at him.

This little reprieve doesn't last long as we're once more interrupted—this time by my cell phone. I recognize the ringtone as the one I'd assigned to my mom. It's close to eleven o'clock. She should be asleep.

I don't waste any time apologizing to Ford for taking the call. Instead, I answer with a breathless, "Mama?"

"*Mija*, everything is okay," she says quickly, obviously aware of how this call will raise red flags for me.

I breathe easier and glance at Ford. He's watching me with concern.

"What's going on? Are you okay?" I ask my mother.

"I'm fine, really. Though, you could say I'm a little confused. See, I got a phone call earlier from a woman named Doris. She apologized for phoning, but said she couldn't find my email address to forward the invitation to attend a *dinner party*—that's the expression she used—on Saturday in honor of my daughter's engagement."

I feel the color drain from my face. Admittedly, I haven't given this whole bizarre scenario with Ford that much thought, but I never considered that my mother would be dragged into it.

"Hang on a second," I tell her. "Ford, who is Doris and why is she calling my mother to invite her to your father's dinner party?"

"Doris? That's my father's secretary."

"Check your—" I stop when I realize his silly flip phone makes normal communication impossible. Instead, I check my work email for new messages but don't find anything personal. My Gmail account, however, has a new email from a woman named Doris, cordially inviting me to attend a dinner party on Saturday at Ford McAvoy Senior's house. The attendee list appears to include me and about fifty others, including, it now seems, my mother.

"Okay, I see the invitation," I say, both for Mama's and Ford's benefit. "Um," I say, "what did you tell her?"

"I told her I wouldn't be able to reply until I checked my calendar," she says with a laugh.

My mother responds with good humor to most things

thrown her way. I've only ever seen her positive outlook on life shaken once, when my father passed away. She'd been broken by it. If I wasn't there to pick up her pieces, I'm not sure what would have happened.

I'm especially glad she's amused by the news traveling so fast to her that I'm engaged, but I'm just as alarmed by this all slipping out of our control.

"So, yeah," I say. "Here's the thing, remember the guy I told you I met in Maui?"

I see Ford raise his eyebrows as he winks at me, clearly delighted at this bit of news. His ego must be inflating by the second as he realizes I'd told my mother about him.

"Yes, of course. You were practically lovesick over him," Mama says.

"*Lovesick* isn't the word I'd use," I say before I can think better of it.

Now Ford laughs. When I scowl at him, he blows me a kiss. I must be drunk because my first instinct is to think how sexy he looks when he's being playful like that.

"What is this all about, Ava?" Mama asks. "Why did some strange woman call me at nine o'clock on a Wednesday night? I was ready to laugh it off and forget about it, but I just had to check with you."

The fatigue in her voice snaps me back to reality. I owe her an explanation.

Taking a deep breath, I release it and say, "The man I met, his name is Ford. And it turns out that he's a lawyer. He doesn't practice anymore, but he's in town. And we ran into each other. Things sort of got out of hand with people gossiping about us. So, we kind of joked about being engaged and now, well, it seems that everyone thinks we're getting married."

I close my eyes tight as I wait for a response.

Thankfully, my mama reacts with grace. "And should I be attending this dinner party, *mija*, with you and your fiancé?"

Opening my eyes, I relax. "Yes, let's plan to attend. I promise, I'll tell you what this is all about before then, okay? Just for now, trust me and roll with it?"

There's only the briefest hesitation before she replies, "Yes, of course, I will. If this is what you want."

"I do. And thank you. Get some rest now. *Te quiero mucho,* Mama."

She tells me she loves me too before we disconnect.

I set down my phone and pick up my drink.

"Things just got more complicated for us, right?" Ford asks with a half wince, half smile.

"More complicated for *you*, actually. Because you're going to be the one to explain all this to my mom."

I'd thought he'd be nervous at the prospect, but instead, he says, "You met my mom. I'd love to meet yours."

Dropping my head into my hands, I mumble, "What is happening?"

"Hey, let's get out of here. Get some air, okay?"

When I look up at him, I see he's already dropped a wad of cash on the table and has his hand out to me. I take it and when he then wraps his arm around my shoulders, I lean into him, grateful that he's taking charge at this moment. It's not that I need rescuing, it's just that I wouldn't mind having a partner, someone I can lean on.

And here he is.

21

The night air has gone cool and I drape my suit coat over Ava's shoulders as we walk down the dark and now empty streets. I don't know where we're going and it's not entirely clear to me that she knows either.

What I do know is that I like the way she wraps her arm around my waist as I hold her shoulders. Her body against mine is a welcome feeling after the events of the past few hours. This day has been nothing what I expected.

Of course, I only have myself to blame for all that. *I'm* the one who claimed to be Ava's fiancé. *I'm* the one who urged her to keep up the story when my father played along. *I'm* the one who asked her to see it through.

The only saving grace to this bizarre situation is that there is no one else I'd rather be pretending with. The side of her I got to know a little in Maui showed me she's fun, sweet, and sexy. Now, it's fascinating to see this other side of her. She's obviously a capable professional if she's been under Randall Miller's tutelage. He's not known for suffering fools, which makes it even more surprising that Manfred Khan rose to partnership level in that firm. It makes me wonder what kind of sleazy maneuvering he might have done to get there. Watching Ava more than hold her own with that jerk was impressive.

And now she's challenged me to make all well with her mother. I like that she's put me up to this. It means she's already opening up her world to me.

"Where are we going?" she asks.

I can hear the alcohol in her voice. It's just a hint of that Old Fashioned, but not enough to worry that she's incapable of handling herself.

Looking down at her, I laugh. "Why are you asking me? I thought you were leading us somewhere."

She pulls away and looks around. We're now on Hill Street, having walked several blocks.

"Oh," she says softly, almost to herself. "I haven't been on that thing since I was a kid."

I follow her gaze to the large tangerine-colored pillars and arch demarcating the entrance for Angels Flight, the historic funicular railway which takes tourists up the steep but very short journey from Hill Street to Olive Street. I know of it, but haven't been on it and tell Ava as much.

She grabs my hand. "We should go on it!"

I let her pull me toward the gated archway, seeing before she does that it's closed for the night. Her disappointment when she realizes we missed the chance to ride it is palpable. The sigh she releases is so heavy that I wonder at the significance this thing has for her.

"Who did you ride it with before?" I ask.

"What?"

Her eyes are fixed on the top of the hill and her mind is elsewhere.

"Was it your father? Did you ride this with him?"

That gets her attention and she looks at me. "I, uh, yeah. He liked to show me around all the old Los Angeles sights. This was one of them."

"Well, let's go to the top, then."

"We can't. It's stopped running for the night, remember?"

I nod to the stairs on the right side of the entrance. "Come on, honey."

This time, I'm the one pulling her. But she soon keeps pace with me as we climb the steps up the thirty-three percent incline.

"Did you know there are one hundred and fifty-three steps?" I ask when we're about halfway to the top.

"You're making that up."

"No, it's true. And you remember that this isn't even the original site? That it was first built and operated about a half a block from here?"

She turns to me, and we stop on a landing, both of us now taking in a little more breath with the effort of the uphill climb. The fact that she's doing this in heels is not lost on me. She's something else.

"I do remember something like that," she says. "But the question is, why do you know that if you've never even been here before?"

"I read about it at some point."

"At some point?"

I shrug. "In eighth grade."

"Why would you remember that from all those years ago?" she asks with a laugh.

"I don't actually remember it. It's just something I can recall."

She fixes me with a skeptical stare. "Explain."

Now I laugh. "I have a photographic memory. Or near-photographic. I've never actually tested to see if it's a true photographic memory. But the point is that if I've read something, I can recall it."

"Is that really true?"

I sigh. "Want to test me?"

"I do."

"Go for it."

"Um, okay. There's a plaque I always remember seeing. It says how many feet Angels Flight runs—"

"Three hundred and fifteen feet."

"And it mentions that the engineer—"

"Was also a lawyer."

"And a friend of—"

"President Lincoln."

"Wow," she whispers. "Boy Wonder."

Grimacing, I start back up the steps. I've hated that nickname for as long as it's been around. I'd enjoyed almost a year without hearing it in some fashion while I was in Maui.

"I'm sorry," she says as she comes up behind me, doing double-time in those heels. "I can tell you hate that nickname. I won't use it again."

We've reached the top and I turn to her just as a breeze picks up and sends her hair flying dramatically behind her. The backdrop beyond her is the lit-up buildings of downtown, peppered by enormous construction cranes. The city's growth has continued while I was away. It makes me ever more confident in my decision to leave. But my eyes are drawn away from the reminder of the city life I no longer want to the beautiful woman in front of me. The woman who keeps letting me chip away at her walls by revealing the thing that still pains her, the loss of her father.

"What would you and your dad do when you got to the top here?" I ask.

She looks surprised by the question, by my interest. But then she gives it thought and I can practically see her reviewing the memories.

"We'd sit over there," she says, pointing to a gated off park-like area. "There's a bench there in the Knoll where we'd eat the *gorditas* he packed while looking out over the city. I can still remember being little enough that my legs would swing. Not touch the ground, you know?"

I smile at that detail and give her a nod, encouraging her to continue.

"He had big plans for me," she says. "He'd wave his arms out toward the city and say, 'All this is yours.'"

When she laughs, I catch the glimmer of tears in her eyes. She looks away quickly and blinks. I step closer to her, but she doesn't meet my eyes.

"I bet he'd be so proud of you, Ava," I tell her, cupping her cheek in my hand.

She catches her breath, her hand flying to her mouth. "I think so. I hope so."

I wrap her into my arms, and she presses her face to my chest. I'm not sure how long we stay there like that, but it seems like a while has passed before we're interrupted by a group of men in suits cutting through. They're talking loudly, likely coming from some after work happy hour.

"Ready to go?" I ask, pulling away from her.

She nods but stops me when I start toward the stairs to go

down. "Would you mind if we caught a cab? My feet are killing me."

"Let's do it."

Turns out my amazing Hula Girl is human after all. I offer her my arm and she takes it, leaning on me once again as we move slowly toward Olive Street.

22

I must be losing my mind. I'm going along with a pretend engagement with my vacation fling and acting like it's real. Acting like he's someone I can confide in.

What other explanation can there be for my now compulsive need to share things with him about my father? I've never felt like I could talk about him the way I have with Ford.

And not only that, but I also thought it was a great idea for him to come up with me to my loft. I'd suggested it as the cab stopped in front of my place and he lingered, obviously assuming he should take it to wherever he was planning to crash for the night.

"Walk me up?" I'd said. Because I didn't want to say goodbye to him. Because I didn't want to go cold after he'd found a way to warm me from the inside out.

It hadn't taken him more than a second to register my request and to slide out of the cab, once again handling the payment with cash.

After surveying the brick walls, large iron-framed

windows facing an interior courtyard, and blond wood flooring, he asked if he could draw me a bath.

"A bath?" I asked with a laugh.

"For your feet," he'd replied simply, as if it was the most obvious thing in the world.

So, that's what he's doing now as I straighten out the less than well-made bed positioned on the far end of the completely open concept floor plan.

"It's ready."

Startled, I turn to see Ford a few feet away, his shirt sleeves rolled up and looking entirely comfortable in his self-appointed role of caretaker for me. I try to imagine Bryce having the instinct to do this but quickly dismiss the thought. That wasn't the kind of relationship we had. Laughing, I realize how deluded I was to have ever thought we had the potential for something more than Netflix and chill.

"What?" Ford asks.

"Oh, um, nothing." I step closer to him. I don't know if his drawing me a bath is purely platonic or if he had hoped I'd invite him to join me. I don't even know if it's a good idea to keep up a sexual relationship with him—though, god knows I'd love to—since we've got this whole fiancé hoax to perpetuate before separating once more. He is, after all, headed back to Maui before too long. "Thank you for this," I tell him.

"Of course."

I step past him and into the bathroom, closing the door only halfway. There's no use in being prudish. I raise my eyebrows when I see that he's thoughtfully attempted to create a bubble bath with my jasmine-scented bath gel.

Stripping, I step into the tub and let out a moan as I sink into the water. It's exactly what I didn't know I needed. I realize too late that I didn't put up my hair and make a bun out of it, holding it with my hand. My choices are to get out and disrupt this delicious relaxation to grab a hair tie or call for Ford to help.

"Ford?" I call out.

My place is not big, I'll admit, but he still pokes his head around the door in record time, making me think he was *very* nearby.

"Yeah?"

"Can you get that hair tie for me?"

He looks at the counter and locates what I've requested, handing it to me.

"Thank you." I quickly secure my hair on top of my head without having to get up from my position of leaning against the end of the tub.

"Sure. I'll—"

"No, stay. Talk to me. Keep me company," I tell him.

His gaze slowly travels over me, moving from my eyes downward to my bubbles-covered chest and to where my knees are just above the waterline before he nods. Grabbing a towel, he places it on the edge of the tub and sits.

"So—"

"Should we—"

We both start speaking at the same time and stop short, watching each other with a smile.

"I thought maybe we could plan what's going to happen in the next few days," I say, ever practical. I am not usually a "wing it" kind of girl. I like to prepare, to study, to have the best sense of what's to come.

"Yeah, sure."

I realize with his distracted response that having a planning session with me naked in the tub may not be the most efficient way of doing things. But here we are.

"I think it's a good idea for us to get to know each other a bit more before I bring you home to my mom," I say. "She'll trust you more if we can show we have some kind of relationship beyond—"

"Beyond hot sex in Maui?"

Smiling, I can't resist the tease of what I say next. "It was hot, wasn't it? Remember out on the balcony of my hotel room?"

He looks pained in the way only a man who has to restrain himself can. "Inside my truck was pretty damn hot, too," he says.

"Or when you licked the tequila off my thigh? That was *really* hot."

To my surprise, he reaches into the water and his hand glides along my inner thigh. "This thigh?" he murmurs.

All I can do is nod, my eyes locked onto his as he keeps his hand where it is but moves to his knees by the side of the tub. He squeezes my leg but doesn't move his hand any farther up, building the anticipation. To spur him along, I sit up just enough for the bubbles to slide down my chest. His eyes leave mine and linger on my breasts, following the trail of suds as they trickle over my nipples.

"Jesus, Ava," he breathes and slides his hand upward. At the same time, he leans in and takes my mouth in his, kissing me with unrestrained passion. His tongue searches mine as our lips crash together over and over.

Whether it's a good idea or not, we both clearly want this.

"Get me a towel?" I ask.

He's thrown by the sudden interruption, but only for a moment. When he stands, I can see that he's just as turned on as I am. His suit pants are straining at the crotch, giving me ideas for how to help him alleviate the situation.

I stand when he holds out a towel for me with one hand and offers his other hand to help me out. The fact that he's both a gentleman and the one who is about to ravage me sends a rush of heat to my core.

Once my feet are on the plush bath rug, he wraps the towel around my body, taking care to smooth it down my arms, back, and butt. There, actually, he takes extra care, squeezing my ass with his strong hands. He sucks in a breath when I, in turn, rub the hard length of him.

"I have missed you," he says softly, lust thick in his voice.

Raising myself onto my tiptoes, I kiss the side of his neck. "How bad?" I whisper.

He pulls my towel open so that it's only covering my shoulders. I watch as his eyes survey my naked body, trailing over every inch of me in the same slow, deliberate way he did when we first met. This time, though, he does nothing to hide the hunger in his eyes.

"I'll show you."

I bite my lip at that and he makes a noise that's part moan and part growl before reaching out and picking me up with his hands around my butt. I take in a sharp breath.

"I got you," he says and I believe him. His strength and confidence are on display as he easily takes me to the vanity countertop where he places me.

When he kisses me, he makes me feel like he can't get enough of me. His tongue is firm and insistent in my mouth, and I wrap my arms around him to pull him closer, feeling the same sense of insatiable need that he does.

Dropping his hands to my breasts, he squeezes me gently before playing his thumbs over my hardened nipples. It's a tease at first but quickly turns more desperate as he pinches and rolls my nipples between his fingers, making me moan into his mouth.

He breaks from our kiss so he can trail his lips and tongue down my neck and to my breasts, taking one nipple into his mouth. I wrap my legs around him as he swirls his tongue over the sensitive bud. When he uses his teeth to nibble, I feel an electric shock run straight down to my core. I'm on fire, so needy for him.

"Ford," I whisper, my voice hitching.

Looking up with his mouth still doing wicked things to me, I start to speak. To beg him to take me to the next level. But I can't get a word out. I'm caught in this state of ecstasy, on the verge of orgasm but wanting this to go on and on.

I don't have to say anything, it turns out, because, though he keeps toying with my breast, he also unbuttons his shirt and dress pants. It's only then that he pulls away so that he can toss his shirt aside and pull his undershirt over his head while stepping out of his trousers.

His chest is tan and so defined by muscles that he should be a sculptor's model. I run my hand over each definition as he fists his cock.

"Do you—I don't have anything," he says.

It takes me a split second to understand what he means. "Oh. Yes, in the bottom drawer, right here." I kick my heel against the vanity.

In record time, he locates the box of condoms stashed at the back of the drawer and rolls one on.

Leaning back slightly on my hands, I open my legs wider for him. His eyes go hooded with escalated desire.

"I don't know whether I want to eat you or fuck you," he says.

"I want both. But if I have to choose," I say coyly, "I need you to fuck me right now like your life depends on it."

And that's exactly what he does. He slides his hand into the hair at the nape of my neck, just as he's done before. But this time, he grabs a handful and pulls my head back so he can suck on the tender skin at the hollow my neck. At the same time, he plunges deep inside me. The vanity is the perfect height for him and I wrap my legs tightly around his hips as he fucks with the kind of intensity that has been built up by our separation. It's the kind of animalistic sex that will leave me sore. And god, is it good.

It doesn't take me long to break, coming with waves that I ride over and over. He slows his thrusts and caresses my cheek. There's sweetness in his face now, the sex god in him having taken a step back as he examines me.

"Just getting started, honey," he says. "Hang on."

I laugh when I realize he meant that literally because he picks me up from the countertop and walks us to my bed while I cover his face in kisses. I want so much of him. I want him to take me with the same kind of passion we just shared all night long. I want more orgasms and to give him as many as he can handle. I want *him*.

Before I can show him that kind of desire, he lays me down and then quickly flips me over, taking me from behind while I'm pressed face-down against my bed. He gets close to his own breaking point before pulling back and flipping me over again so he can tease his tongue over my clit until I'm coming so hard that I'm pulling his hair. With incredible stamina, he then pulls my legs over his shoulders as he pushes so deep inside me that we're both moaning from the exquisite pleasure of it. Finally, he pulls me into his arms and holding me close against his spent body while kissing my temple over and over.

I'm drifting in this lovely aftermath when he speaks and pulls me from sleep.

"Do you have to go to work tomorrow?"

"What? Uh, yeah," I reply. I slip my arm around his naked hip so I can snuggle closer to him.

"Maybe you can take a half day? It'd be good for us to, you know, work on getting to know each other."

I look up at him but he's got a far-off expression on his face, even as he's repetitively stroking my hair.

I mentally check my calendar. I know my day is full of meetings, some more flexible than others. "I can try. Off by two o'clock at the latest."

"That'd be perfect."

23

AVA

I sleep so hard that when my alarm goes off at the usual time of five-fifteen in the morning, I have no idea what is making such a horrible racket. Once I come to my senses, I turn it off and lie on my back. After a moment I turn toward Ford but he's not there.

I hear noises in the kitchen and sit up. Ford is there, with just the stove range light on as he makes a cup of coffee. He's shirtless, wearing only his boxer briefs, making me want to pull him back into bed with me. But I have other obligations to attend to, especially if I'm to cut my work day short.

Pulling on a white silk kimono patterned with colorful flowers, I join him in the kitchen. I inhale the scent of my shampoo as I wrap my arms around his waist from behind. He's not only been up long enough to make coffee but has also taken a shower. It's a reminder that he has his own work to get to today. His desire to avoid selling his shares to his father had struck me as a bit of silly revenge, especially given that he's already moved on and found his happiness. But he seems determined.

"Good morning," he says. He squeezes my arm before turning to face me. "A little bit of milk, right?"

The coffee cup he holds up has just the right tone. I gratefully take it from him.

"How did you know? This is perfect."

He shrugs. "I saw the way you take it when we had breakfast at your hotel."

I arch an eyebrow. "You are a quick study."

"For things I'm into, absolutely. Especially you, Hula Girl."

I catch myself from falling for this flattery. After all, we may have had an amazing time together in bed last night, but this whole thing with us ... it isn't real. I have to remind myself—and him—of that.

"Listen, you can't do that," I say.

He squints at me. "What do you mean?"

"I mean, we can't really do this. We can't *invest* in each other. As much fun as last night was, this thing with us, it isn't real."

"Uh oh! There they go!" He starts looking around like there's a swarm of wild butterflies he's trying to keep his eye on.

I can't help but laugh. "What are you talking about?"

"There they go!" he repeats before leveling his gaze on me. "There go your walls. Right up to your normal don't-fuck-with-me levels."

I drop my eyes from his, sensitive to this criticism. I've already told him once that this was the point Bryce tried to make with me and that it doesn't sit well. Taking my coffee to the bar-height dining room table in front of the windows, I stand rather than sit.

"Hey," he says as he joins me. "I was just trying to make light of it."

I don't look at him. Instead, I keep my eyes focused out the window, watching the sky lose pigment as the sun rises. "Yeah, sure. It's fine. Um, but maybe we should just backup a little with the stuff that's not part of our mission."

"Mission?"

"The fake engagement. You know, pretending that we have a relationship so you can screw over your father?"

"Oh shit," he says softly before laughing. "You went there, didn't you?"

I regretted the words the moment they came out of my mouth. But I don't know how to fix that. I glance at him and then away again. "I just—I told you I'd go along with this thing, and I will. But we shouldn't pretend to be something we're not with each other."

"Got it. Yeah, okay." He runs his hands through his hair. "Well, I'm not pretending when I say I'm into you. But if you'd rather keep me at arm's length, I'll have to respect that."

Now I turn to him. "Ford, I *don't* want to fall for you. I *can't.*"

"Because?"

"My life is here. My world—my *real* world—is here. Yours is in Maui. We just aren't ... compatible."

"We were pretty fucking compatible last night. Pun fucking intended."

I shake my head. "That's all it ever was with us. There's no option for more."

He watches me for a long moment, studying me until I look away. "I understand, Ava. I do." He takes a deep breath and slowly releases it. "I'll pick you up at your office at two o'clock. Bring some casual clothes to change into, okay? We've got our *mission* to work on."

Before I can reply, he walks away. I watch as he dresses in

his crumpled suit from last night. Once he's done, he goes straight to the front door and slips out without so much as a wave goodbye.

I'm left wondering whether I was premature in shutting down any possibility of us beyond this week. In the end, I just don't see what opening my heart up to someone I can never really be with will get me. It can only lead to disappointment. Better to pull back now and get into protective mode before it's too late.

With a nod to myself, I start to get ready for work.

24

FORD

Yes, my ego was a bit bruised when Ava said we should back off, but I'm good now. I've spent the morning at the firm, sourcing everything I can find to help me with my shares dilemma. In the back of my mind, I've also been thinking of how she shut me down this morning. She was right to remind us both that we don't have a chance of lasting. Admittedly, I got carried away. There's something about her that keeps drawing me further and further in. But, now that I've been reminded that there's no point in pursuing anything meaningful with her, I'm good with this hands-off approach.

Not that that stopped me from buying her a ten-thousand-dollar ring. We have appearances to keep up, and even though I've ditched all my high-priced lawyer trappings for the simple life in Maui, I still have a good deal of money in the bank. It wouldn't do to grab some small, temporary ring. I selected a four carat, emerald cut solitaire surrounded by pavé diamonds on a platinum band with more diamonds lining the band three-quarters of the way around. It's beautiful, elegant, and a little flashy all at the same time, and I think it perfectly suits Ava. I did my best with the guess on the size and hope it's not too far off, and in any case, it only needs to last for a week.

I've never proposed to a woman before. Never even got close. In both high school and college, I dated widely, had a few long-ish relationships, but nothing ever really stuck. I was always so ambitious, so eager to accomplish the next step that would get me closer to becoming a part of my father's firm. And I got what I wanted, only to discover within a few short years that it had all been one bad decision after another. I'm just grateful that I didn't let my whole life go by before rectifying the situation.

And now I've got a beautiful fiancée; a fake one, but a beautiful one, nonetheless. I guess I won't be formally proposing to her in any case. But now that I think of it, I like the idea of making some grand show of it just to bug her.

Guess I'm not entirely over how quick she was to say that we are *incompatible*. I mean, I get what she's saying. I get that this game we're playing will only be trickier if we allow real emotion into it, but how about just going along for the ride to see where it takes us?

Clearly, she's not a roll-with-it kind of woman. Though, isn't that what she told her mother she should do? Just roll with it. Seems like she might want to take her own advice.

Especially this afternoon. I've just arrived at the offices of Miller, Newell & Kahn to pick her up.

The receptionist, a bright young thing who probably took the job in the hope of gaining real world experience while studying for the bar exam, looks up as I approach. Her eyes widen as she takes in my less than professional attire. I'm back to my beach standard: Well-worn T-shirt (this time a Billabong), hybrid shorts that can pass for regular wear and that can also work in the water, and flip-flops. My sunglasses are up on my head, helping keep back my hair.

I give her my most charming smile. "I'm here for Ava Ruiz."

"Oh," she says, her surprise escaping her before she can contain it.

"Don't worry. She's expecting me."

"Uh huh. I mean, no problem. Have a seat, and I'll call her office. "

"Great. My name is Ford McAvoy. In case you needed it."

She blushes bright red. "Thank you, Mr. Ford. I mean, Mr. McAvoy."

When I give her a wink, her blush only deepens. I step away from the reception desk, not wanting to further fluster her. I'm much more interested in seeing Ava. In seeing her reaction when I slip the ring on her finger.

I feel that familiar invisible pull when Ava pushes through the glass door toward the lobby. She's wearing a white skirt that stops well short of her knees with a white and black patterned silk top. The black heels she wears accentuate those gorgeous legs of hers, and like Pavlov's dog, I feel myself salivate at the sight of them.

"Hi, babe," she says with a big smile. She greets me with a hug and a quick kiss.

It takes me a second to recover from her calling me *babe*. This is now the second time she's used that term of endearment. The first was when we were playing off our engagement with my father and her boss.

"Hi, honey," I say, forcing the stiffness out of the greeting. "Ready to go?"

She looks back at the glass door, and I see a man standing

there. He's towheaded with bright blue eyes that are wide as he watches us, mouth agape.

"Yeah, but first, I want to introduce you to my good friend Tyler." She waves the man over, and he joins us eagerly.

Ava laces her fingers through mine, playing the part of happily engaged girlfriend beautifully as she makes the introductions.

"And here I was telling her last night," Tyler says, "that *I* was going to introduce *you* to her. What a poker face you have, Ava."

The look on Tyler's face is pure skepticism, telling me he's not quite buying this whole story.

"Well, it's good to meet you in any event," I say, shaking Tyler's hand.

"I've been apologizing to him all day about the fact that we kept our engagement secret, even from him," she says with a laugh.

"Yeah, sorry about that," I say.

"He understands now, of course," Ava says.

"I do," he confirms. "Sort of, anyway. I guess since it was such a quick engagement, coming straight out of a vacation fling and all, you were trying to take your time sharing the news."

Ah, so that's what she's told him. Looks like I'll have to go with it. "Yeah, some people can get funny about how quickly things moved. You know, all judgmental about it. But when you know, you know."

"That's beautiful," Tyler says, and I believe he means it, which tells me he's a romantic, just like Ava.

"Oh, speaking of which. Ava, honey, I got the ring back from being sized. It should be perfect now."

Her mouth drops open, and I can tell she has to force it

closed as I pull the Cartier ring box out of my pocket. I slip the ring from its velvet confines and onto her left hand before she can instinctively pull away. The fact that it fits perfectly has me breathing a sigh of relief. It looks gorgeous on her hand I have to say.

"You are *not* serious," Tyler says, staring down at the fine piece of jewelry.

Ava raises her now shaking hand to her chest. "It's overwhelming, isn't it?" she asks and gives me the side-eye.

I laugh inwardly. Might as well enjoy all the absurdities of this thing.

Tyler takes her hand into his and whistles. "Girl, you done good," he says.

"My Surfer Boy did good," she replies, and I take pride in the fact that the style of ring I chose is something she truly likes.

"Now you can wave that thing in Bryce's face," Tyler suggests, finally releasing Ava's hand.

"It's not about him," Ava says quickly.

I suspect, though, that she doesn't mind proving to him that she *is* the type of woman a man would want to marry. That she is capable of both marriage and a career.

"And where are you taking your fiancée?" Tyler asks me.

"It's a surprise," I reply with a wink. "And we'd better get going. You do have something more casual to change into, right?"

"Yes, I do. My bag is back in my office. I'll run and change. Won't take long."

Tyler and I both watch her hurry away. I have my eyes on her swishing skirt and tan bare legs, while it seems Tyler is still eyeing that ring.

"So, you created quite a stir last night," he tells me. "First with your unexpected return and then with this unbelievable engagement."

"Yeah, well," I say with a sigh. "I've always been a little unconventional."

"Small world that you and Ava would meet up—and *fall in love*—in Maui when you're both based here in LA."

He's fishing. And he's clearly smart enough not to believe the story. But I have to respect the fact that there's a reason why Ava hasn't confided in him, even though they seem to be pretty close friends.

"Just makes our story all that much more romantic, doesn't it?" I grin when I see this explanation affect him. I was right. He is a romantic. And when his lingering gaze trails over me from head to toe, I know he appreciating me in another way.

"Certainly makes me swoon," he replies conspiratorially, and for a second, I don't know if he's talking about the story or me.

"I'm ready," Ava calls as she moves toward us.

She's changed into a black one-piece shorts and top thing. The deep V-neck of the top hints deliciously at her cleavage, and the shorts expose even more of her legs than the skirt did. The high heel sandals lengthen those lovely legs even more. Damn. How am I going to keep my hands off her? That's what she was hinting at when she said we should back off, right? Or maybe we can still have sex but just leave any feelings out of it.

I'm lost in these thoughts while she's saying goodbye to Tyler. And then she takes my arm like it's the most natural thing in the world, and we're off.

25

AVA

An engagement ring.

I can't believe he bought me an engagement ring.

"Wait a second," I say and stop in my tracks. We're somewhere in the subterranean parking garage, going to his car.

"What is it?"

I hold up my left hand. "Is this thing even real?"

He laughs. "For ten grand, it better be."

"Oh, you're funny. That's good."

"No, that's the truth. Thought it best to really look the part, you know? I mean, if I were actually to buy a ring for the woman I was going to marry, that's the one I would pick."

"Ford, this is crazy."

He shrugs. "Makes me look crazy in love, at least."

I laugh. "Don't tell me you're a Beyoncé fan."

"Who?"

"Never mind."

I hear the chirp of a car unlocking and see that we've arrived at Ford's ride. It's a BMW M3 convertible in electric blue and so not what I expected of him. His beat-up Chevy truck in Maui is much more of who I thought he was. This .... is kind of disappointing.

"This is from my old life," he says, clearly reading the expression on my face. "You'll need to know—for our mission —that this is my car and that I have a townhouse in Brentwood."

I raise my eyebrows at this bit of information.

"Yeah, I know," he says with a sense of resignation. "But I did tell you that I was an asshole for a good number of years when I bought into all this stuff."

With this admission, he comes around to my side of the car and opens the door for me. The thing with him claiming to have lost his way is so at odds with who I've known him to be that it's hard to imagine the other version of him. Although, the car helps.

He takes the bag containing my work clothes from me and puts it in the trunk before sliding into the driver's seat.

"Where are we going?" I ask.

"It's a surprise."

I wrinkle my nose. "I don't really like surprises."

He glances at me as he sets the car into gear. "Too bad, Hula Girl. I'm not telling."

His smirk says he's getting a kick out of annoying me this way, so I pretend disinterest in the drive and focus on his profile as he confidently steers us through the mid-afternoon traffic.

"So, tell me about your day, honey," I say woodenly.

"My day," he says slowly. "Well, it started all right. Woke up in bed with a beautiful woman. But then it took a turn when she told me to fuck off. Still, I went to work, got in a few hours of what I needed, and then bought that woman a ring. So, not bad, all in all."

"I didn't tell you to fuck off," I protest. "I'm just trying to be realistic about who we are and what we're doing."

He glances at me. "It's all good. You were right. There's no need to *invest* in each other. Our time is limited. Once we've gotten through my dad's dinner party, we'll be done."

A rush of tears stings my eyes, and I turn away from him as I try to blink them back, confused by the sudden emotional reaction. But now that he's made it clear that he is on the same page as me with thinking there's no point in trying to be anything special to each other, it's the last thing I want. Not that there is anything I can do about that.

"How was your day, honey?" he asks casually.

Grabbing my phone, I study it intently to shield my still-wet eyes from him. "Um, it was good. I had a talk with Randall, gave him the same love-at-first-sight story I gave Tyler. I don't think he believes me, but he didn't question it too much."

"So, you have a special relationship with him?"

I look up at him quickly, my defenses raised. "What makes you say that?"

"Just—"

"Because of what Manny said about me being under his protection?"

"No, not because of that creep," he says. "Because of how you described him to me. You said he was like family. And because of the way he looked at you at the event last night. He clearly cares for you."

My tense shoulders sag in relief. "Yes, he's like a grandfather to me."

He nods. "How did that come about? He's the managing partner, and you're still a little green there, aren't you?"

"I've been there six years, and I'm a senior associate."

Holding up a hand, he says, "I meant no offense. I have no doubt that you're a damn good lawyer and have worked your ass off for everything you've got."

"That's exactly right," I tell him quickly, firmly.

Silence fills the car, and I look down at my phone again. Before long, my assumption that he was suggesting something improper with my relationship with Randall abates. He's never given me any reason to think he would jump to such conclusions about me. In truth, he's only ever listened to me with incredible generosity.

"I, uh," I start, "we became close, actually, really quickly."

He looks over at me and we get locked into each other's gaze. Before I tell him more, his eyes soften, and it feels like he somehow understands why I'm so protective of Randall. When he reaches out and rests his right hand on my thigh, using his thumb to gently stroke my bare skin, it's a warm comfort that I gladly accept. It gives me a sense of safety and security that I can be completely honest with him.

And so, I confess to him the story of my interview and how I helped cover for Randall when he fainted. I've never told anyone that story. Not even my mom. I've always kept it in the strictest confidence, somehow thinking absolute silence is the best way to protect Randall. I also tell him why I'm so touchy about it. That it's not just Manny who insinuates that I've gotten special favors because of Randall, that I've had to weave between actively fighting against rumors and ignoring them for the last six years.

"It's such bullshit," Ford says and squeezes my thigh. "I'm sorry you have to deal with that."

I put my hand over his, linking our fingers. "There are so many politics in this field it's crazy."

"Well, it's easy enough to see that Manny's gunning to take over."

"Oh, he definitely wants to take over. In fact, he was in the middle of trying a power play on Randall about the time I interviewed. I sensed that his motives weren't exactly above-board when he came in after Randall fell. It made me want to protect him all the more. And Manny's been stymied about it ever since. For the last six years."

Ford laughs. "Serves him right. But he will pounce, that's clear. Is Randall in good health?"

I nod. "He's definitely slowing down, though. He doesn't play tennis anymore, which drives him crazy. But he still gets into the office, sometimes even by six-thirty in the morning like me."

"Maybe we can get Manny and my father to start a new firm together."

I laugh. "Why's that?"

"They both want to push out the old men who built their firms."

"Really?"

He then tells me his own secret, sharing how he overheard his father plotting to take over the controlling interest of the firm by, not just sidelining him, but pushing out his own father.

"Thing is, I don't have the genuine relationship with him the way you do with Randall. He's never had any interest in me. Not until I could do something for the firm. So, while I don't like the idea of what Senior is trying to do, I'm also not driven to protect my grandfather. It's a weird thing to have no feelings for him."

"Do you have a relationship with your mom's parents?" I ask, looking for something positive to focus on.

"Yeah, I do. I mean, I did. They passed away, one after the other, a few years ago."

"Oh, I'm so sorry, Ford." I squeeze his hand where it still rests on my thigh.

"Thank you," he says on a sigh. "It still catches me by surprise to think of them as being gone. They visited us a lot in Maui when I was growing up. My grandmother was always thinking of me. She used to send me clippings from the newspaper whenever she thought I'd be interested in something she saw. My grandfather used to take me out to fly kites. They were good people."

I take a lesson in how he's responded to my condolences. He not only accepts it with thanks, but shares his feelings about them and about having lost them. That's what he had urged me to do with my father. And when I allowed myself to do that, I did feel better. It seems the alternative is to sort of push those feelings aside and that's not fair to yourself or to the memory of the person you lost. It makes me realize what a special person Ford is.

Releasing my hold on him, I sit back and try to shake off this sentiment. It's only going to get me into trouble to dwell on what a gorgeous, smart, amazing person he is. Not to mention how incredible he is in bed.

"Finally," he says, and flicks the turn signal to exit the freeway. "I do not miss LA traffic, I can tell you that."

I'd been so caught up in either focusing on him or pretending to look at my phone that I haven't kept track of where we're going. Looking up, I see that we're taking Dodger Stadium Way exit, and tears fill my eyes once more.

"Are we—" I can't get out the whole question because I'm too choked up.

We're stopped at a red light when he turns to me. "Listen, I want you to know that I'm not trying to replace the memories you have with your father by taking you to a game for the first time since he passed. I hope coming back today is a way for you to honor him. To honor the closeness you had with him. And also, maybe, to experience this all anew. To create new memories and know that he would probably really like that for you." He takes a deep breath and winces a little on the exhale, as if he's not sure he said the right thing. "What do you think?"

What do I *think*?

I *think* it's the most wonderful thing any man has ever done for me.

I *think* he's exceptionally thoughtful and sweet.

I *think* that there's absolutely no way I can keep from falling for him.

And here's what I *feel*: To hell with holding back. To hell with trying to protect my heart. Because there's no stopping how good he makes me feel. I just want more of this. I want more of *him*. Even if I know this is going to end.

Unless ….

Unless I start using the huge backlog of vacation time I have and make regular visits to Maui.

That's something I can figure out later. For now, I throw my arms around his neck and kiss his mouth and his cheek over and over, all while he smiles broadly and tries not to run off the road when the light turns green and I don't stop my attack on him.

26

I'd wanted Ava to experience the Dodgers in a different way from how it had been with her father. She had said they sat in the nose-bleed seats when they came to the stadium. I've arranged for the very opposite. We're not only sitting on the field level, but it's VIP all the way before that.

We're directed to the parking lot right next to the Players' Lot, and the look on Ava's face is priceless. Her eyes get even bigger when we enter the stadium by the outfield and keep walking toward home plate, only to then head downstairs to the Dugout Club.

"I've only ever heard of this place," she says excitedly as she holds onto my arm with both hands.

Her response is exactly what I hoped for. She's ecstatic by the very prospect of what she's about to see with this exclusive access. Her eyes are wide as we walk through the hallways showcasing to glorious effect Dodgers baseball history, including photos of Hall of Famers, framed jerseys of players whose number has been retired, World Series trophies, Golden Glove awards, Louisville Silver Slugger awards, and Cy Young awards. Knowing I had a part in putting that expression of awe on her face is such a good feeling. Almost as good as when she threw her arms around me in the car and covered my face in kisses. That was some kind of shift. She had been trying so hard to guard herself against letting me in, not realizing that it was too late. She'd let me in when we were in Maui. She let me see her. Know her. But she convinced herself that being free and open with me was safe since it was only temporary. Thing is, I'm not willing to let her go. I'm not willing to act as if we don't have something incredible together. And it feels like she's closer than ever to admitting the same thing, too.

I stand back and watch when she lingers at Fernando Valenzuela's Cy Young award. The pitcher is originally from Mexico and became a hero to his countrymen as well as Latinos here back in his heyday of the 1980s. Odds are good that he was a sports idol for Ava's father, too.

That seems to be confirmed when she turns to me with tears shining in her eyes. "This is so incredible, Ford," she says. "Really, it's more special than you can even imagine."

I wrap my arm around her just as she leans into my chest and kiss the top of her head.

This is a much better feeling than where we were this morning. We both know there aren't any answers to this thing we're doing, but I think we're agreed on allowing ourselves the chance to enjoy it while we can.

"You want more time here?" I ask.

"I'm good. And ready for a Dodger Dog."

Laughing, I steer her to the Dugout Club restaurant where there is indeed a Dodger Dog station with special add-on toppings, but also higher-end offerings like a prime rib carving station and a full bar. But Ava walks past it all without registering the lavish displays. The sound of batting practice has lured her out toward the field and our seats.

I watch as her hand flies to her mouth at the wonder of being this close—no more than a few yards—to the players.

"Jesus, they're big in real life, aren't they?" I ask as I come up behind her and wrap my arm around her chest.

She laughs and squeezes my forearm. Looking back at me, she whispers, "Where did you come from?"

"All I know is I'm right where I want to be," I tell her, and she practically swoons, leaning into me.

When she looks back at the field, I can feel her release any worries she's had with a deep exhale.

"This is the kind of romance you like, isn't it? Good seats at a baseball game is all it takes," I tease.

"You have no idea."

"No?"

"You've just swept me off my feet, Surfer Boy."

Smiling, I lean down and kiss her, soft and slow. Pulling away, she turns around and looks up at me. We share a silent moment, each of us with a small, satisfied smile on our faces. Then I stroke her cheek before cupping it.

"Are you ready for this?" I ask and glance at the field.

She places her hand on my hip, her fingers slipping just inside the waistband of my shorts. "I'm so ready it scares me," she says softly.

Squinting at her, I try to make sense of that.

"They've got to win, right?" she says quickly.

Now I get it. I was asking about the game, and she was replying about something completely different. About us.

But the admission spooked her, and now she's brushing it off. I'll let her off the hook on it—for now. This afternoon is supposed to be all about her experiencing her beloved Dodgers in a new way, after all.

OUR SEATS ARE FIRST ROW, with the protective foul ball netting the only thing between us and the field. With drinks, Dodger Dogs, and a competitive game, we've got it made.

Ava is very serious about her baseball. She knows all the players, including their strengths, shortcomings, and quirks. We talk easily as we watch the game, and I share with her my history of playing in high school.

"Oh god, I'd love to see you in a baseball uniform," she says, turning to me with a wicked gleam in her eyes.

"I'll do that when you wear a hula girl outfit."

"Be careful what you wish for." She raises her eyebrows at me playfully.

Because I find it very hard not to do so whenever I possibly can, I slide my hand into the hair at the nape of her neck, pull her to me, and kiss her deeply. She's sexy and fun, and I don't want this to end.

I pull away from her abruptly when I realize what I've just thought. She looks at me with a mixture of confusion and amusement before shrugging off my sudden withdrawal and turning her attention back to the game.

Gulping down the rest of my beer, I finally understand what she was trying to do by saying we shouldn't get invested in each other. There are consequences to this. It's temporary pleasure with the promise of future heartache, because neither of us is willing to change our lives. Hers is here, pursuing her career. Mine is in Maui, pursuing my peace.

Thing is, I'm already a goner for this girl.

27

AVA

I can't get used to the weight of this ring on my finger. It's distracting me from focusing on the conference call blaring from my office speakerphone.

It is a stunning piece of jewelry. I've found myself gesturing an awful lot with my left hand ever since he slipped the ring on me yesterday afternoon.

That it was only yesterday that this happened is hard to believe. Taking me to that Dodgers game is just as hard to absorb.

Our hometown boys won and to celebrate, I had Ford take us to my favorite taco food truck near the stadium. We ate one taco after another, standing under a streetlamp in the street, until we were ridiculously full.

Afterward, we went to my place again, not even making it as far as the bed before we pulled each other's clothes off. I can't get enough of him and it seems he feels the same way.

He woke me before my alarm went off in the morning and made slow, sleepy love to me.

And then he got up and started the coffee maker before

hopping into the shower. Still in a post-orgasm daze, I curled up in bed and inhaled his scent. As I listened to the water from the bathroom, I marveled at how quickly we've become comfortable with each other. It felt like this in Maui, too. Like we needed no separation from each other, that we simply *fit* together.

Later, I kissed him goodbye at the door when he was leaving to go to his firm. And then I kissed him again. And again, until he stepped back inside, kicking the door closed behind him as he pulled his fly open with one hand and pulled up my dress with the other.

I've never been so relaxed about being late to the office. How else could I be when I'm so intensely sexually satisfied *and* falling so hard for him?

"Are you still there, Ava?"

Sitting up straighter, I zero in on the voice and wonder how long I've been checked out.

"Ah, yes. Sorry, I had someone here in my office," I say, thinking quickly. "Can you please go over that last point?"

From then on, I return to my usual laser-like concentration. I have work to do, after all, since this time, I'm picking Ford up from his office later today so I can take him to meet my mom.

I THOUGHT MILLER, Newell & Kahn was a nice law firm, but it's nothing in comparison to McAvoy & Partners. The elevator ride to their offices takes an obscene amount of time, but I suppose that's what's to be expected when you're going all the way up to the forty-sixth floor.

When I enter the reception area, I'm greeted by not one, but two pert, smiling blondes behind a huge shared desk.

"Hi," I say, not sure which one to look at. I finally pick the one on the right at random. "I'm here to see Ford McAvoy."

"Senior or Junior?" she asks.

"Oh, um, Junior."

"Your name?"

I straighten my spine and give her my name.

"Have a seat." She nods to the sleek leather settee by the wall of windows showcasing the city.

As I start to do as I'm told, I wonder why I didn't just have Ford meet me downstairs instead of doing this formal pickup at the office thing. A part of me wonders if he was hoping to impress me, but I dismiss that idea. He's not the type to want to show off. Or if he did, it would be about catching waves. A vision of us together on his longboard flashes in my mind. That was such an incredible experience. Gliding on those waves felt heavenly. And then, lying on the board with Ford, feeling his heartbeat somehow sync up with the gentle lapping of the water was the most soothing feeling. For a moment, I wish we were back there. I wish we were spending lazy, long warm days together at the beach and having poke at Makai's before stumbling tipsy back to his little shack on the sand.

"Ah, there you are, Ava."

The voice interrupting my little fantasy isn't Ford's. At least not *my* Ford's. I look up to find his father coming toward me with open arms as if we're old friends.

Standing, I smooth down my dress and smile at him. "Looks like you've been troubled by mistake," I say. "I asked them to let your son know I'm here."

"Oh, don't be too hard on Emily." He stops himself and

glances at the reception desk. "Or was it Emmaline?" he asks with a shake of his head. "I can never keep them straight. I mean, who can when they've got such similar names?"

"Yes, well—"

"That is an impressive ring, Ava," he says, taking my left hand into his.

"Thank you. I ... well, I really love it."

"I imagine you do."

I'm not sure what to do with that response, so instead, I skirt past it. "It was very kind of you to come out to get me. Maybe you wouldn't mind showing me to Ford's office?"

For a moment, he just watches me. *Examines* me.

I imagine most people would be intimidated by this close inspection, but I've had more than my fair share of successful older white men like him assessing me in this way. Instead of wilting the way I'm sure he'd intended I do, I wait him out.

"Yes," he finally says. "Shall we?" He holds out one arm to gesture toward the door and uses his other to guide me by the small of my back.

His presumptuous touch puts a pep in my step, and I move through the expansive office space to create some distance between us. I don't know where I'm going as I pass by rows of secretaries directly outside of glass offices, none of which contain Ford.

"Why don't we step in here," he says, stopping at an empty conference room.

Before I can question why we'd make this detour, he pulls open the glass door and steers me inside. It's a mid-size space with an oblong table large enough for ten padded-leather chairs. There are two seventy-inch plasma screens on the wall at one end of the room and what appears to be a catering spread of sandwiches and beverages leftover from an earlier meeting on a built-in countertop at the opposite side of the room.

"I'm glad we have a minute here, Ava," he says.

I've turned my eyes to the view of the city through the floor to ceiling windows. It's an impressive sight. I'd guess that's at least part of why we've ducked into this space. He wants to show me his success. But he wasn't counting on the sour smell of the roast beef sandwiches in the corner. The contrast feels very like my understanding of who he is through Ford's description. He's preoccupied with appearances, and yet refuses to acknowledge what's right under his nose.

"You went to Southwestern, is that right?" he continues.

Turning to him, I fix a blank expression on my face. His knowing which law school I went to is probably only the tip of the iceberg. He's probably done more research on me than that. I keep my own counsel, as the expression goes, by remaining silent.

"Yes, well, that's what I hear anyway," he continues. "It's a nice success story for a disadvantaged girl from Boyle Heights." He tries for an amiable smile, but it does nothing to offset the condescending remark he tried to pass off as a compliment.

There's nothing *disadvantaged* about me. I didn't grow up with the wealth he has, but I had what matters—a loving, supportive family. Still, I don't strike back. Instead, I keep biting my tongue, letting him reveal more of his motives in diverting me to this meeting room.

"Randall sure speaks highly of you." He chuckles. "And he's tickled that it seems he's to thank for you and my boy getting together. I mean, if you hadn't tripped up in that deposition, you'd never have even gone to Maui."

Wow. He went right for my weak spot.

Or at least, that's what he thinks my weak spot is. That I made one error—and not even a significant error in the grand scheme of things—at work is not something he can hurt me with. What kind of lawyer would I be, after all, if I wasn't able to recover from that?

"It was definitely ... fortuitous," I say.

He raises his eyebrows at my choice of words. And it was a deliberate choice. He thinks he has the upper hand here, but I can see where he's going. I can see it a mile away.

"You do know about Ford's plan to resign, don't you?" he asks.

I nod.

"So, then you know that the very generous paychecks of this firm will cease."

And there it is, just as I suspected. He thinks a *disadvantaged* girl like me can only want one thing from his son: money. Never mind the fact that I have my own successful career.

"I don't want or need his paycheck," I say.

"Is that so?"

"Not that I need to share this with you, but I make a good living."

"I'm sure you do ... fine." He says the word "fine" as if it leaves a bad taste in his mouth. "But he will soon have nothing from this firm. No income, just so we're clear."

I've had enough of his emphasis on this point. Time to disabuse him of the antiquated, sexist notion that all I'm after is landing a rich husband.

Just then, Ford—*my* Ford—pulls open the door and steps in, eyeing us both warily as he tries to assess what he's interrupted. But I don't let that stop me from what I say next.

"It's okay if he's penniless," I say. "I'm not after his money, after all."

"No?" Senior looks skeptical.

"Nope." I shrug. "I'm after his phenomenal legal mind. You're really going to miss his skills once he and I partner up."

"Partner up?" he asks with an arched brow.

"Marriage is a partnership, isn't it?"

"I—"

"Oh, sorry, I know you've never actually been married. But Ford and I, our relationship is a true partnership. And the natural thing would be to take that into a legal practice, too. We'd make a very tempting alternative for some of the clients Ford still has here, don't you think?"

Senior's mouth drops open for just a moment before he recovers himself. "Wait a minute. Are you saying—" he starts, but Ford interrupts.

"Ava, we have to go."

I make a show of looking conflicted over cutting things short. Then, I shrug with a small smile. "Gotta go," I say, and wink at Senior.

I've played it cool, but as soon as Ford pulls me out of that meeting room, I can feel my heart beating wildly. Ford's got my hand and is leading me through the expansive office. I feel all eyes on us. Suddenly, I can't contain a giggle. It turns into real laughter that I can't even muffle with my hand to my mouth.

I don't know what came over me.

But damn, it felt good to see Senior's shocked expression.

Ford pulls me into a side room, and before I know it, he's closed the door and pushed me up against it, his body pressed to mine.

He's grinning.

"What was that all about?"

"I, uh …" Looking around, I see that the room is a study space. It's small, with a table and four chairs and a library reading lamp atop it. There are several law texts, a copy of the *Los Angeles Times*, and a legal pad scattered there. Otherwise, we're alone. "I don't know."

"Not many people can do what you did just now to my father." He draws his fingers through my hair gently, his eyes full of admiration.

"What did I do?"

He laughs. "You caught the bastard flat-footed."

"Oh," I say.

"You want to partner up with me, huh?"

"Um, that just kind of came out," I say. "Seemed like the way to throw him."

"It sure as fuck did. But you gotta watch it, honey. He can be vicious." He touches my chin, making sure our eyes meet. "I don't want you getting a target on your back out of all of this. I couldn't stand it if he went after you."

I like that he's protective of me. But despite all the years of Randall trying to do the same thing, when it comes down to it, I know no one takes care of me better than me.

Grabbing his hip, I pull him closer. "I know how to handle myself."

"Hell, yeah you do," he murmurs as he presses his lips to mine, kissing me tenderly at first. That quickly escalates to kisses that are so heated that we're pawing at each other at the same time.

"Hey," I say breathlessly as he kisses my cheek and neck, getting rougher and more desperate. "I was thinking about your shares issue."

He pulls away for a second and looks at me quizzically. "You were?"

"Yeah, a little."

"Jesus, that turns me on."

I laugh and then kiss him, pulling on his bottom lip with my teeth as I pull away. "Have you looked into whether the bylaws have ever been amended regarding shares transfers? You know, special circumstances you can use as precedent for doing something different with your shares?"

"I, uh ..." he starts, and I can see his mind working.

Now I'm the one to kiss his neck, biting at his skin, wanting to take this into something that will satisfy us both. We get lost in each other, but when I reach down and stroke him, he pulls away and goes to the table, leaning over.

"Are you okay?" I ask.

He looks up at me with a smirk. "I will be. I just need a minute."

I realize he's being prudent to stop things given where we are. Still, I can't help but ask, "Probably not a good idea to have sex in the office?"

"There's nothing I'd rather do." He sighs regretfully. "But you're right. Probably not a good idea. The whole floor saw us come in here. I don't think we need that story going around."

I nod. But then say, "Hey, what does it matter to them? We're engaged, aren't we?"

Meeting my eyes, he shakes his head with an appreciative smile. "You better believe it," he says and quickly closes the distance between us.

28

This girl. Man, she's something. I'm watching her from the backyard of her mother's small home. She and her mom are just inside at the kitchen counter, pulling together dinner. Ava is lightly frying corn tortillas before dipping them into enchilada sauce whereupon her mom takes them and fills them with a combination of cheese, onions, and chicken. Pretty soon, we'll have plates filled with those enchiladas, topped with fresh avocado along with rice and pinto beans to go with it. My mouth waters, both because it smells so good and because I worked up an appetite back at the office. That quickie was phenomenal.

Yeah, we had the office talking. But we walked out of there on a cloud. It's hard to care what people think when I've got Ava by my side. Nothing else matters.

That feeling lasted the whole car ride here. I should have been worried about what her mom would think of me, but all I could do was stare at my Hula Girl in amazement.

I needn't have worried about Rafaela, Ava's mother, anyway. She greeted me so warmly and with such generosity that I immediately felt welcome. After giving me a bottle of Pacifico beer, she suggested I enjoy the breeze in the backyard while they finished up dinner. I've been out here, sitting at the wrought iron table, nursing my beer, and musing on all of this.

When they join me, loaded down with food that looks so delicious I know I'll want to lick the plate clean, I realize I should have been thinking of exactly what I'll say to Rafaela. Especially when after we've all enjoyed the meal with superficial conversation, she looks at me expectantly.

"You're up, Surfer Boy," Ava teases.

"Oh, I, uh …" I say before taking a deep breath and starting fresh. "So, first, you should know how much I adore and respect your daughter."

Rafaela nods cryptically. Doesn't look like I'm going to be able to soft-pedal my way out of this.

"And I'm just going to be brutally honest," I continue. "This all started as a way to sort of mess with her ex, Bryce."

With that, Rafaela raises her eyebrows and looks at Ava.

"I knew from Ava that he didn't truly understand what a remarkable woman she is. So, when I saw him approaching her, and frankly, getting kind of handsy with her, I interrupted and said I was her fiancé. Just to make him back off and prove him wrong about what Ava was capable of."

Glancing at Ava, I see she looks embarrassed by me sharing all of this. I figure, though, that the only way to get Rafaela on our side is to tell her everything.

There's a tense moment of silence.

Finally, Rafaela says, "I never did like that Bryce."

I laugh. "See," I tell Ava, "mothers *know*. They just know."

Ava smiles, giving in to that notion without objection.

"Then, my father came around, and I urged Ava to keep up the ... lie—let's just call it what it is."

"Why?" Rafaela asks simply.

I struggle for a moment to explain this part. How honest should I be? Should I tell her that if my father thought he was being toyed with over something like this that it's possible he could do something to hurt Ava's career? Wouldn't she instantly dislike me for putting her daughter in this precarious position?

"I just, uh, truthfully, it was the path of least resistance. My father is a very powerful man. He hates to be caught by surprise. If he were to think he'd been duped as part of a joke, well, no good would have come from it. So, we just need to play along with this whole thing until I can finish up my business here."

Rafaela nods thoughtfully. "When you finish your business, you'll do what?"

"I'll go home to Maui."

She looks at Ava. To my disappointment, Ava is quick to reassure her, saying, "I'm not going anywhere."

"You could always come." The words come out of my mouth before I can process what I'm saying. "You could get out from under the corporate legal machinations with all its sexism and racism and open up your own practice. Be your own boss. And have all the control over your career. In Maui."

I watch as Ava's eyebrows come together in confusion. "Ford, that's crazy."

"A little," I admit. "But—"

"We *just* met," she says.

Shit. What have I done? Did I just suggest that Ava move to Maui to be with me? In front of her *mother.*

I laugh, and it comes out forced, even to my ears. "I was

just throwing out possibilities. You should come, too, Rafaela."

I pat my stomach. "I clearly cannot get enough of your enchiladas."

Rafaela's mouth quivers, telling me she's fighting off a laugh. And that's when I know I've screwed up. She knows her daughter well enough to understand that my attempt to backtrack isn't going to get me anywhere.

"*Possibilities?*" Ava says, incredulous. "No, what you're doing is casually suggesting I give up my whole world. For a man I barely know. You're seriously suggesting that I give up on the place I've earned at my law firm? I have put my *life* into this career."

It's irrational, but I can't help how much her quick dismissal of me as someone she "barely knows" stings. Yes, this thing of ours has been a whirlwind, but it was more than some surface-level connection almost as soon as we met. We've shared *real* confidences with each other. And now she's ready to disregard all that. She'd rather pull up her walls and close herself off than give it a chance to be something real.

Because I have that annoying habit of saying things when I shouldn't, I push the issue, focusing on the thing I know she cares about more than almost anything else: her career.

"And you're saying that there's no other way to have a career, but there is. You don't *have* to follow that path to be satisfied with your work."

"Says the man who walked away from everything in order to do nothing," she snaps back.

"Ouch," I half-moan, half-laugh. That characterization hurts, but at the same time, I can't help but admire her fighting spirit. She's tough and sexy at the same time. That combination has left me hesitating to respond, even as we stare at each other.

"*Mija*, did I ever tell you how I met your father?"

Ava and I break eye contact as we turn to Rafaela, her apparent non-sequitur catching us both off-guard.

"Uh, yeah," Ava says, clearly confused. "You met him in Mexico. In Zacatecas, the town where you're both from."

"*Si*, very much by chance, in fact. We were both at El Jardín—" She stops and looks at me. "That's a sort of town square, near the church. There are some nice trees for shade, and everyone ends up there as the evenings cool off. It becomes a marketplace for homemade food. The kids run around and play. The adults gossip and hope to run into friends."

"It's a very nice spot," Ava agrees. "But, I'm not sure—"

"Your father and I ran into each other. Like, actually bumped into each other as he was turning away from getting *horchata* as I was passing by. He spilled it all over me." She laughs at the memory. "He was always a little clumsy."

"Oh, *that's* why you'd always joke with him about not spilling the *horchata!*" Ava says.

"Oh yes. That was our running joke."

"I love that," I say.

Rafaela smiles, acknowledging me. "That's all it took for us, is what I'm saying. He spilled the *horchata* and spent the rest of the night apologizing and somehow convincing me not to run home to change. We were ... drawn together after that. It was truly hard to pull us apart."

"Aw, that story makes me so happy," Ava says, her eyes shimmering with tears.

"The only problem was that he was planning on moving to America less than two weeks after we met. I thought we had no chance."

"No, but you moved here together. After you were married

in Zacatecas," Ava says, clearly trying to sort out her recollection of her parents' love story.

"That's true," Rafaela says. "But only because he broke down a few days before he was due to leave and told me he thought the universe had put us in each other's paths, *horchata* and all." She laughs. "He said it was crazy, but he was sure he had fallen in love and that if I took a chance by marrying him and coming with him to America, he would make me happy for the rest of my life."

I hand Ava a clean napkin to wipe the tears she's no longer able to fight.

"And so, I did. I loved him, too, of course. But I also knew that he used the word 'chance' well, because isn't that what we all do when we fall in love? We take a chance, hoping that our hearts will be cared for by that other person." She takes a deep breath and stares up at the sky. "I'm so glad I took that chance. It wasn't the longest life with him, but I can't imagine ever having a better one."

"Oh, Mama," Ava says and scoots her chair closer, so she can hug her.

I sit quietly as they hug and murmur comforts to each other. Looking up at the night sky, I watch as a commercial airplane slowly makes its way past and contemplate Rafaela's purpose in telling us the story of how she and her husband met. She sure seems to be on the side of doing the unexpected for the sake of love. Could she be in favor of Ava trying to work something out with me? The idea tugs a smile from my lips.

But then Ava's accusation that I'm doing nothing reasserts itself and I slump in my seat. If I'm not one of those manipulative bastards in the glass offices at work, then apparently, she thinks I'm not doing much with my life. How do you get around that? As much as I like her, I can't imagine having to convince her that my life is meaningful. Because if you have to make a case for something like that, you've already lost.

NOT MUCH LATER, I help clear the dishes. I start to wash them, but Rafaela won't hear of it. She's made flan, and we sit at the kitchen table to eat it. It's the thickest, creamiest flan I've ever had. Much more like a cheesecake than the watery, Jell-O style flan usually found in restaurants.

"What do you do for work in Maui?" Rafaela asks casually.

"I help my mom with her music school. There's a group of students that I've taken on. Ava saw them perform when she was there."

"Really?"

"There's one boy who is something else," Ava says. "What's his name? The clarinet player."

"Eli," I offer. "Yeah, he's a little mixed up on what constitutes confidence. He's got this whole wise-beyond-his-years-thing. We're working on that."

"Ford is really good with the kids. And you can see that they all look up to him. It's very sweet."

"And would you consider moving back to Los Angeles?" Rafaela asks, throwing us both again with her way of suddenly changing the topic.

"Mama," Ava says reproachfully.

"Well, we do have children here in need of a good music teacher," she says, putting on a face of innocence.

I laugh and shake my head. I really like this woman. She's insightful and clever. I can see that Ava gets those traits from her.

"I'm committed to Maui and to the kids at my mom's school," I say. "We've come a long way together, those kids and me. I think we've both benefited from our work."

Rafaela watches me for a moment before nodding. Then she looks at Ava and says, "So, he doesn't really do *nothing*, does he? Seems like he's making an impact in the lives of children."

Ava looks confused. "What?"

"Earlier, you said he left everything, so he could do nothing."

Her hand flies to her mouth and she looks regretful. "I, um, I shouldn't have said that. It's not what I even believe. I'm so sorry."

I wave it off. "It's okay. I understand that we have different views on the place work should have in our lives."

She drops her hand and lifts her chin. "What is that supposed to mean?"

"Just that your commitment to work is your only priority."

"*Only* priority?"

I shrug. "You had to be *forced* to take a vacation by your own boss. You have a generic apartment in downtown LA of all places, because you spend more time at the office than at home. It's pretty easy to see that you've let work define you."

"That's not true."

"It's a little true," Rafaela says just as she rises to clear our plates.

Ava gives her mother the side-eye and crosses her arms over her chest. She practically huffs but holds back when Rafaela stops on her way to the sink and squeezes her shoulder. It appears that they've talked about this sort of thing before. When Ava squeezes her mother's hand in return, I can see their unconditional support for each other. It's nice. It reminds me of my relationship with my mom.

"Okay, it might be a little true," Ava concedes to me. "But I have been trying to figure out a better balance, I swear. You have been a big part of that lately."

She's got the cutest impish smile on her face. I can't resist leaning over the small kitchen table and giving her a quick kiss.

"Ford," she whispers, and glances at her mother.

Rafaela still has her back to us, but leaning back, I can just make out a pleased expression on her face.

"It's okay," I whisper back. "Your mother loves me."

"Ha! Don't you think you're jumping to conclusions there, Surfer Boy?" Ava says with a laugh.

"Ford," Rafaela says as she turns to us. "*Una quesadilla?*"

"*Si, por favor. Muchisimas gracias,*" I reply.

That gets a huge smile out of Rafaela. I watch as she looks at Ava and imagine she's silently telling her, *yes, I do love him.* In turn, I give Ava an *I told you so* expression, and she just shakes her head.

29

AVA

I'm up in the morning before Ford. We'd gone back to my place after Ford ate not just *una quesadilla* but *tres quesadillas*. He was so full, but so happy.

Now he's lying on his stomach in my bed, his bare tanned back exposed all the way to his beautiful pale butt. His face is turned away from me as I quietly go to the kitchen to start brewing coffee. As I watch the drips of the dark brew drop one by one before becoming a steady drizzle, I try to sort out my conflicting feelings.

We hadn't talked about Ford's surprise suggestion that I move to Maui. I sputtered out a quick and harsh rejection of that, after all. And he had made clear to my mother that he was committed to returning to Maui. Neither of us made any attempt to talk about the fact that as of now, we are set to go our separate ways in a few days with no plan to see each other again. Instead, we're living in a weird state of denial where we're sleeping together, enjoying each other's company, and playing each other's fiancée. It's that whole *investing* in each other thing that I had tried to avoid before throwing caution to the wind when he took me to the Dodgers game. There's no doubt in my mind that I'm going to get hurt with this thing. Because there's just no good answer for how we can make it work.

With a sigh, I do my best to pull together breakfast for us but have to use what I've got, including bagels pulled from the freezer and bananas that are more brown spots than yellow.

"I'll understand if you want to call off the engagement because of this paltry offering," I say when Ford has roused himself and joined me at the dining table.

"Nope, not a deal-breaker. Especially knowing my future mother-in-law is so talented."

"That was such a smooth move last night, speaking in Spanish to her like that."

He laughs. "What? It was totally appropriate in the moment."

"Speaking of appropriate … what should I expect with the party tonight?"

Taking a contemplative sip of his coffee, he thinks about my question for a moment. "Here's how I expect it to go: Just like any other dinner party my father typically throws. Which means, a very nice catered event where the conversation is focused on him, and with guests that literally line up to tell him how wonderful he is. And I'd guess that after dinner but before dessert, he'll do some sort of toast to us. That'll be about the gist of our 'engagement party' since he never really intended to do this at all."

"Oh," I say with relief. "That sounds bearable."

He rubs my hand. "We're almost to the finish line with this thing."

"Yep." I force levity I do not feel into my voice. "Mission almost accomplished."

"Honey, I know it's been a bit of a roller coaster these last few days. But I sure have enjoyed taking this ride with you."

I smile at that. I know he means it sincerely, but I can't take any more of his sweet talk, so I steer my response toward something I know he's happy to indulge.

"You never did make me scream your name," I tell him and arch a brow.

He laughs. "That is so not true. You have screamed it plenty."

I shake my head with mock solemnity. "Nope."

"Oh, I see." He stands, and I watch him warily. "Challenge accepted."

When he reaches for me, I dodge out of the way while scrambling to my feet. He lurches left, and I go the opposite way. He lurches right and I go left. Then he comes straight for me and I let out a playful yelp and turn to run toward the other side of the apartment.

Of course, he catches up to me almost right away. He grabs me around my waist and lifts me in that way that he can, making me feel like I'm light as air as he carries me to the bed.

"What I am going to do to you," he says into my ear, his voice a sexy growl, "is going to make you scream so loud the windows will shatter." He drops me unceremoniously on the mattress. "You have homeowner's insurance?"

I'm laughing so hard that tears come to my eyes. At least, that's what I tell myself—that the tears are from laughing. But a part of me knows this reaction is because I know that I'm going to miss him and that my life will be dimmer without him in it.

I WANTED to spend the day with Ford, but he had to go back to his place where he has the proper clothes for tonight's party and I need to spend an hour or so at the office since I have uncharacteristically neglected my work this week.

I've been at my desk for almost two hours when the rumbling of my stomach motivates me to get up and go to the communal kitchen. It's always well stocked with fresh fruit, granola bars, nuts, crackers, and even assorted cheeses in the refrigerator. I make myself a plate that includes a sampling of all of these things, grab a bottle of Pellegrino, and am on my way back to my office when I hear rustling in Randall's office.

"Couldn't stay away, either, could you?" I ask, smiling as I push open the door.

I expect to see Randall, my mentor and boss. Instead, I see Manny Kahn.

I'm frozen in place as I take in the scene. He's crouching down behind Randall's big desk, almost completely hidden. Except I can see the top of his balding head, the long strips of hair that he combs back from his forehead greasy from product meant to stick it in place. And I can also see that he's been rifling through the cabinet behind Randall's desk.

"What's going on?" I ask.

Manny stiffens before slowly straightening up.

My hands are full of the snacks I'd helped myself to for brunch. His hands are full of papers he clearly shouldn't have helped himself to.

"Oh, hi, Ava," he says.

I arch a brow. "Seriously?"

"Don't let your suspicious nature run wild," he says with a breezy smile. "I was just retrieving some papers of mine."

"Papers that were stored in Randall's private cabinet?"

He takes a long moment to ignore me while he straightens

the papers into a neat stack. Then he folds them in half and sticks them under his arm before kicking closed the cabinet door and heading toward me.

He stops when he's just inches away. It's uncomfortably close, but I don't let him intimidate me. I stand my ground.

"I'll be on my way now, and I'll expect you to say no more of our little ... meeting."

I scoff. "That's what you'll *expect?*"

He had started to walk past, but now, he rears on his heel and stares daggers at me. "You would do well to remember your place, Ms. Ruiz," he says. "An employee in your position should not question a partner as often as you do. Anyone else would see this as insubordination. It's only because of Randall that I'm willing to let this go."

"I am only ever looking out for Randall's best interests," I say. It's the truth. When I go at Manny, I know that I'm teetering on the line of professionalism. Well, okay, I'm falling right over it. But it's only because I have a fierce sense of wanting to protect Randall. Even if that ends up being to my detriment.

Manny studies me for a long moment. I lift my chin, waiting for him to tell me once more that I'm talking out of turn.

But he doesn't admonish me. What he says instead takes things in a direction I hadn't anticipated.

"Listen, I know you revere Randall." He pauses, hesitating for a moment. "I want to be candid with you because of that. But in doing so, I need you to keep this in strict confidence."

"Of course," I say, snapping into professional mode.

"This may not even be news to you, I suppose. I'm sure you've noticed how he's diminished in the last few months, right?" He doesn't let me respond, which is probably good, because I would have rejected this and revealed my denial over the matter, which is not a good look for a lawyer who should be able to assess the facts of any given situation. "He's been on a downward trajectory," he continues. "I don't like to see it. But it's true. And if you want to help him, if you want to look out for his best interests, you'll convince him to step down and let others carry this firm on in good stead."

I can't see past the logic in this, not when my instinct is to protect Randall. "Others? You mean *you*. You've been gunning for power since before I started here."

"Be that as it may," he says, exasperated, "this *isn't* how I wanted it to end. Open your eyes and look at Randall's recent history. He's not himself."

I still don't want to accept what he's saying. I'd rather deny it, or laugh it off, or accuse him of the lowest kind of subterfuge. I open my mouth, but Manny cuts me off.

"And don't be naive about how others will use this against him."

"What do you mean?"

"This is exactly what your ex Bryce was doing when he tried to speak directly with your client. You know, when you were off in Maui getting insta-engaged?"

I'm completely thrown and only manage to stutter out, "Wh-what?"

He sighs with impatience. "He was trying to get our client to admit that Randall wasn't competent to represent the case in your absence. *He's* the one going after Randall. *I'm* trying to protect him."

"But, I still don't understand. Randall may be a little forgetful, but he's still capable."

"He's been coming in to the office less. He's less involved in cases. He only took on your case because he saw fit to spend firm money on an all-inclusive vacation for you. That alone, is evidence—"

"Manny, please." Everything he's said is true. So, too, is the fact that Randall has been withdrawn. More often than not, when I've seen him in the past few months it's when I've caught him staring off into space. Engaging him in conversation had been difficult, but I'd attributed that to him having things on his mind. I hadn't inquired after him when he stopped coming into the office on Saturdays or started coming in later and leaving earlier during the week. I'd built him up as not just a brilliant legal mind, but an indestructible surrogate grandfather all these years.

The truth is, what I can only see now is that I didn't want to absorb all the changes. I didn't want to acknowledge any kind of decline. It was too painful. And now that I realize what I had willfully denied, I feel incredibly guilty. I should have been helping him, not ignoring the signs I was too afraid to accept.

Manny meets my eyes. Neither of us looks away for a long moment. Finally, his shoulders sag.

"I take no pleasure in this, Ava," he says. "I know you don't believe that, but it's true. Yes, I have believed I have the better instincts for running this firm for quite a long while, but that doesn't mean I ever lost respect for Randall. I only want to see him off in a way that pays tribute to everything he's accomplished. I would be grateful if you could help me do that."

"Me?" I ask with a startled laugh. I have to blink back the tears that have once more filled my eyes. My emotions have been doing overtime today, starting with Ford and now with Randall.

"Yes. He adores you. You are one of his greatest achievements, to be honest."

"Wait," I say. "You're giving *me* a compliment?"

He hesitates before giving in and laughing. "Ava. I can admit that Randall made the right decision in hiring you."

I take in a shaky breath. "Thank you, Manny."

"You'll do what you can?"

"I, uh, yes. I will."

He purses his lips together before giving me a nod. And then he walks out, and I'm alone in Randall's office. My hands are still full. But I stay in the same spot, taking in everything anew. Randall's big desk is the perfect reflection of the man I always thought him to be: sturdy, high-quality, comforting. But looking closer, I can see that the corners are scuffed from years of use. The wood is worn where Randall leaned his forearms on it as he engaged in heated debates with other lawyers in the firm, including me. If it's to keep being a useful piece, it will need a little more TLC than it's seen in recent times.

So will Randall. He deserves to have the time and freedom to enjoy a true retirement. Resolved that this will be my mission going forward, I nod to myself and then head back to my office.

30

FORD

In one of my last acts of deference to my father, I've dressed up for his dinner party, wearing a slim fit navy-blue Hugo Boss suit paired with a starched white shirt, no tie. I'm standing on the second-floor balcony of his Pacific Palisades home, taking in the last sherbet hues of the sunset over the ocean in the distance. But I'm also keeping an eye on the arrivals in the circular drive below where a valet service has been set up.

The cocktail hour started fifteen minutes ago, and most guests had arrived on time. But Ava and her mother are not yet here. I'm contemplating calling her when I spot her white Acura RDX pulling into the drive.

I turn away and step back into the great room being used for cocktails, intending to rush downstairs to greet them. There are bistro tables scattered around a full two-sided bar in the center of the space. Senior has invited fifty people to this dinner, and it doesn't appear that anyone has declined. The chatter is loud, overpowering the cellist and violinist in the corner who were meant to provide elegant background music. Dinner will be served downstairs in the garden. It's been set up by the catering company with long tables, and Italian bulbs have been strung overhead, making this look more like a wedding reception than a simple dinner party. I might be suspicious of this decor, fearful that Senior wants to push this into something more than a spontaneous engagement party, but I know that his girlfriend *du jour* has a flare for event planning. She was probably tickled to help organize this soirée.

"Ah, there you are."

I turn to see Randall Miller and a woman I assume is his wife ambling toward me. I stop and shake his hand, though I wish I had waited for Ava and her mother at the valet rather than risk getting caught up like this. With no other choice now, I wait for an introduction.

"Yes, this is …" he says, hesitating. "This is … my wife."

"Alice," she says, offering her hand.

She's small in stature with a tidy gray bob and a ready smile.

"It's a pleasure to meet you," I say. "Ava thinks the world of you both."

"Oh, we just love her right back," Alice says. "But it was a surprise to hear about this engagement, I have to say."

"Surprised us, too," I say with a grin I hope is charming.

"Made me wonder if I had forgotten something along the way, there," Randall says. His eyes go wild for a moment, as if he's struggling with something only he can discern.

"Of course, you hadn't," Ava says, joining us with her mother by her side.

She looks radiant in a baby-blue off-the-shoulder dress that has large-print flowers on it and conforms to her delicious curves. Her hair is down but pulled back above one ear with a clip that glitters with Swarovski Crystals. Her lips are tinted dark red, making me think they must be the same color of the apple that tempted Adam once upon a time.

"Hi, babe," she says breezily, before kissing me quickly.

The touch of her lips on mine is too brief, but leaves a lasting sensation. I force myself to greet Rafaela. She's well turned out in a crimson dress and sensible heels. It seems she's met Randall and Alice before as they all greet each other familiarly.

We chat genially for a few minutes, standing in a little circle together. I take the opportunity to put my arm around Ava's waist, and when she leans into me in response, I wonder if it's genuine or for show. She has been very good at playing the part, complete with dropping "babe" into the mix.

"What a lovely night," Manny says, as he joins us.

I tense at the sight of him, my last interaction when he not only demeaned me, but suggested Ava was flighty, still at the forefront of my mind.

"Hi, Manfred," I say. "I was just going to show Ava and Rafaela the grounds. You'll excuse us?"

He smirks but doesn't reply, instead turning his attention to Randall.

Ava touches Randall on the shoulder and makes eye contact with him. "I'll be back in a few minutes."

"Sure, take your time," he replies. His eyes express his affection for her the same way I had noticed they did before at the American Bar Association event.

I offer both women an arm, and they take me up on the offer to escort them out to the garden. "You both look beautiful tonight," I say. "I am the envy of all the men here, that's for sure."

Rafaela laughs. "Such a charmer!"

I raise my eyebrows. "I do hope so."

Ava leans into me again, and this time I know it's genuine. This time, it's not pretending, but rather, it's her letting down her guard and it warms me from the inside out.

The garden is large with a manicured lawn, bushes, fruit trees, and fragrant flowers. And then there is the stunning ocean views. My father bought this place after I had gone away to college. He never had any other children, and he's never been married. It's a genuine shame to have such a large home and no one but a rotating series of girlfriends to share it with. But it's the life he's chosen.

"Girl, you are looking fabulous!" Tyler says as he meets us at the fountain in the center of the garden. He's directed this comment not to Ava, but to Rafaela, and she laughs with delight.

It's nice to see that Ava has acquainted her mother with the people whom she's closest with, even if they are all work friends. Ava had insisted that my father extend an invitation to Tyler, saying he would be a good companion for her mother when we were busy making the rounds with guests.

"You're such a flirt, Tyler," Rafaela says.

"Only for you," he replies and takes her arm. "Come with me. You'll love the raw bar. It's set up inside a custom ice carving in the shape of an enormous oyster!"

"Oh my," she says, and waves as he leads her away.

"Alone at last," I say, and Ava smiles. "You do look exceptionally beautiful tonight."

"Thank you." She smooths down the lapel of my suit coat. "You look very handsome."

"Can I tell you a secret?"

She laughs. "Of course."

"I think there's a reason why we've been so good at playing the part of a couple."

"And what would that be?"

I pull her to me, my arm around her waist. "There's just something about us together. It can't be faked. And we shouldn't just let it go."

She stares into my eyes for a moment before breaking the connection and putting her hand on my chest to push away.

"But we have no other option," she says. "You know that."

"I—"

"At the end of tonight, you'll walk me out and I'll give you back this gorgeous but ridiculously expensive ring."

"No, you have to keep it."

"I don't, and I can't."

"Ava, at least to keep up the pretense for a while. That's what we said we'd do, right? To make this seem real? A 'long engagement' and then subtly let people know it didn't work out. You need the ring for that."

"But, how will I get it back to you then?"

"Come visit me," I tell her.

She shakes her head, her eyes filling with tears.

"Ava, promise me you'll visit. Promise me one visit."

The struggle for how to reply maps itself across her face. Finally, she shakes her head a little in capitulation. "Sure, if I can get away for a few days, I will."

Not the most enthusiastic response, but I'll take what I can get. "Okay, I understand."

"It's just," she starts and leans in closer to me, "I think I'm going to be needed at the firm. I learned something today that means I'll have to put in even more hours than usual."

"Is it Manny? Did he—"

"No, it's not him. He and I are actually on good terms right now."

I squint at her, trying to sort out what she isn't telling me. But she doesn't offer anything more. And before I can push her, the catering staff has begun walking through the crowd, chiming little bells to signal that it's time to sit down for dinner.

"I'm going to go find my mom," she says before slipping away, and leaving me both curious and concerned about what will be taking up her time at the firm.

Perhaps it's a good thing. Perhaps she'll be getting a promotion, or the opportunity to take the lead on a big case. That would indeed be a good thing for her. She'd love the recognition and challenge. But it'd stack the odds against me having her in my life, and that is the last thing I want.

31

AVA

At dinner, I'm glad that Randall is seated to my right as it gives me the chance to subtly test the bombshell Manny dropped on me earlier. Ford is across from me with my mom next to him. There are low candles and a mixture of tiny vases holding one or two colorful flowers each and small potted succulents lining the center of the table. Those combined with the overhead string lights give the still warm evening a charming feel. Rather than bask in the lovely event, I repeatedly try to connect with Randall.

"Randall, I was in the office today," I tell him, "catching up on the Flores case."

He nods, but I see no recognition in his eyes.

"Hey, now that I'm back from vacation and all caught up, let's start up our lunches again."

"Oh, sure," he says.

"You missed the last few before I went away," I remind him. We've had a standing bi-monthly lunch date to catch up on both personal and work issues for years. But he hadn't shown up for the last two we had, claiming after the fact to have been caught up in work. It's only after my talk with Manny that I've taken this into account as another sign that he's slipping.

"I'll have your secretary do a better job of reminding you," I say.

He nods but it doesn't seem like he's absorbed this conversation. And then he surprises me with what he says next.

"Ava, is this boy, is Ford's boy really the one for you?" he asks.

I'm torn. I don't want to lie to him. He deserves nothing but my honesty. But his voice and his eyes are so hopeful that I feel like I have no choice but to keep up the ruse.

"Yes, he really is," I say.

He smiles. "It's important that all my girls are happy, you know?"

"Oh, uh, that's so sweet." I realize this isn't him being mentally unclear, but rather his way of saying how much I mean to him, that he considers me part of his family.

"He seems like a good boy," he continues. "They say he's whip-smart. And anyway, the thing that matters most is the way he looks at you."

He nods across the table and I follow his gaze. Ford had been watching us and he doesn't look away now. We lock eyes, and he gives me a wink.

There's a tapping of metal on glass and all conversations slowly hush.

Ford's father is standing at the head of the table, patiently waiting for everyone's attention to be focused on him.

"I want to thank you all for being here," he starts. "And big thanks to Paige for putting together such a lovely evening."

Paige must be Senior's girlfriend. She half stands to acknowledge the polite applause from the crowd. She's about my age with long blonde hair, a thin frame, and large breasts —the definition of an LA social climber, in other words.

"Tonight, is actually a very special occasion," he continues, and I cringe. This is going to be the toast that Ford predicted would happen. I brace myself for some insulting reference to my rise from Boyle Heights, but to my surprise, he passes on the chance to announce the engagement, instead saying, "Ford, come on up here, won't you?"

Ford looks at me and must see a still-worried expression on my face, because he winks before getting up and joining his father at the head of the table.

"I thought it would be more appropriate to have Ford share his news rather than me," Ford's father says and takes a step back.

It dawns on me that his father has done this not out of respect for it being Ford's moment, but because Ford hasn't spoken to him about me. He doesn't know anything about our "story" and so can't begin to tell it.

Ford glances up at the expectant crowd before meeting my eyes. I have no idea what he'll say, and my stomach tightens in anticipation.

"Well, quite a few of you have heard the news about my engagement to Ava Ruiz," Ford says, and the crowd murmurs before settling back down. "But I'll tell you all a little more now. She and I met by chance in a totally unexpected place. In fact, if it wasn't for a wild chicken, of all things, running her off the road, we'd never have met." He pauses to let the laughter die down. "The thing is, as odd as that circumstance was, I think the universe put us in each other's paths, *wild chicken in the road*, and all. I know it's crazy, but I fell for this woman that first day we met. And I've kept on falling ever since."

I've got tears in my eyes, and my heart has twisted and tightened along with my stomach. His choice of words is not lost on me. If I could manage to look across the table at my mother, I imagine she would recognize it too. He's repurposed the story she told us about meeting my father.

"And so, I had to ask her," Ford continues, his eyes still fixed on mine. "I had to tell her that if she would just take a chance on me, on *us*, I'd promise to make her happy for the rest of her life."

The audible coos this receives soon gives way to applause. But I'm so confused. On the one hand, Ford just made an incredibly romantic and seemingly sincere grand gesture with what he's said. I want to believe he's genuine. I want to believe that he really feels this way. But on the other hand, I know—he and I *both* know—that we don't have a future. That there's no chance of him making me happy for the rest of my life. Not when we're both standing our ground in refusing to completely change our lives to make something work between us.

"So, please join me in raising a glass to my lovely fiancée," Ford says, holding up a flute of champagne.

I hadn't even noticed the catering staff delivering glasses to everyone, including me. There's a glass on the table in front of me, and I pick it up automatically. Still willing and able to play the part he had asked of me.

As everyone holds out their glass and choruses "cheers!" and "congratulations!"

When I pull my eyes away from Ford and look across the table at my mom, I see that she understands my conflicting emotions. I may be holding it together on the outside, but Mama always knows.

She gives me a warm smile and a little nod of her head. It's her signal for me to hang in there. To roll with it, just as I had asked her to do with this whole crazy scenario.

And so, I do. I play the part of the love-struck fiancée as Ford and I mingle among the party guests for the rest of the evening, accepting their well wishes and fending off questions about when the wedding will be.

If I didn't know none of this was true, I'd be just as dazzled by this version of a love story as everyone else is.

32

AVA

When it finally feels reasonable to leave, I tell my mom that I'll just say my goodbyes to our host and meet her at the front of the house.

I find Senior with my Ford. They're standing near the ridiculous ice sculpture, deep in conversation.

"I'm sorry to interrupt," I say, and they both turn to me. "I just need to get my mother home. But I wanted to thank you so much for this evening. It was lovely."

Senior nods slowly, his eyes leaving mine to scan my body.

It's been such a draining day. I'm emotionally exhausted from everything I've learned about Randall. I don't have the patience to endure this casual disrespect.

"Hey," I say sharply, and his eyes bounce back up to mine. "That's better."

Ford laughs. "She doesn't tolerate creeps," he explains with a shrug when his father glares at him.

"Anyway, thanks again," I say.

"I'll put you in touch with Paige," Senior says. "I'm sure she'd love to help plan the wedding."

"Uh, sure." I look at Ford. "Can you walk me out, babe?"

"Of course." He looks at his father. "I'll be back in a few minutes."

"What were you talking about?" I ask when we're far enough away not to be overheard by his father.

"Nothing."

"Nothing? Seemed like you had an intense conversation going on there."

"No, not really."

I look up at him to find his face frustratingly impassive.

"Ford," I say, but he doesn't look at me. We've stopped walking and are alone on the first of two landings on the wide staircase that leads up to the house. "Listen, I'm tired. Today has been ... a day. So, please don't play games with me. What is going on?"

He sighs. "I was just trying to assure my father that what you said yesterday at the office wasn't true. That you and I *aren't* plotting to take business away from the firm."

"Oh."

"Yeah, oh. That's all he cares about."

He rubs the back of his neck before pulling his tie loose. Though he seems agitated, he's never looked sexier.

"Hey, how about you leave with us?" I say playfully. "After we drop off my mom, we can go back to my place. As hot as you look in this suit, I'd love to get you out of it."

There's a twitch at the corner of his mouth before he shoots me down. "I, uh, should probably go back and reinforce what I already told him. I just need to be sure he chills out. He's kind of agitated about it."

"He'll be fine," I tell him dismissively. It's odd to see him so preoccupied by what his father thinks. All he's ever wanted is to be free of him. "Let's go."

He hesitates, looking around, looking anywhere but at me. We're alone, with most guests having left and the remaining dozen or so clustered with their backs to us as they stand at the bar down in the garden.

"I just need to be sure he's good, okay?" he says, still distracted.

I wait a beat. Wait for him to say that he'll meet me at my place later. Wait for him to make some sexy suggestion for what we'll do together. But his head is somewhere else. He doesn't say a word.

I can't help but feel rejected. He's leaving LA soon. We both know it's unlikely we'll see each other again. The fact that he's not interested in spending every spare second with me before then is a rude awakening. It feels like now that I've served my purpose in this fiancée game, he has no use for me.

"Yeah, well, you gotta do what you gotta do," I say and start up the steps once more.

"Ava," he says, his voice flat.

That inflection tells me he doesn't want to fight about this. That he doesn't want to put in the effort to make this better. So, I don't turn back, and I don't stop walking. I do, however, start to feel deep regret over how I allowed my heart to be toyed with by this Surfer Boy.

"Stop," he calls after me.

I make it to the top of the staircase and he's just a half-step behind. He grabs my hand and pulls me so that I twist toward him, and he wraps his arms around my waist and shoulders, bringing me in close against his body. I lower my gaze to his chest, not wanting him to see the hurt in my eyes.

"I want to be with you, I do," he says urgently into my ear.

"I just need a minute to deal with him, to make sure that he's not going to do anything—"

But the damage has already been done, and I suddenly feel cold. Suddenly feel rejected by his clear lack of interest in me now that we've pulled off the fake fiancée ruse. And I lash out.

"Yeah, sure," I say. "Go ahead and work on that grand plan of petty retribution against the man you're suddenly so concerned about. That's time well spent, I'm sure."

"Why do you care so much about what I do with him, anyway?" he snaps back.

"Because it's not who you are. It's not the man I met in Maui. The man who told me about directing *mana* in a positive way."

"You don't understand."

"I've got to go."

I start to move toward the house.

"This is all you finding an excuse to walk away," he says and I stop. But I don't turn around. I just listen as he continues. "You just can't stand to let me in, no matter what I say or do. Called it right from the start, didn't I? *Closed off.* That's safer than letting me really know you, isn't t?"

My chin is trembling from trying to stave off tears. I'm so hurt and angry. He knows this is the way to get to me. He knows that the loss of my father is why I might be "closed off" and that I've spent a lot of years trying to protect myself against a similar kind of hurt. And then the minute I do let someone in—because that's *exactly* what I've done with him— he uses it against me.

"But the thing you need to know," he says before I can respond, "is that you don't have to put up your walls." I feel him wrap his arms around me from behind, holding me tightly. "I'm the same guy from just a little while ago who made that toast about taking chances, about falling for you no matter how crazy it seems. That wasn't pretend. I don't want to pretend with you, Ava. I want reality. Even if it's complicated and hard. I want it as long as you're along for the ride with me."

I want to sink back into him. Sink to the ground with him. Just to feel his strong and reassuring arms around me. But that would require taking a chance. Something I just don't think I'm capable of doing right now.

Instead, I say, "I have to go. My mom is waiting." And I pull away from him, hurrying into the house.

33

AVA

The minute we drive away, leaving Ford behind, I feel cold. I hadn't realized what a warm, bright presence he has been in these last few days. I mean, there's no doubt that I've had a good time with him, but I hadn't understood how much space he had taken up in my life. In my heart.

"You don't have to stay, *mija*," Mama tells me when I follow her into her house. "It's okay if you want to go be with Ford."

I take a deep breath to try to clear away those unwanted pangs of missing Ford. "No, I want to. I'm going to find some clothes to change into. We can get cozy and watch something on TV."

She nods, unconvinced by my forced enthusiasm.

In my old bedroom, I keep a stash of emergency clothes for when I decide to stay over at the last minute like this. It includes shorts, sweats, T-shirts, and even some work clothes. I may have officially moved out years ago, but I've never really left. I feel safe here. And being here for Mama always feels good.

It strikes me that I feel the same way about my firm. I feel safe there. And I like being there for Randall.

At the same time, I imagine that neither Mama nor Randall would want me to feel obligated to stick around for them.

But that's too bad, because I'm not going anywhere. I'm definitely not running away from my life like Ford seems to want me to do.

With that thought, I sit heavily on my bed, focusing on that word: safe. It's the same word Ford used in accusing me of not letting him know me—because I thought it was *safer* to protect myself. He's right, of course. Because I've operated out of that sense of wanting *safety* above all else for so long. Financial safety for my mom and me after my father passed away, work safety with my loyalty to Randall, emotional safety with only allowing so much intimacy in my relationships. Until Ford came along, that is.

I want to scream into my pillow to relieve the frustration and heartache I feel. Instead, I change into sweats, a T-shirt, and a Southwestern Law hoodie. When I return to the living room, I find Mama setting out a bowl of freshly popped popcorn sprinkled with spicy *Tajín* seasoning. This snack was a staple of my teenage years, whenever I was heartbroken either by a boy or by less than perfect test results. It meant sitting on the couch with Mama, snacking, and vegging out while we watched telenovelas. And it was always the perfect remedy to take my mind off things. She knows me too well.

I sigh and plop down on the couch. Grabbing a handful of popcorn, I know it's no use to pretend that everything's okay. Mama knows better.

She sits next to me and pulls my left hand toward her,

looking at the ring I'm still wearing. The weight that I'd earlier lamented has gotten comfortable surprisingly quickly.

"Is it real?" she asks, and I laugh.

"I asked the same thing. He says it is very real. He said it cost him ten thousand dollars."

She gasps. "Why would he do that? Can he return it?"

"I don't know, Mama. I don't know why he's done a lot of things, honestly."

Sitting back against the cushions, I close my eyes. A blur of images comes to mind. Not the sexy moments we've had, but the moments of genuine connection. The times when I opened up to him about my father, about how hard I worked to help keep my mother from falling apart after he passed, about how I've dedicated my life to finding success in my career. And all the while, he listened and offered gentle support. More than that, actually. He gave me big gestures like with the Dodgers game, and even with this ring. Why did he buy me a real ring? He didn't have to do that. And why did he say that I haven't let him in. Doesn't he know that I've let him in more than I've let any other man in? Though my eyes are closed, I have to open them to blink away the tears that are forming.

"There isn't a lot of 'pretend' in this thing you're doing with him, is there?"

"What?" I sit upright and try to put on a blank mask.

"Ava," she says softly. "It's okay that you feel something real for him. I can see why you would. He's very good looking."

That makes me laugh, which I know was her intention.

"But also, he seems to feel something for you, too."

I shake my head. "It's no use, that's the thing. He's going back to Maui. I'm staying here."

"That's the end of the story?"

I nod. "That's the end of *our* story."

"There's no chance one of you can move to be with the other?"

"No, it doesn't seem so." I laugh in frustration. "I just—I really don't discount the work that he does at the music school, but I just wish he was open to moving here. I mean, why can't *he* be the one to give up his life to be here with me? Why does the woman always have to make the sacrifice?"

"Like I did to be with your father?" Mama asks gently.

"No, I didn't mean it like that. That was different. You chose that, right? You didn't feel like your hand was forced, did you?"

"No, not in the way you're thinking. I mean, it was hard to leave Zacatecas. I had my family and friends there, of course. But with your father, I got so much more. He was what I *needed*. I'm not ashamed to admit that."

"And I love that. But I need more than a man. I need my job. I need to feel like I'm accomplishing things."

"You deserve every happiness, *mija*."

I lean into her, and she wraps her arm around me. "Thank you, Mama."

"Just don't let the happiness of your heart suffer by thinking it shouldn't come first."

"What are you saying?"

"This man, he cares for your heart. That makes him a chance worth taking."

"This isn't the same as it was with you and Papa," I say, suppressing a yawn.

"No, not the same," she agrees. "But not all that different from what I can tell."

"You just like him because he ate *six* of your enchiladas the other night."

She laughs. "Probably so, *mija*."

AFTER WE CLEAN out the popcorn bowl and shut off the TV, I go to bed. As tired as I am, though, I can't sleep. Instead, I lie on my bed, staring up at the ceiling. I wonder what Ford is doing. I wonder if he'll want to see me again before he leaves for Maui.

Purely as a thought-exercise, I try to envision what it would look like if I did as he suggested and moved to Maui. I'd be walking away from all the years I invested in Miller, Newell & Kahn. I'd be walking away from a clear career path. I'd have to study for and pass the Hawai'i bar exam. And there's no guarantee that I would be able to create a successful practice. I also wouldn't have my mother close by. And I'd never see the Dodgers play in person.

It sounds terrible so far. Turning on my side, I try to focus on the positives instead of the negatives. I'd live on an island paradise without all the Los Angeles drawbacks like smog, and traffic, and crime. I'd have complete control over whether I succeed or fail with my career if I had my own practice. I might even be able to make my own hours and create that elusive work—life balance I keep saying I want but haven't managed to find yet. I'd watch every Dodgers game on TV, just like I have for all these years. I'd bring Mama over to visit, and maybe even convince her to retire there and live a well-deserved life of leisure. And, I'd have Ford. Ford, the man who has turned my world upside down and shown me an incredible amount of caring in such a short time.

I don't get to an alternative thought-process whereby Ford is the one to give up everything and move here because my phone buzzes and I'm shocked by the text message that comes through.

It's from Ford. He must have spent an hour keying in his message on that old flip phone of his.

I was wrong. You have let me know you. And you are the most amazing woman I've ever known. I love everything about you. I love the way you've shared your life with me. I love the way you put me in check. Seriously, everything. I don't want to hurt you. I'm sorry.

I feel myself go warm with his words, with his presence, even if it's only by text. I don't play any games by waiting to write him back.

I'm sorry, too. I hate to leave things like this.

I want to add more. I want to tell him to think about moving to Los Angeles. To sort out a way where I don't have to be the one to give up everything. But I don't. Because I know that being back in LA wouldn't make him happy. Not even if it was for us to be together. The Maui *aloha spirit* is his happiness.

Bfast? 9 am?

I laugh at his abbreviated invitation to breakfast. His phone is practically useless. I text him back quickly, suggesting a place in Santa Monica, over on his side of town. Maybe we can have a real talk then.

34

FORD

I've been up for hours by the time I get to Ava's chosen spot for breakfast, The Penthouse restaurant in the Huntley Hotel. True to its namesake, the restaurant is on the top floor and offers sweeping views of the Pacific Ocean and the city of Santa Monica.

That's the ocean I was in not long ago as I tried to find some waves. It felt good to be back in the water, though it didn't offer the same warmth and clarity as back home.

Being here in Los Angeles again has been a reminder of all that I don't need. I don't need the hustle and bustle. I don't need the traffic. I don't need the palpable anxiety of how most people live as they strive to make themselves look better, get richer, or accumulate more things.

A year in Maui was enough to reset the easy-come, easy-go mind frame I had once known so well. Everything moves at a slower pace there, which can sometimes be frustrating, but that lifestyle forces you to focus on what's really important. In my mind, what's important is the quality of life you get when you drop all the ambition and truly live the *aloha spirit*. Los Angeles could do with some of that.

Looking around the restaurant, with its white leather club chairs and mini crystal chandeliers, I see a mixture of well-dressed tourists and locals, and I once more feel out of place. I've spent a lot of years struggling to fit in, first in Maui as a non-native white boy before Pika and Hiro befriended me, and then in my father's world as a wild child who spoke before thinking. The thing is, Maui is the only place where I've ever really felt at home. It's the place that makes the most sense for who I am and what I need. It's why I blurted out that night at Ava's Mom's that she should move there. Because I don't want this thing with her to end. But the only way I can see it continuing is if she's able to come to me. To take that chance, like her mother said.

As if in tune with my thoughts, I see Ava making her way through the restaurant toward me. She's wearing a short olive-green dress and brown sandals with her hair up in a high ponytail. I stand to greet her. She offers me her cheek.

"Hi," she says as she pulls away.

I don't let her go, pulling her back to me with my arm around her waist. "Missed you, Hula Girl," I tell her.

She smiles and touches my cheek and then my still damp-from-the-shower hair. "Me too."

"Me too, what?"

"Hmm?"

She's playing dumb. She knows I want her to say the words. I want her to open herself up and tell me she missed me too. But I'm just glad she's here. I won't push her.

Releasing her, I pull her chair out for her and she sits. When I've joined her, our waitress arrives with the coffee and a basket of freshly baked banana poppy seed muffins I had ordered after I had been seated.

Once we're alone, I tip just the right amount of milk into her mug and she smiles her thanks.

"It's a beautiful day," she says, taking in the view.

It's sunny but a little hazy. Not bad, but it doesn't compare to the views I have back home. "I was in that ocean this morning," I tell her.

"Surfing?"

I nod. "Pretty good waves."

"But not the same?" she guesses.

"Of course not. Nothing can match Maui."

"Yes, you are certainly Maui's biggest advocate."

I squint at her, trying to understand whether she's teasing me or rebuking me. In the end, our waitress returns before I can decide how to respond.

She tells us about the seafood eggs Benedict special, suggests a mimosa, then slips away after we order.

"So," Ava says, "it seems all went well last night."

I give her a *you can't be serious* look, and she laughs.

"I meant as far as the whole fiancée thing goes," she continues. "If your father is offering up his girlfriend to help with wedding planning, then he's convinced it's all real, right?"

"Oh. Yeah, that part was ... good."

"And I assume you were able to smooth things over with him after I left?"

"Yeah, it's all good now." What I don't tell her is that my main concern in staying behind to talk to him wasn't so that I could assure my own petty retribution, but so that I might deny him his. He was peppering me with far too many questions about her saying she and I would be partnering up and potentially taking his clients. I had to make sure he knew she was just joking. That it was just her sense of humor to throw him off balance since she was nervous in his esteemed presence. Yeah, I played to his ego and it worked. Thankfully, he finally let it go.

"When do you go home?" she asks.

"The board meets tomorrow. I'm resigning on Tuesday. I have a flight booked for eleven that morning."

"And you've sorted out the issue with your shares?"

She's all business now, her walls back up. It's a shame to see her revert to those instincts. As if she needs to protect herself from me. I sigh, suddenly weary. There's only so many times I can convince her she doesn't need to pull away from me.

Left with no other choice, I snap into the same impersonal mode she's put on. "I have. I'll submit the paperwork along with my resignation. I found a creative solution. You pointed me in a very helpful direction, so thank you for that."

"Great."

Her short reply and unfocused eyes tell me she's not listening.

It feels like our time is slipping by. I can see it draining away along with the easy intimacy we once shared. I have to do something to make her understand that this—*us*—is worth fighting for.

Leaning across the small table, I tell her, "Let's cut the bullshit and really talk. We need to figure out how to make us work."

She looks wary. "What do you suggest? I mean, honestly, we both know it would be me moving to Maui just like you said at my mom's, wouldn't it?"

"It's an option." When I see her exasperation, I continue,

"At least say it's an option. I'm not saying it's the *only* way, but it has to be an option."

"Ford, you're asking me to compromise. You're saying you want me, but only if *I* change my life and give up on my career."

"No. I'm asking you to take a chance on us," I counter.

She lets out a pitiful laugh. "How do I get to have you *and* my career?"

I'm silent because I haven't figured that out. I don't have all the answers. But at least I can admit that. And I can admit how much I want her.

But my silence only intensifies her frustration. So much so that tears form in her eyes. And then, to my surprise, she slams her fist against the table.

"Damn it," she says weakly. "*You* are my fairy-tale romance."

"Then—"

"And you're also proof that I *can't* have it all."

"You can. We both can. We can figure it out," I say but she just shakes her head.

I'm hyper aware of the other diners sitting too closely. I don't want to be here in this restaurant where we have to force ourselves to have a meal together. I don't want the fire we had together to burn out in this way. I want to stoke it, to bring it back to life and feel the heat of *us* once more.

Abruptly, I stand and take the money clip from my pocket. I throw down three twenties, my best guess for the cost of the meal we had ordered plus a tip.

Then, I hold out my hand to Ava.

"Let's get out of here." When she hesitates, I add, "*Please.*"

"And go where?"

There's futility in her voice, as if it's already clear to her that there's no point to us anymore.

"Anywhere," I say. "Down to the beach. We can explore the pier, go for a ride on that big old Ferris wheel, I'll win you a giant stuffed animal at one of those rigged games—whatever you want. But let's just go." I just want some of our spontaneity back. I want that promise that when we're together, anything's possible. That there *could be* a point to us spending time together.

As soon as she tentatively takes my hand, I pull her up and with me through the restaurant. I don't take her to the main hotel elevators, but to the single glass elevator attached to the front of the building that offers ocean views during the descent. We catch it just as an older man and a much younger woman step off.

Once the doors close, I slide my hand into the hair at the nape of her neck. But I don't kiss her. Instead, I press my forehead to hers, willing her to take a chance. For a moment, we stay just like this, both of us with our eyes closed, breathing each other in with perfect synchronicity. And then I kiss her. It's a searing, searching, desperate kiss that she returns with the same passion.

"Just give me one more day," I whisper into her ear before meeting her eyes. "Give me *you* today."

Her eyes fill with tears, and she shakes her head. "I don't know what you want."

"I just want to be with my Hula Girl one more time. I want *you*. I want *us*. The way we were in Maui. And have been here until it changed last night."

The elevator is slowing to a stop and I'm desperate for her to understand. To answer me. To say that she will do as I ask.

"Ford—"

I can tell by her tone that she's going to argue against it. She's going to say that the real world has made all that impossible. That there's no point since neither of us is willing to change our lives, including where we live. So, I speak before she can finish because I don't want to hear her say it aloud.

"Don't give up on us, honey," I tell her.

"I ... can't do this. I'm sorry."

My chest tightens with this rejection. She's just made it clear there's nothing else I can do. She's not willing or able to take a chance on us.

The elevator doors open and the people waiting to board force us to step out into the lobby. I follow her out onto the street. The hazy sunlight is too bright for my dark thoughts and I laugh.

She looks at me quizzically.

"I don't know," I say in defeat. "I just—fuck it. I love you, Ava. Yeah, it's crazy. Yeah, it's impossible. But it's fucking true. I love you. And I'm just so ... sad that this is where it's ending."

Her face is full of the same regret I feel. Reaching up, she touches my cheek. "I knew you were a romantic," she says, and I laugh weakly. And then she adds, "I love you, too, Surfer Boy."

The nickname makes me smile, but now, it's so fucking bittersweet. I've never felt more conflicted in my life. Not even when I had to move away from Maui at my father's insistence. Because now, the choice is completely mine. No one is forcing me to give up the thing I want most this time.

No one but me.

35

Tequila is my friend!

That's what I declared at some point to the bar full of strangers at the cheesy "cantina" not far from my townhouse. I'd gone straight there after Ava left me standing on the sidewalk. As I sat by myself, I looked around at the garish decorations that were a ridiculous approximation of Mexican culture and wanted to laugh. Ava would have rolled her eyes at it.

And she really wouldn't have enjoyed the less than top shelf tequila they had on hand. Even as I drank, I knew I'd regret it in the morning. There would be no getting up early to hit the waves, no coconut water hangover cure could erase the damage I was intent on doing.

I remember calling the bartender Makai a few times, as if I was back home. This guy looked nothing like my friend Makai, though, he did have the same epic level of patience. He listened to me as I confessed that I was heartbroken because my fiancée (yes, I called her that—it was easier than explaining the whole backstory) claimed she loved me, but she obviously loved her work more, because she wasn't willing to move to Maui to be with me. My fake Makai checked on me throughout the afternoon, but eventually, he eased me out to the street and watched as I got in an Uber.

Now I'm in my bed, staring up at the ceiling as it spins, thinking that I must not be as smart as I've always thought, because I still can't figure out how to make things work with Ava. I want her. Jesus, I want her so much. But, giving up my life in Maui is simply inconceivable. I think of being out on the waves there, feeling the magic of that surreal flow and force of nature. At first, I ride the motion in my mind. But then, I feel the vomit rising and I scramble to the bathroom to get sick.

A real class act, I think, after I've given all I've got and am sitting on the cold floor.

Look at what Ava's missing out on.

No wonder she loves me. I laugh at that.

She loves me.

I love her.

What the hell are we doing?

I don't get any further in this grand debate with myself as I soon pass out, cuddling with the towel I'd used to clean the sick from my mouth.

IN THE MORNING, everything hurts.

Everything.

But I have no choice but to dress in a suit and head into the office. There are tedious board meetings to sit through for most of the day, which I do without complaint. I'm only biding my time, anyway, until I can resign.

All goes smoothly. I make no objections to the issues raised. I vote with whatever my father wants, which happens to align with what my grandfather advocates for, too. Today is the first day I've seen him in over a year, and he barely acknowledged me. I'm guessing it's because my dad told him my decision to leave the firm was final. It's of no concern to me anymore. Going through the motions is all I can muster, anyway. All I can think about is Ava.

I'm so lost in thoughts of her, that when the day of meetings is finally over, I'm still in my seat at the board table after everyone has left.

"Well, that wasn't exactly the performance I'd hoped for to boost the board's confidence, but it'll do."

I'm slow to look up in response to my father's words. He's loosening his tie. It was a good day for him, and now he's ready to unwind. Well, as much as he ever does.

"I did what I had to do," I reply, standing.

"So, you did. And what now? I suppose you have plans with your fiancée?"

I hesitate, wondering what lie to tell him. In the end, I say the thing that I think is closest to the truth.

"No, we don't. She's caught up at work."

"Ah, right. I suppose Randall's issues mean everyone over there has to step up and put in even longer hours."

I have no idea what that means. But I do know how to ask probing questions. I'm a lawyer, after all. "Right, there's a bit of a panic over it. How would you handle something like that?"

Senior raises his eyebrows. "Well, I should hope I'll never have to deal with that. I mean, it's a delicate thing, dementia in the managing partner."

Dementia? Holy shit. Is that what Ava meant when she said

she was going to have to dedicate herself even more to her job? And why didn't she tell me about Randall? She must be devastated.

"There are a lot of public relations issues to take care of with that," Senior continues, "let alone the internal factions lining up to go at it once he's stepped down." He takes a deep breath and lets it out as a whistle. "Something like that is another reason why it's all the better that I'll have your shares tomorrow to bolster my position here."

I don't reply to that. Even without my shares, he'll still be the managing partner. That wasn't enough for him, though. He wanted the controlling interest of the firm, simply for his ego's sake. Being king of the castle was worth pushing his only family out of the way. As much as I once strove to be like him and bought into all the power plays, I'll never understand his desire to consolidate all the control at the expense of those he's supposed to love.

"Anyway," he says, "we meet with Legal at eight tomorrow morning. Then you'll be free to ... what will you do?"

"Hmm?"

"I assumed you were going back to Maui. But with this fiancée of yours in the picture, what's the plan? I hear she's fiercely dedicated to Randall's firm."

"We're working it out. Probably do some sort of splitting of our time between L.A. and Maui."

He nods, but it's clear he's not convinced. It doesn't matter, though, because he's lost interest.

"Tomorrow. Eight o'clock," he reminds me before taking his leave.

As soon as he's gone, I pull my phone out from my pocket and start the laborious process of texting Ava.

Not trying to interfere, but I heard about Randall. I'm so sorry.

Please let me know if there's anything I can do to help. I mean it. I just want to help if I can.

By the time I hit send, my thumbs are practically numb. And Ava responds so quickly that I have to laugh. Maybe a smart phone isn't such a bad idea.

I really appreciate that. The best help would be to try to kill the gossip going on about this very personal issue. Otherwise, I've got things handled. Thank you.

So, that's it. That's the extent of our relationship now. Impersonal but still gracious.

And over.

IT'S seven twenty-three the next morning when I hear from her again. I've just gotten into my car to make the drive to the firm when my cell buzzes. I flip it open and have to scroll through the tiny screen to read the full message.

Good luck today. I know it's a big day and that you'll feel relieved to have it behind you.

While it's nice that she's thought of me and remembered my task for the day, I don't know what to do with it. I don't want to get sucked into feeling like I've got a place in her life when I know that's not the case. I decide to keep it simple with my reply.

Thx

IN THE OFFICE, I go straight to the conference room that had been set aside for our purposes and find the table full of suits. My dad, my grandfather, and four people from legal who might as well be replicas of each other, are all there. And, as luck would have it, they're all wearing some variation of a charcoal-gray suit. I've opted for jeans and a T-shirt again, wanting to feel like myself as I make this move.

"Gentlemen," I say and get a scattered chorus of replies. I take the open chair across from my father. My grandfather is sitting at the head of the table, stoic.

"Larry, pass down the paperwork," Senior says to one of the legal clones.

I ignore the shuffling of paper coming my way, and instead, reach into my messenger bag. I pull out a manila folder.

"I'd better get this to you first," I say, proffering the formal resignation letter I'd written up and signed yesterday afternoon.

"Noted," Larry says. Looks like he's the lead for the legal team.

My grandfather picks up the resignation letter and scans it before shaking his head mournfully.

"Such a waste," he mutters.

There's no use in trying to make him understand the value of living your life to your own standards of happiness, not anyone else's. I pull out a sheaf of papers from the folder next.

"You'll want to review this, but you can also trust that it is completely in order," I say.

"What is it?" Senior asks.

"It's how I've decided to divest my shares."

My father scoffs. "There's only one choice in the matter. The bylaws are clear. You must sell to the managing partner."

"Well, that's the thing," I say. "It's not as clear as you think. There is a clause that I am taking advantage of."

Senior snatches the paperwork I had prepared and scans it.

"What is this? Charitable giving?" He looks up at me, fury in his eyes. I don't look away, and after a moment he turns to Larry. "What is this bullshit?"

Larry has a fine layer of perspiration on his upper lip. He opens his mouth to speak, but nothing comes out.

My grandfather snickers. "Does this clause reference the change that happened around 2001?"

I nod, impressed that he's put it together so quickly. It took me days of research to sort out how I might do this.

"What does that mean?" Senior asks, his voice betraying his panic. "Dad? Answer me."

My grandfather can't keep from smiling. "It means that your *Boy Wonder* has bested us all in this little scenario."

Senior stands and rests his hands on his hips. "Someone better explain this to me right now."

I look up at him and lean back in my chair, crossing my legs, ankle over knee. "What it means is that I have taken advantage of the one time this firm decided they'd better do some charitable giving. That was right after September eleventh happened, and everyone seemed to want to do good. Funny that it doesn't ring a bell, but I guess the press release you and Grandfather put out at the time was as far as it all went, anyway."

Recognition slowly dawns on him and I can tell by his face that I don't need to go into detail. I don't need to explain that after that tragic event, the firm had set up a way to transfer the revenue gained through shares, up to 100 percent, to a charitable cause. As far as I can tell, no one took advantage of it. But the firm sure did make a splash in the media with the announcement of their "giving back" program.

"You'll see here in the paperwork," I say, "that revenue of one hundred percent of my shares will be transferred, in perpetuity, to the Inner-City Music Project here in Los Angeles. Of course, I reserve the right to extend this to other cities once I see that it's making the impact I hope for. It should go a long way, though. Those kids are in desperate need for new instruments, good instruction, and even funds to go on tours to different parts of the state. Maybe they'll even get the chance to travel the country. It'll be incredibly enriching. At least, I hope so."

"And so, what is this, Ford?" Senior says through clenched jaw. "Your way of saying *fuck you* on your way out the door?'

I lean forward and make eye contact with him. "It started that way, to be honest. I didn't want you to have those shares because I knew you'd just turn around and push your own father out—"

"I wouldn't—"

"I think we all know your intentions. Nothing is ever enough, is it? Anyway, I realized that sticking it to you wasn't going to make me happy. In fact, I didn't need that to be happy because I've already found what I truly needed. All I had to do was return to being the person I was before I ever got sucked into your world. And so, I thought about what I could do to help others with it. I want to make a positive impact in people's lives, not just work the loopholes and flaws of the law to my own advantage. *This* is meaningful. *This* is going to change people's lives."

"*This*," Senior says, "will be challenged in court."

I sigh and shake my head. "You'll lose. You're fighting against your own rules. And you'll lose in the public eye, too."

"What does that mean?"

I make a show of looking at the watch on my wrist that

isn't there. "A press release is being issued in about two minutes explaining the donation."

My father's face goes red.

"But it's to your benefit to let it stand as is, Senior. I've put this out as being in the firm's name. It's got McAvoy & Associates as the backer. That's fantastic PR for you. You'll get *more* business because of it. So, really, it's a win-win. The firm will do well, and the kids who need it will get a helping hand."

With that, I stand. "Well, fellas. That's it for me. I do appreciate the education and the opportunity. This was just never my place. I'll leave it to you and trust that your dedication and passion for this will continue as it always has."

Before I can get to the door, my father comes to me and stabs his finger into my chest. "You have *always* been a disappointment."

"Leave him be," my grandfather says sharply.

Senior looks startled and backs away.

"It's okay," I say. "I can live with that. We've never seen eye to eye. That's just the way it is. For the first time in my life, I understand that accepting that is better than fighting it. That goes for both of us. Give it a try, and you might find some peace."

He raises his eyebrows, not with some miraculous epiphany, but with frustration. "Get out," he says.

I flash a hang loose sign. And then I walk out.

I've never felt freer in my life.

36

AVA

I'm at my desk in my office when Tyler comes breezing in, looking like he's bursting at the seams, eager to share one of his gossip scoops.

"What?" I ask.

He sits in the chair in front of my desk. "Your Ford has to be behind this, right?"

My eyebrows come together in confusion. "Behind what?"

"Girl, please stop hiding things from me! This whole secret love story and engagement is one thing, but to keep pretending—"

"Just tell me what you're talking about. I'm busy, Tyler."

He rolls his eyes. "The press release from McAvoy & Associates. The one about their charitable endeavor."

"I have no idea what you're talking about."

"Really? Like Ford didn't tell you about this? Ford, your *fiancé?*"

I sigh and do a quick Google search. It shows me the latest press release detailing a rather extraordinary and ongoing donation to a music organization for underprivileged kids.

My eyes fill with tears as I read. This is what Ford did with his shares. This is how he managed to transform something negative—his disdain for being a part of McAvoy & Associates—into something positive. And not just positive, but life altering for kids in need. At the same time, I feel guilty for accusing him of wanting nothing but petty retribution. My heart feels too big in my chest. I press my left hand against it, trying to ease the emotion I'm being overwhelmed by.

"Damn, that ring," Tyler says with a whistle. "When is the wedding, anyway?"

I look down at the ring. It's odd how quickly it's become a part of me.

"I, uh, I don't know."

"Well, fear not. Paige and I were talking, and we've got tons of ideas for the reception."

I don't register what Tyler says. My mind is still stuck on the awful feeling of Ford slipping away. He'll soon be on a plane to Maui. I have no idea if I'll ever see him again.

"She's actually not as awful as you might think," Tyler continues.

"Who?"

"Paige," he says with exaggerated patience.

"Oh, okay."

I look at my computer screen and click through to my calendar. I have multiple meetings throughout the day. But the most important thing I have scheduled is lunch with Randall. This is my opportunity to suggest to him that he step down. I'm going to as gently as possible point out the ways in which he's lost a step and steer him toward understanding that his time is better spent in the company of his wife and family. That I, and others here at the firm he started, will be good stewards of all that he created.

While I want to be the person to put these things to him as plainly as possible because I believe he'll take it best from me, I am at the same time tempted to postpone the lunch so that I can run to the airport like some lovesick heroine in a *Lifetime* movie of the week special. I want to catch Ford before he even makes it through the security line, throw myself into his arms, and tell him he's right. We *can* figure out a way to be together. That the universe *did* put us in the same place. That we're meant to be with each other.

I'm startled out of this fantasy when Randall walks through my office door. Tyler stands up and stares down at his phone.

"Ah, yes, I have to get going," he says. "Busy, busy."

I smirk at him as he backs out of the office with his hands raised in a helpless gesture. He's never lost his healthy respect —and fear—for Randall like I have.

"Randall, how are you?" I ask.

"Good, good." he hesitates. "Well, actually, I'm going to have to postpone our lunch."

I try to keep an impassive expression. "Really?"

"I'm, uh, well, I'm not feeling great. I—I didn't sleep well. So, I'm going to take some files home and work there. Maybe for the rest of the week."

He looks pained with this admission. I go to him and wrap my arm through his. "You know what?"

He pats my hand and smiles at me affectionately. "What?"

"I would love nothing more than to help you with those files. And how about I follow you home? I bet Alice wouldn't mind the company. The three of us can have lunch and catch up."

I see his face light up at the idea. And that's all I need right now. I just need to be able to help this man who has done so much for me, who has become so much to me.

"Well, if you're sure you have the time," he says.

"For you, Randall, I absolutely do."

AND SO, I don't rush to the airport to intercept Ford. I don't make a wild, romantic gesture to declare my love for the man who so suddenly and completely won my heart.

The best I can do is text him from the car while driving to Randall's.

I heard about the charity initiative. Well done. You are a hell of a lawyer. Anyone ever tell you that? Well, anyway, I'm proud of you. Hope you make it home safe and sound.

Once at Randall's, I watch the clock, watch the minutes tick by as they get closer to Ford's eleven o'clock flight.

In exchange, I get time with Randall. *Real* time. It's the exact right opportunity to speak honestly with him and his wife, Alice. It's when they both share that he has been diagnosed with Alzheimer's. I let them talk through all their fears and hopes in how they'll deal with everything in the coming years. Years, that is, if he's lucky. He's got the best medical care and a great support system, so there is a good chance that he'll be able to extend his quality of life. I steer the discussion toward next steps with the firm. It's hard, I'm not going to lie. Randall is torn up about stepping down. But he's also realistic. Together, we work out a plan that he seems to find comfort in. In the end, that's the best that I can do for him.

It's late by the time I say my goodbyes to Randall and Alice, but I don't want to go home. Instead of heading to my place, I drive to my mom's.

When she answers the door, she's already in her pajamas. But she doesn't hesitate in ushering me inside.

I sit at the kitchen table while she makes *Tajin* popcorn as I tell her all about my day.

"I'm sorry, *mija*," she tells me as she joins me. She puts her hand on mine and gives me a smile that says so much more. I don't need words. I know she understands how I feel.

"Did you know," Mama says thoughtfully, "that when your father asked me to take a chance on him, it was in that same countryside you've been to?"

This sounds familiar, but I can't quite square it with the story she had told Ford and me about how they met at El Jardín.

"Remember, *mija*, we told you before that he proposed to me under the shade of this big Encino tree out in a pasture. Though it was barely spring, the day was warm. There wasn't a cloud in the sky. It was so quiet. Well, except for the birds. And the wind in the tall grass. But besides that, all I could hear after he asked, after he gave me his theory about us and the universe, was my heartbeat. It was … unforgettable."

"I love that image. Oh, you and Papa were so perfect."

"Surely not perfect. But perfect for each other, I think."

I scoop another handful of popcorn into my mouth and nod. "Mama?"

"Yes?"

"Why did you bring that up?"

She shrugs. "I suppose I've been thinking of your father a lot more than usual lately. It's nice to share these stories. To keep the memories alive. To cherish what a special thing we had."

We both have watery eyes.

"But I'm not the only one who has been thinking of him more lately," she continues.

Tilting my head, I realize she's remembering that I've confided in Ford about my father more than once. First, on our first date at Makai's. Then, during our first night in LA when we stumbled upon Angel's Flight.

"It feels good to share those memories with someone you can trust, doesn't it?"

"I ... it does," I admit.

She's gently nudging me to understand that in Ford I have found an exceedingly rare thing—someone I can trust. Of course, she knows that I've spent a lot of years keeping that kind of intimacy at arm's length, and now she seems happy to see that I've let down my guard. Let down my walls, as Ford would say. I've never done that with anyone else.

All this makes me wonder if I could ever look back at the time Ford and I had together with as much satisfaction as she does the time she had with my father. Granted, it's not the same. She had seventeen years with the love of her life. I didn't even have seventeen days with Ford. Thinking of him makes me smile, but that soon fades because I know that we haven't had enough time together. Our story *isn't* over. I don't know exactly how the next part of us will play out, but I do know that it has to.

It has to.

37

AVA

That certainty that Ford and I aren't over hasn't faded, but I haven't come up with any grand idea for how to act on it. The next few days go by as I put in long hours at the office. Between my normal case load and working with Manny on the succession plan for Randall, I'm swamped. Being busy helps to avoid thinking about Ford as much as possible. It's only when I return to my generic home, as Ford called it, that I disconnect enough to let my mind wander to him.

He never did answer my text telling him I was proud of him for the way he handled his shares. I understand that he might need to take a step back. But it still hurts every time I look at my phone with the hope that he might have responded.

I'm on the verge of sleep when I hear the chime signaling an incoming text. Exhausted, I almost don't bother to look. But hope springs eternal, as the saying goes, and I groggily grab my phone.

It's from Ford.

I laugh in surprise when I see that he's sent a photo, because that means he's given in and gotten a smartphone.

I quickly click on the photo, and it comes into focus. He's taken a selfie of himself holding the photograph of us that I had printed and mailed to him as soon as I returned from Maui. I had sent it to his mother's music school because he doesn't have an actual address. He must have only just now gotten it. In the picture he sent, he's shirtless, his hair is wild, and his smile is wide. He looks like he just came from surfing. And he looks like he's in his happy place, even if he does text:

Miss my hula girl. Thanks so much for sending the photo.

I'm smiling through tears. And also kicking myself over this being the only selfie we've taken together. How did that happen? How didn't we think to take a photo of us when we were together here in LA? I should have at least gotten one of us at his father's party when we'd accidentally dressed so perfectly to complement each other with him in his navy suit and me in that light-blue dress. And now there's a very good chance that I'll never see him in a suit again.

Not that seeing him in a bathing suit is a bad thing …

Sighing, I turn onto my belly and try to think of what I should reply. I miss him. I could tell him as much. But where would that get us? I'm still no closer to figuring out where we go from here.

I finally decide to keep it neutral.

You got a smart phone! Welcome to the present.

His reply comes back in mere seconds, almost as if he's showing off his new phone's capabilities: *This is strictly my "In case of Ava emergency" phone.*

His reply makes me laugh and I can't stop myself from replying:

I'm glad to know I can still reach you.

I watch as the little bubbles appear, showing that he's typing his reply. I bite my lip, anxious for his next text.

Always.

I take an involuntary, gulping breath when I read that. I want to believe him. I want to believe we have all the time in the world to figure this out. But I'm realistic enough to know that life—and love—doesn't wait forever.

WE KEEP up texting each other sporadically over the next couple of weeks, usually light banter about the Dodgers or surface-level updates on our days. I've let him know that I'm committed to being Randall's advocate as he steps down, and he's fully supportive. It's nice to still feel some kind of connection with him, but that doesn't stop me from aching for him each night as I go to bed alone.

Randall doesn't want a lot of fuss for his retirement, and so when the time comes, it's marked by a simple champagne toast in the main lobby of our office with all the staff gathered around. So that he doesn't go off script, or forget the script entirely, Randall has written his speech on an index card.

I watch him give it with mixed feelings. I love him dearly and respect all that he's accomplished, but I'm sad that it's come down to a three by five inch piece of paper. Still, he is dignified and says all the right things as he hands off the managing partner duties to Manny.

As soon as he's done, everyone raises their glass to him and shouts out their thanks and congratulations on all that he has accomplished. That part is nice. I can see tears in Randall's eyes at this and know it's not spurred by helplessness, but at having done something truly meaningful with his career. He has inspired a lot of lawyers, not the least of whom has been me. I've told him before what an incredible impact he's had on my life and how grateful I am, but when I see an opportunity to steal him away from the group, I grab it.

Looping my arm through his, I steer him toward the wall of windows that showcases the Staples Center and LA Live entertainment complex. This area has become a much different place than it was when Randall first took a single suite four decades ago. It used to be on the edge of downtown Los Angeles with not a lot of hustle and bustle. Now, he has three floors in this high-rise, and the area is a huge attraction for locals and tourists alike. The times and environment may have changed, but Randall never has. He's always been someone I can admire for the way he treats the law and his clients with respect and integrity.

"Randall, before everyone tries to get a word with you and I lose my chance," I say, "I just want to thank you. Thank you for every—"

"Alice will be here to take me home soon," he says, looking at his watch.

I'm thrown by the interruption but understand that I have to be flexible and let him express himself in whatever manner makes him comfortable. And obviously, his comfort level right now is not in listening to me blather on once more about what a great mentor he's been.

I smile and decide to take a different tact. "Well, I'm sure—"

"What I mean to say, Ava," he interrupts again, "is that my time is limited, so let's not waste it with platitudes. Though, I know you mean them and I appreciate the sentiment."

Now I'm thrown by his purposeful tone. I don't try to

guess how I should handle the moment, and instead, let him speak, which is clearly what he wants.

"I want to say a few things to *you*." He takes a deep breath and I try to steel myself, suddenly fearing he will have changed his mind about the retirement plan I helped engineer. "I know you have great loyalty to this firm. I know you've found a way to get along with Manny. And that both of these things compel you to stay in a situation that isn't necessarily to your benefit."

"I, um, what do you mean?"

"I mean, that as decent as Manny is now being to you and me, that doesn't mean he will ever allow you to progress in this firm. Certainly not at the pace that I have encouraged."

"Oh, I see." I hadn't thought much along these lines. I've been so busy with this transition process that it hadn't occurred to me what my future might be here.

"I'm telling you this because you and I have always been honest with each other," he says and levels a meaningful look at me. "And because you're family."

I nod and manage a smile. But the idea that my career path at this firm is likely stagnant at best has left a sour taste in my mouth.

"I appreciate that, Randall."

"I'm not saying it's fair. I'm not saying it's right. It's just the way it is." He takes a deep breath. "Now, the question is, how do you manage this reality?"

"I will have to take some time to consider that."

"That's the thing, Ava. There's never as much time as you think there will be."

My eyes fill with tears, and I try to look away from him to hide the sadness I feel for him with those words. But then he touches my chin and forces me to meet his eyes again.

"That doesn't just apply to this old guy," he says with a laugh. "I'm not done yet, but I have had a great life. I've had a great career. But I sure wish I would have found more time for my family along the way."

I swipe the tears from my cheeks, unable to keep them at bay.

He takes my left hand in his and toys with the engagement ring. "I don't know the whole story of you and this Ford fellow," he says, "but I can see there's something real there. My last bit of advice to you, Ava, is to not settle. Not in work. And not in love. And you certainly don't have to stay at this firm to find success. Know that all I want for you is to be happy."

There's no concern about office decorum as I throw my arms around his neck and hug him tightly.

"Thank you, Randall. Thank you so much."

"It's been my pleasure. Now, get me to the elevator banks so I don't have to schmooze with anyone else. I'd rather just go gently into that good night, if you don't mind." He winks at me, and I laugh.

"I'd love to."

38

AVA

I don't rush out of there, pack a bag, and hop the first plane to Maui. I don't call Ford and tell him that Randall has finally been the one to push me into deciding to follow my heart. I don't do anything out of the ordinary at all, in fact.

Once I've seen Randall off into Alice's good hands, I return to the office. I bypass the remnants of the party and go straight to my office. To anyone watching, I will be doing what I've done for the last six years here at this firm: working longer and harder than just about anyone else.

But what I'm really doing is methodically reviewing each of my open cases and making detailed notes. They are notes for whichever attorney will be taking my place. That's not to say that I'm about to burn bridges here. No, I'm preparing to take a cue from Ford's playbook and availing myself of the firm's leave of absence plan. It will give me just enough time to plan my next move. I know it will be a move away from this place where I've been so comfortable and had such high hopes for advancement. But I don't know anything more than that. And I'm just too damn practical to not have some kind of a plan.

Once I've written a letter to human resources and copying Manny explaining my need for time away, I schedule it to deliver tomorrow, after I'm well gone.

I run by my place and toss bathing suits, sundresses, and other warm weather clothes into a suitcase while I talk to my mom on the phone. I tell her everything I'm thinking, and she doesn't hesitate in encouraging me. She's genuinely excited for me, not just because I've told her that I'm hoping to surprise Ford with a grand gesture, but because she believes great things will come out of this—both in work and love.

"So, I don't know exactly what happens from here," I say.

Mama laughs. "And isn't that wonderful?"

"It's terrifying," I reply. "But I think I can do this."

"I know you can, *mija*. Enjoy yourself. Promise me."

"That's the plan." I hesitate. "Um, and I wanted to ask you, well, whether you've ever thought about living in Maui? I mean, not that I know that I'll be living there, but just in case that's what ends up happening?" I close my eyes tightly.

"Oh, Ava," Mama says. "I appreciate the thought, but you don't need to worry about me. You have spent too many years taking care of me—or thinking you need to, in any case. But I want you to know that I am fine. I have been for a long time now. You don't have to be that brave little thirteen year old who took on way too much anymore. You always want to take care of others. Me. Randall. Your clients. But Ford, he knows how to take care of you, doesn't he?"

"Yes, I think he does."

"*That* is a wonderful thing."

I take in a breath, and when I let it out, it's shaky. But I nod to myself, grateful for the sense of release I feel.

"Don't think I wouldn't be visiting all the time, though," she continues, making me laugh. "And if grandbabies come into the picture, you'll get sick of me."

"Okay, let's not go overboard."

"I'm just warning you, *mija*."

"*Te quiero mucho*, Mama."

She tells me she loves me, too. I end the call with the promise to tell her how everything goes.

With my suitcase and carry-on bag now packed, I hesitate at the door of my loft. Looking around, I realize Ford was right. There's no character here. No life. Not even a single potted plant. I never had time to invest in this as a home.

Now, I'm excited to make a different kind of life.

39

FORD

"Let's call it a morning and go get breakfast, yeah?"

I look over at Pika. He and Hiro are straddling their boards in the water just like I am. We came out here to Honolua Bay this morning, hoping we'd get lucky with a big swell, but nothing has materialized. We knew it was a long shot, but when it comes to catching waves, we're eternal optimists.

"Yeah, sounds good."

After carefully extricating ourselves from the water byway of the rocky coastline, we follow each other up the dirt trail. Once in the parking lot, I can't keep from thinking of Ava. I'll never be able to disassociate her from this spot.

I figure I can text her in the car on the way over to one of the little dives we like to go to for a spam, sticky rice, and egg breakfast. I know she had a big day yesterday with Randall officially stepping down. We've kept in touch but just enough to know the broad strokes of each other's lives. I assume with Randall leaving, she'll be in line for a step up at her firm, something she'll be thrilled about.

I've been thinking about the Inner-City Music Project I worked with in Los Angeles and their offer for me to be more directly involved as they start to implement the funds they'll be receiving. It wouldn't be a full-time job, but rather more of a consultant-type relationship. It would be the kind of meaningful work I crave. And it would give me good reason to be in L.A.

My offhand comment to my father that we'd split our time between L.A. and Maui when he asked how Ava and I would make things work is the most promising solution. It's been weeks now since we parted ways, both of us thinking we were at an impasse. But now, as I load my surfboard into the back of my truck, I realize that was us being too cautious. We're two intelligent people. Two people who love each other. We can work this out.

We have to.

In my truck, I send Ava a text on my fancy new smartphone.

Good morning. I want to hear all about how things went yester-day. But I also want to talk to you. Really talk. Let me know when you have time.

With that, I nod to myself before putting the truck into gear and driving on.

THE BREAKFAST PLACE we go to is a walk-up counter rather than a restaurant. It's no more than a shack off the side of the road, but it offers tasty local options and outdoor picnic tables in the parking lot with a view of the ocean beyond the sporadic traffic going by. We've just sat down with our food, when out of nowhere, Hannah, Hiro's stalker ex-girlfriend, sits down with us.

All three of us guys jump at her sudden appearance. The worst part is how casually she makes herself comfortable by leaning over and snatching one of Hiro's spam musubis to take a bite.

"Hannah," I say, "how are you?"

"Good," she replies.

We all sit in awkward silence for a minute. I'm giving Hiro the stink eye, silently urging him to once again break up with her.

Hiro clears his throat. "Uh, listen—"

"Let me go first," she says. "I know you'll be devastated. But there's nothing that can be done about that. I've met someone else."

All three of us guys let out an audible sigh of relief with that news.

"I know," Hannah says, looking at Hiro with unwarranted sympathy. "It's a terrible way to end things. But, what can you do? If I don't follow my heart, I'll be missing out on really living my life, right?"

"Uh, yeah," Hiro says, eyebrows raised. "You're right. I mean, I'm sad." He's scrambling to project the right tone, afraid of provoking her into changing her mind. "But I just want you to be happy."

"Aww," she coos. "You're the sweetest. I'll take the rest of this, okay?" She holds up the spam musubi as she stands.

"Of course, yes. Here, take the rest of my plate," he says eagerly.

She eyes him with a sad shake of her head. "Sorry, Hiro. You can't win me back with yummy snacks." Taking a deep breath, she lets it out and shakes her head. "Well, see you around, guys."

"Yeah, see you around," Pika says, grinning.

Hiro punches him in the arm.

We wait a respectable amount of time before bursting into laughter.

"Holy shit," I say. "You dodged a bullet with that one."

"What a trip, dude," Hiro says in wonderment.

"That was the best thing I've ever seen," Pika says and goes about mocking Hannah's sweet, clueless demeanor. *"You can't buy my love with yummy snacks."*

I'm distracted from joining in when my cell phone buzzes with an incoming text.

You're right, we should talk.

Ava's reply sounds ominous, setting my nerves on edge. Maybe she's ready to cut all ties. She doesn't have time for a text relationship with some guy she met on vacation. Because that's all it turned out to be, right? With her in LA and me here, what else can she think?

Another text comes through before I have a chance to swallow my pride and truly let her go. This one is a photo.

The image stops my heart.

Which is fitting because it's a photo of Heart Rock at Nakalele Point. It's the spot I had told her she'd love the same day she left Maui. I never had a chance to take her there. But, what is she suggesting? I hesitate to get my hopes up that this means she's planning a trip.

And then another photo comes through that has me standing abruptly and climbing out from the picnic bench.

This photo is a selfie. It's Ava in front of Heart Rock, a gorgeous smile on her face as she flashes a hang loose sign with her left hand. The left hand that still showcases a sparkling engagement ring.

"Where are you going?" Pika asks.

"I gotta follow my heart, like Hannah said," I reply, leaving them both calling after me for an explanation.

I DRIVE WAY TOO FAST. Especially as I while I do so, I text her back:

Do not move.

But stay away from the blowhole. Seriously. It's dangerous.

I'm not kidding about that. More than one tourist who got too close to the geyser which erupts every few minutes at the same spot as Heart Rock, has been sucked in and quickly drowned. Its blasts of seawater of up to one hundred feet in the air are a magnificent sight to behold, but only at a safe distance.

Thankfully, our breakfast spot wasn't all that far away, and I'm soon parking along the road at mile marker thirty-eight-point-five. I rush along the trail toward the water, my mind racing with questions about what all this means.

But the only answer I need is the one I find when I see Ava standing by Heart Rock, looking at me expectantly. She's wearing a short yellow sundress and has a matching hibiscus tucked behind one ear. I stop several yards away, taking in the sight of her. Then I laugh when she raises her arms and sways her hips just so. She's my perfect Hula Girl.

I go to her, and before either of us can say anything, I slide my hand into the hair at the nape of her neck, pull her body to mine, and kiss her.

I kiss her like she's mine.

Because that's what she is.

I know that both from how I feel and from how she returns the kiss. It's full commitment on both sides.

When we finally pull away, she looks up at me and says, "Missed you, Surfer Boy."

"Where did you come from, Hula Girl?"

She smiles at me, her eyes sparkling in the sunlight. "All I know is I'm right where I want to be."

Just then, the geyser goes off, and we both turn to look at it. The water shoots high into the air, fanning out slightly. The sunlight is just right to create a rainbow in the spray of water.

"How's that for romance?" I tell her, grinning.

She looks into my eyes. "Total fairy tale, babe."

I get all that she means with that. I get that this means we're really working on being together. That she believes in us. And that we'll figure it all out.

"You better believe it," I tell her, and lean in for another kiss.

She surprises me by putting her hand to my chest. I watch as she looks around, taking in our surroundings. The wind is whipping the ocean against the rocks. Wandering Tattler birds are making occasional calls. Mercifully, we've found a brief time when there isn't anyone else here. The geyser is bound to go off again, giving us another private show.

"What is it?" I ask.

Her smile is beautiful, serene. "All this," she says, gesturing around us, "and all I can hear is my own heartbeat."

I cock an eyebrow. "And is that a good thing?"

"You better believe it," she replies and leans in for another kiss.

40

So, what happened after the fairy-tale reunion at Heart Rock? Did everything just magically fall into place? Not exactly. Instead of jumping right into the logistical and practical matters of it all, we reverted to vacation fling mode. We created our own little world, either at his place, or in the water, or at Makai's. Then, we spent time with his mother, Rebecca, which allowed me to get to know her better. She's very sweet and welcomed me warmly, especially when she understood that the sudden seriousness of our relationship wasn't based on an accidental pregnancy. Pika and Hiro have become my good friends, too. So has Makai, though I suspect he loves to play up our friendship as a way to tease Ford since he likes to pretend that he's just a customer to him.

It was after almost two weeks of living in the moment like this that we started talking about what our future would look like. Ford was quick to suggest that we work out a way to split our time between Maui and Los Angeles, saying he wanted to take up the offer the Inner-City Music Project had made for him to come on as a consultant. That would require him to be in LA. for a good chunk of time every quarter. I loved that he was showing me that he was willing to compromise. It meant that I wasn't the only one willing to change my life for our relationship. But I had to figure out what I would do with my career. Unlike Ford's generous leave of absence policy, mine was finite. I had a total of four weeks before I had to return.

One lazy afternoon after spending too much time in the sun and ocean, we sought refuge under the shade of a palm tree to let the saltwater evaporate on our skin. I dug my toes into the soft sand and closed my eyes, trying to let the rhythm of the waves and the gentle breeze rustling the palm fronds relax me.

"Honey," Ford said.

"Hmm?"

"Let's talk. Time to dig deep. And I don't just mean your toes."

Turning toward him, I cracked one eye to give him a quizzical look.

"Take me back to why you pursued the law," he said.

Ah, so it was going to be that kind of conversation. I knew this lovely state of denial I was living in would have to come to an end at some point. On a deep breath, I realized what it meant to have him initiate this talk, though. It meant he was going to be right there by my side, being my partner and support system as I sorted it out. As I released my breath, I turned onto my side and rested my head on my hand. I was right to have taken that big leap of faith at Heart Rock, the one where I'd trusted that he would care for *my* heart. He started doing that almost as soon as we met, and he hasn't stopped since.

"It was twofold," I said. "I wanted to have a career that guaranteed financial security, and to also feel like I was having a direct impact on the lives of those who really needed help."

"You got the first part. How often did you get to do the second?" He laced his sandy fingers through mine.

"Not often enough. I mean, the rare pro bono case was the most satisfying, of course."

"What if you negotiate with Manny to take the lead on those cases for him? That way the firm still gets the goodwill that comes with those cases, but he doesn't have to deal with it. And then you can also have the time to study for the Hawai'i bar exam. You know, just to have the option here."

"Why would Manny do that? Keep me on for just those cases?"

"Because he still needs you. You're still his conduit to Randall. He may have stepped down, but there's a lot that he still needs to be involved in. He's too big of a force to make a clean break."

"That's true." The more thought I gave it, the more I liked it. I also knew that Randall would back me up. I'd called him a few days after I got here to let him know that I was away but that he could reach me whenever he needed to. When he heard that I had taken a leave of absence, he was delighted that my version of managing the reality of my weakened position at the firm was to withdraw for a time. He chuckled and said that Manny was probably scrambling to cover all the things I had managed to do in the long hours I had put in on a regular basis. And then he told me he'd make sure Manny didn't push me to return too early, that I should enjoy my time with Ford. "I could plan my trips to LA for when you go, too," I said, warming to the idea.

"Perfect. We'll have a place here and a place there."

I smiled. "About that … your place here, well, no offense, but I need a little upgrade."

He laughed. "Come on, I know it's not much, but it's on the sand. How can you upgrade that?"

"Well, I was looking into the legality of that real estate."

He winced. "I told you it's not really legit."

"Turns out that's not exactly true."

"No?"

"I mean, it's definitely not up to code and wouldn't pass inspections for habitation, that's for sure. But it is zoned under some odd exception that's hard to understand. The point is, if your mom's boyfriend will sell it to us, we can renovate, and we won't have to live like outlaws."

He laughed. "You're kidding."

"Nope," I said with a smile.

Leaning forward, he kissed me and I felt the familiar heat in the connection of our lips. This man had done more than make me fall dizzyingly in love with him. He had taught me to slow down and enjoy the simple things in life, including, to my everlasting pleasure, the sensual kisses he gave me every chance he could.

IT'S BEEN ALMOST six months now and the renovations are done. This timeline is exceptional given Maui's famed "island time" which can see projects drag on and on. Pika and Hiro did a lot to help, dedicating themselves to a rigorous schedule motivated by promises of me cooking them Mexican food at the end of each week. What we have now is a 950 square foot place that is more cottage than shack. The outside is painted turquoise, we've added a screened-in front porch, created a separate bedroom, living room, and kitchen, and upgraded the bathroom to include an indoor shower. We've kept the outdoor shower on the side of the house as an easy way to rinse off the saltwater. Inside, it's clean and simple, but with touches that reflect who we are, including artwork from both Hawaiian and Mexican cultures.

Once the last of the workers leaves, we look at each other in wonder. Then Ford takes my hand as we stand with our backs to the ocean and stare at the cottage in front of us. It's a home. A *real* home unlike any I've had in my adult life. There's nothing generic about it.

As I'm thinking about how far I've come in less than a year, I'm suddenly lifted off my feet as Ford picks me up.

"What are you doing?" I say with a laugh.

"We have to make it official," he replies.

"Make what official? Us living together?"

He's always carried me with such ease that I never worry that he might let me slip. It turned out that when he told me "I got you" that first night we were together and he helped me down the rocky inlet, he didn't just mean at that moment. He's had me ever since then.

Climbing the three steps up to our porch, he deftly swings open the screen door and carries me through. Next, he takes me over the threshold of our house before gently lowering me to my feet just as he drops to one knee at the same time.

"Ava," he says, and I watch him, paralyzed and wide-eyed. "I don't have the ring for this because you haven't taken it off since I first gave it to you."

I laugh and looked down at my left hand. The ring he had given me for our faux engagement sparkles. It somehow hadn't seemed right to take it off. We never talked about what we meant to each other or how we should define us. We just existed, happy and focused on making our lives together.

"But," he continues, "I know that you deserve a real declaration from me about what I want from you and for us." He takes my hand and kisses it sweetly as I inhale a measured breath, trying to absorb everything about this moment. "Who would have believed I found my soulmate all because of a chicken?"

I laugh and use my free hand to stroke his cheek.

"I have the feeling that every once in a while, the universe does something right. It worked for your mom and dad. And it's worked for us. Because, Ava, there is no other woman in the world who can do what you do for me. You have helped me complete this journey I've been on to find my sense of self, my sense of peace, again. You are truly my happiness, my love, and the one I hope to have hot sex with for the rest of our lives."

"Ford," I whisper with a smile.

"Honey, you should know that I really liked it so I put a ring on it. Will you marry me?"

I gasp. "You *do* like Beyoncé!"

"Who doesn't?" he says with a laugh. "Answer me, though. Will you marry me?"

There's no hesitation now as I tell him, "Yes, I'll marry you, babe."

He smiles widely and mimes putting the ring on my finger before I pull him to his feet and throw my arms around his neck so I can kiss him all over his gorgeous face. And then I jump up and on him and wrap my legs around his waist.

"Time to break this house in," he murmurs between kisses. "Where do you want to start?"

I pull away enough to look into his eyes. "It doesn't matter. Because as long as I'm with you, I'm right where I want to be."

That gets a smile out of him. "I love you, Ava."

"I love you, Ford."

EPILOGUE

AVA

"It's not too late, you know? You don't have to do this."
I look around at the view as the wind whips loose tendrils of my hair against my face. It's early morning, just past eight. The full heat and humidity of the day is still an hour or more away. Still, the sun shines down, warming my bare shoulders. There are only a few big puffy white clouds in the otherwise blue sky. Just beyond the red-dirt road and down the cliffside is the blue-green water of Honolua Bay. There aren't any surfers out there, even though it's late February and still big wave season. Instead, they're seated in the backs of the trucks they have strategically parked to create an aisle.

"I mean it, Hula Princess. Say the word, and I'll take you out of here."

I smile, giving the gorgeous surroundings one more look before focusing on Eli. He's here along with the other kids from Ford's music class, and they're all wearing matching outfits of aqua and white Aloha shirt with khaki shorts.

"Thanks, Eli," I tell him. "But don't you have a job to do?"

He takes a deep breath and puffs out his cheeks as he glances toward the spot where his fellow musicians are setting up.

"Forty-five degrees," I remind him, pulling his hands out in front of him as a reminder of where he should hold his clarinet.

Although his playing has improved quite a bit since I first saw him perform, he still gets anxious when in front of a crowd.

Not that this is much of a crowd. It's purposely a small affair. Turns out Bryce was right about one thing. I'm not interested in a flashy ceremony. What we have planned here is perfect. It's all about Ford and me being surrounded by the beauty of Maui, and supported by the people we love. In a few minutes, I'll walk down this makeshift aisle with my mom. I'll walk toward the ocean, meeting Ford at the arch that Pika and Hiro handcrafted out of driftwood and we've had covered with a mixture of hibiscus and plumeria flowers.

I'm wearing a white dress that has spaghetti straps, a fitted bodice and a flowing chiffon skirt that moves nicely in the breeze and exposes my right thigh at the slit there. I chose it with that in mind, knowing the peek at my leg would make Ford happy.

I smile thinking of his perfect proposal. It was simple but so suited to us. Just like this ceremony. Although, the part about this not exactly being a legal venue for a wedding isn't really me. But I'm learning to roll with things. Our service will be brief. Afterward, Pika and Hiro will load the arch into one of their trucks and take it to Melissa's house. She has a large backyard and is hosting a luau for our reception. The Kalua pua'a—roasted pig—has been in the ground since yesterday. Loads of people from the community have been invited to join in the celebration, and I'm almost as excited to experience it as I am to get married.

"*Mija*," Mama says as she joins me, "you are the most beautiful bride." Reaching out, she smooths a stray strand of hair behind my ear, just like she's done for me since I was a little girl.

My eyes tear up. I'm so glad to have her here. She's visited twice before this and each time she's here, I try to convince her to move. But she's content to give Ford and me the space to focus on building our lives together. Although all that could change, she still none too subtly hints, if a grandchild comes into the picture.

Kids are definitely in the near future. I've got a few things I want to accomplish first, though. I'll be taking the Hawai'i bar exam in a few weeks. I've decided to try my hand at having my own small practice here in addition to returning to California on a regular basis for the pro bono work Manny agreed to. Everything is falling into place. While I'm still ambitious, I no longer feel the need to set the relentless pace I once did. I understand now that there is a time for everything, it's just a matter of where you place your focus. And my focus is finally in balance, thanks to Ford. I only wish my father could have met him.

"Mama," I ask, "do you think Papa would have liked Ford?"

She smiles as she thinks about that. "I think he would. I think he'd be impressed by his intelligence—in picking you, that is."

I nod and laugh.

Mama takes my hand in both of hers, squeezing me tight. "He would love that you've found a man who loves and supports you for exactly who you are. And who knows? Maybe he had a hand in pushing that chicken into your way?"

Laughing, I blink rapidly and dab at my eyes, careful not to smudge the light makeup I have on.

"Wouldn't that be something?" I say and glance heavenward.

The music, a variation of the song "Lovely Hula Girl," starts, and my heart flutters. Ford has had his kids working on this song since before he proposed. I've heard snippets of it when I dropped by the music school, but haven't heard the whole thing. And whereas I thought it would be a simple acoustic version, it seems he's added a vocalist.

I laugh out loud in shock and joy when I see that Eli has put aside his clarinet in favor of powerfully emoting the lyrics. The song was our cue that the ceremony was beginning. I put my arm through Mama's and we start down the aisle. I can't keep my eyes off Eli as he sings the title lyrics with surprising depth. It seems he's completely lost his stage fright. Our small group of assembled guests loves it as much as I do.

When I reach Ford, he gives me a wink before kissing my mother's cheek. Mama then embraces me before finding her place amongst the others standing nearby.

"Did you like that song?" Ford whispers to me.

I smile and then laugh before cupping his cheeks in my hands and telling him, "I *like* you. I like you so much."

He grins. "Good thing. Because I'm about to officially make you *my* Hula Girl."

"There's nothing I want more, babe."

The End

ACKNOWLEDGMENTS

I am enormously grateful to these readers who so generously gave me their feedback on early versions of *Hula Girl*:
Kathy Aronoff
Jennifer Hayes
Samantha Richman
Karen Cimms

ABOUT THE AUTHOR

Lara Ward Cosio is the author of contemporary romances
that are raw, realistic, sometimes funny, and always feature
swoon-worthy men and strong-willed women.

If you enjoyed this novel, please share your thoughts in a
review on Amazon or Goodreads

To learn more about the author, visit:
LaraWardCosio.com

ALSO BY LARA WARD COSIO

The Rogue Series is my Rock Star Romance Series. It follows the lives and loves of an Irish rock band called *Rogue*. The "boys" of the band are charismatic, sexy, and flawed. They'll make you swoon while frustrating you at the same time. Ultimately, however, you'll root for them to figure their sh*t out. It's a roller coaster ride but an addicting one!

While each book focuses on one band member, all characters appear in the whole series as their stories continue to develop.

Tangled Up In You

Playing At Love

Hitting That Sweet Spot

Finding Rhythm

Full On Rogue: The Complete Books #1-4

Looking For Trouble

Felicity Found

Rogue Christmas Story

Problematic Love

Rogue Extra: The Complete Books #5-8

Made in the USA
Columbia, SC
23 July 2021

42290947R00185